# Take a Chance

D0038586

## ALSO BY ABBI GLINES

### The Rosemary Beach series
*Fallen Too Far*
*Never Too Far*
*Forever Too Far*
*Twisted Perfection*
*Simple Perfection*
*Take a Chance*

### The Sea Breeze series
*Breathe*
*Because of Low*
*While It Lasts*
*Just for Now*
*Sometimes It Lasts*
*Misbehaving*

### The Vincent Boys series
*The Vincent Boys*
*The Vincent Brothers*

### The Existence series
*Existence*
*Predestined*
*Ceaseless*

# Take a Chance

*A Novel*

## Abbi Glines

**ATRIA** PAPERBACK

New York • London • Toronto • Sydney • New Delhi

**ATRIA** PAPERBACK

A Division of Simon & Schuster, Inc.
1230 Avenue of the Americas
New York, NY 10020

First Atria Paperback edition February 2014

**ATRIA** PAPERBACK and colophon are trademarks of Simon & Schuster, Inc.

For information about special discounts for bulk purchases, please contact Simon & Schuster Special Sales at 1-866-506-1949 or business@simonandschuster.com.

The Simon & Schuster Speakers Bureau can bring authors to your live event. For more information or to book an event, contact the Simon & Schuster Speakers Bureau at 1-866-248-3049 or visit our website at www.simonspeakers.com.

Interior design by Dana Sloan

Manufactured in the United States of America

10 9 8 7 6 5 4 3

Library of Congress Cataloging-in-Publication Data

Glines, Abbi.
    Take a Chance / Abbi Glines. — First Atria Paperback edition.
        pages cm. — (The Rosemary Beach series)
    Summary: "A new adult romance novel set in the author's Rosemary Beach series" — Provided by publisher.
    1. Love stories. I. Title.
    PS3607.L59T35 2014
    813'.6—dc23
                                                    2013047307

ISBN 978-1-4767-5654-7
ISBN 978-1-4767-5656-1 (ebook)

*To my Uncle Gerald. Thank you for all those summers you took us to the beach, the lollipops you always had in a bowl at your front door when I came to visit, and for believing in me. You were ornery and grumpy but your heart was big. I will miss you and I will never forget you.*

# Grant

Why was I here? What was the fucking purpose? Had I gotten this bad? Really? In the past, I'd been able to shake her loose and walk away. Nannette had been my go-to fuck for years, but then she'd gotten needy. And I'd liked it. Somehow, she had managed to get under my skin. I had wanted to be wanted—I was that pathetic. My dad rarely called me; my mom had decided she preferred French models over me years ago.

I was screwed the hell up.

It was time I let this go. Nan had needed me for a time when she felt like she was losing Rush, her brother and safe place, to his new life with his wife and child. Not that Rush wouldn't welcome her with open arms—it was just that she was such a bitch. All she had to do was accept Rush's wife, Blaire. That was it. But the stubborn woman wouldn't do it.

Mine had been the arms she'd run into, and like a fool I had opened them up for her. Now, all I had was a lot of damn drama and a slightly damaged heart. She hadn't claimed it. Not completely. But she had touched a place no one else had. She had needed me. No one had ever needed me. It had made me weak.

To prove my point, here I sat in Nan's father's home, looking for her, waiting on her. She was running wild again, and Rush wasn't coming to the rescue. He had hung up his Superman cape and decided his days of coming to Nan's side were over. I had wanted that. As sick as it was, I had wanted to be her hero. Damn, I was a pussy.

"Drink, kid. Fuck knows you need it," Kiro, Nan's father, said as he shoved a half-empty bottle of tequila into my hands. Kiro was the lead singer of the most legendary rock band in the world. Slacker Demon had been around for twenty years, and their songs still skyrocketed to number one whenever they released a new album.

I started to argue but changed my mind. He was right. I needed a drink. I didn't think about where the dude's mouth had been when I touched the rim of the bottle to my lips and tipped it back.

"You're a smart boy, Grant. What I can't figure is why the hell you're putting up with Nan's shit," Kiro said as he sank down onto the white leather sofa across from me. He was in a pair of black skinny jeans and a silver shirt, unbuttoned and hanging open. Tattoos covered his chest and arms. Women still went crazy over him. It wasn't his looks. He was too damn skinny. A diet of alcohol and drugs would do that to you. But he was Kiro. That was all that mattered to them.

"You gonna ignore me? Hell, she's my daughter and I can't put up with her. Damn crazy bitch, just like her momma," he drawled before taking a pull off a joint.

"That's enough, Daddy." The musical voice that was finding its way into my fantasies lately came from the doorway.

"There's my baby girl. She's come out of her room to visit,"

Kiro said, grinning at the daughter he actually loved. The one he hadn't abandoned. Harlow Manning was breathtaking. She didn't look like a rock star's kid. She looked like an innocent, sweet country girl, with long, dark hair and eyes that made you forget your fucking name.

"I was going to see if you planned on eating dinner at home tonight or if you were going out," she said. I watched as she stepped into the room and purposely ignored me. That only made me smile.

She didn't like me. I had met her at Rush and Blaire's engagement party and then spoken to her at their wedding reception. Both times hadn't ended well.

"I was thinkin' of going out. I need to party a little. I've stayed inside this house too damn long."

"Oh. Okay," she said in that soft voice that I swear was intoxicating.

Kiro frowned. "You lonely? Locking yourself away in that room with your books getting to you, baby girl?"

I couldn't take my eyes off Harlow. She rarely came around when I was here. Nan wasn't exactly kind to her. I got why she didn't like Harlow. She was eaten up with jealousy where Harlow was concerned. Even if it wasn't Harlow's fault that Kiro loved her and didn't seem to give a shit about Nan. Harlow lit up a room when she walked into it. There was a peacefulness about her that was hard to explain. It made you want to get close to her and see if you could soak it in. She made it easy for someone as selfish as Kiro to love her. Nan made it hard for normal people to love her—much less someone like Kiro Manning.

"No, I'm fine. I was just going to wait and eat with you if

you planned to eat here. If not, I'll just eat a sandwich in my room."

Kiro started shaking his head. "I don't like that. You're in there too much. I want you to stop reading for tonight. Grant is here and he needs some company. He's a good guy. Talk to him. You can have dinner together while he waits for Nan to return."

Harlow stiffened and finally glanced my way, but only for a moment. "I don't think so."

"Come on, don't be a snob. Grant's a family friend. He's Rush's brother. Have dinner with him."

Harlow's spine stiffened even straighter. She went back to not making eye contact with me. "He's not Rush's brother. If he were, it would be even more disgusting that he's sleeping with Nan."

Kiro grinned like Harlow was the funniest person in the world and he was proud of her spunk. "My kitten has claws, and apparently only you bring them out. Sleeping with the evil sister has put you on my baby girl's shit list. Now that's funny as hell." He looked extremely amused as he took another long draw from his joint.

I wasn't amused. I didn't like the fact Harlow hated me. I wasn't sure how the hell to fix it, though. Turning my back on Nan wasn't possible. She wouldn't be able to handle someone else dropping her. Even if her slutty ass deserved it. I wouldn't let myself think about the boy band she was currently sleeping with. Guess I was wrong about those guys. I thought for sure they were sleeping with each other. Instead, they were all sleeping with Nan.

"Have a good night, Daddy," Harlow said, then turned and

walked out of the room before Kiro could demand she stay with me.

Kiro laid his head back and closed his eyes. "Shame she hates you. She's special. Only known one other like her, and it was her mom. Woman stole my heart. I adored her. Worshipped the fucking ground she walked on. I would have thrown all this shit away for her. I had planned on it. I just wanted to wake up each morning and see her there beside me. I wanted to watch her with our baby girl and know that they were mine. But God wanted her more. Took her the fuck away from me. I won't ever get over it. Never."

This wasn't the first time I had heard him ramble on about Harlow's mother. He did it whenever he got high. She was the first thing that came to his mind. I hadn't known that kind of love. Scared the shit out of me, though. I wasn't sure I ever wanted to know it. Kiro had never recovered. I had met the man when I was a kid and my dad had married Rush's mom. Rush had begged his dad, Dean Finlay, the drummer for Slacker Demon, to take me with them on one of his weekend visits.

I had been in awe. It had been the first of many weekends. And Kiro would always talk about "her" and curse God for taking her. It had fascinated me, even as a child. I had never witnessed that kind of devotion.

Even after my dad's short marriage to Rush's mother, Georgianna, I had remained close to Rush. His dad still came to pick me up sometimes when he got Rush. I had grown up personally knowing the most legendary rock band in the world.

"Nan hates her. Who the hell can hate Harlow? She's too damn sweet to hate. Girl hasn't done anything to Nan, yet

Nan's mean as a goddamn snake. Poor Harlow stays away from her. I hate to see my baby girl so defenseless. She needs to toughen up. She needs a friend." Kiro set his joint down in an ashtray and turned his head to look at me. "Be her friend, kid. She needs one."

I wanted to be a lot more than Harlow Manning's friend. But she wouldn't even look at me. I had tried more than once to direct one of those earth-shattering smiles my way, but she hardly glanced at me. Prove me nuts. "Not sure I can be her friend and Nan's at the same time."

Kiro frowned, then sat up and leaned forward. "Three kinds of women in this world. The kind that suck you dry and leave you with nothing. The kind that only want a good time. And the kind that make life worth a damn. That last kind . . . the right woman's the one who gives as much as she takes, and you can't get enough. She's the kind . . . if you lose her, you lose yourself."

His bloodshot eyes told me he hadn't just smoked a joint today. But even high, he made sense. If anyone knew about women, it was Kiro Manning.

"I've had all three. Wish like hell I'd stayed away from the first. The second is all I touch anymore. But that third one . . . I won't ever be the same. And I wouldn't take back one minute I had with Harlow's mom."

He ran his hand through his stringy hair. "Nannette, she's the first kind. Be careful of the first kind. They will fuck you over and walk away laughing."

# Harlow

**Three months later . . .**

Only nine months. Just nine months. I could make it nine months. I would hide in my room and only come out when she wasn't here. Classes would start soon and I would have my courses to distract me. Then Dad would be home and I'd leave this place behind me. I could do it. I had to. Dad hadn't given me any other option.

The house was quiet. The loud sounds of Nan having sex with some idiot had woken me up around two this morning. I had put on my Beats and cranked up my favorite playlist. At some point I had fallen back to sleep. Because the music had been pumping in my ears when I woke up this morning, I wasn't sure if I was home alone or not. It was after ten and the house was so quiet, I was pretty sure no one was here. Besides, Nan didn't seem like the kind to have a sleepover this late.

She screwed them then tossed them.

I threw back the covers and ran my hands through my hair to tame the tangles before stepping into the hallway. Silence was all that met my ears. I was safe. I could eat. Nan hadn't been here when I arrived last night, but I knew she must have noticed my car outside. Dad had an Audi waiting on me when I had landed at the airport.

After finding the house, I had gone to buy some groceries, then unloaded my food and luggage. Dad had bought this house for Nan with the understanding that I would stay with her for nine months while he was on tour with Slacker Demon. She wanted a house in Rosemary Beach, Florida. He had supplied a big one. Dad did everything big. Which was good for me. I could hide from her more easily. Unfortunately, there was only one kitchen.

I walked down the hallway and headed down the winding staircase, which spiraled past the top two floors before ending at the bottom floor. My bare feet made very little noise as I walked across the hardwood planks. I had just opened the fridge to get my organic milk when a door opened and closed somewhere in the house.

I froze and considered shoving the milk back in the fridge and hiding. I wasn't ready to face Nan yet. I needed coffee before I dealt with her. The heavy footsteps on the stairs weren't Nan's. Which made me even more nervous. Facing some strange man wasn't appealing, either. I wasn't dressed. I still had on my pajamas. Pink satin polka-dotted shorts and a matching tank top were all I had on. I glanced around for a hiding place, but before I could figure out what to do the footsteps landed on the bottom floor.

I was stuck . . . unless I hid behind the counter while he escaped. Maybe he wouldn't come this way. The front door was past the kitchen, but the back door was just as close to the stairs. I set my milk carton on the copper countertop and waited. The footsteps weren't heavy anymore. I barely heard them. Straining my ears, I tried to figure out where they were going.

It wasn't until it was too late to hide that I realized he was barefoot and headed my way. My eyes locked with Grant's as he stepped into the kitchen wearing nothing but a pair of black boxer briefs. He stopped when his eyes met mine. We stood there silently, staring at each other. The realization that he was the one who had woken me last night made my stomach knot up. I didn't want to think about him in bed with Nan.

But the realization doused me like a bucket of cold water. Grant was still sleeping with Nan. All that stuff he'd said to me was a lie. He had made me a promise, one I hadn't asked for and he had never intended to keep.

"Harlow?" he said, his voice thick from sleep. He'd been up most of the night. He must've been exhausted.

I didn't respond. I couldn't think of anything to say. I hadn't expected him to even be in Rosemary Beach. But he was here . . . and he was sleeping in Nan's bed.

I was an idiot.

**Three months ago . . .**

A knock on my bedroom door interrupted my favorite scene in a book I had read at least ten times. Annoyed, I laid down my Kindle. "Yes?"

The door opened slowly and Grant Carter stuck his ridiculously beautiful head into my room. His long hair, which curled at the ends and tucked neatly behind his ears, made a girl want to sit and just play with it for hours. I often wondered if it was as soft as it looked. His eyes twinkled as if he knew exactly what I was thinking, so I forced a scowl on my face. I never scowled, so it was a new thing that I reserved just for him.

It wasn't really fair. I disliked him on principle. He had been nothing but nice to me, but the fact he was in a relationship with Nan was enough for me to not like him. If a guy could like Nan then something was wrong with him.

"I ordered Chinese. Want to help me eat it? I got way too much." His blue eyes were so hard to look away from. They had been my downfall since the first time I laid eyes on him. That had been before I knew he was Nan's Grant.

"I'm not hungry," I replied, hoping my stomach didn't growl and give me away. I had been meaning to fix myself something to eat, but the book had sucked me in. Seeing Grant always made me want to escape into one of my stories where guys who looked like him fell in love with girls like me. Not girls like Nan.

"I don't believe you," he said, pushing my door open and walking into the room with a tray covered in boxes from the little Chinatown place my dad loved so much. "Help me eat. Just because I dated Nan doesn't make me tainted. You act like I've got a damn disease—and I'll be honest, it hurts my feelings."

Really? Was I hurting his feelings? I hadn't meant to. I didn't think he would really care. Besides, he was the one who ran off cursing the night we met when he found out who I was after he had made a move on me.

"*Dated?*" I asked, surprised with myself. "You're here waiting on her to show up. I don't think that's past tense." I sounded like a schoolteacher.

Grant chuckled and sat down beside me on the bed and set the tray down on the bedside table. "She's my friend. I'm checking in on her. Not dating her. Besides, I just got word that she's back in Rosemary."

See, *that*. Just that. He was her *friend*. What normal person was Nan's friend? None I knew of. "She's sleeping with the members of Naked Marathon. Surely you've seen her in the gossip magazines on Sellers's arm. Last week she made the news with Moon, and there was all kinds of talk about her breaking up the band. Which isn't going to happen."

Grant opened a carton of sweet-and-sour chicken and stuck a pair of chopsticks in it, then handed it to me. "Sweet-and-sour or honey chicken? You pick."

I took the sweet-and-sour. "This is fine. Thank you," I replied.

His smile grew. He hadn't expected me to take it.

"Good, I wanted the honey," he replied with a wink. I hated that my stomach fluttered. I didn't need that to start happening. Grant was on the other side of a line that I wasn't going to cross.

"It isn't my business who Nan is screwing. That's over between us. I'm just checking in on her. Making sure she's not about to go off the grid again. She's home now, so it's all good."

Why would he do that? What had she done to earn that kind of protectiveness from someone like Grant? "That's nice of you," I said because I didn't know what else to say. I took a bite of my chicken.

"You're gonna hold that against me, aren't you?" he asked, studying me in a way that only made me want to squirm.

"You can protect who you want, Grant. We're just sharing

some Chinese food. Doesn't matter what I think." I replied before putting more chicken in my mouth.

Grant frowned and then a small smile touched his lips. "I feel like we're doing this crazy-ass dance around each other every time I get around you. I don't play games. It ain't my thing, sugar. So let me be blunt," he said, setting his food back down on the table and turning his body so that he faced me completely. I tried to calm my racing heart. What was he doing? What was I going to do if he got any closer? Guys didn't flirt with me. They didn't come into my room. I was Kiro's weird, awkward daughter. Didn't Grant get that?

"I don't want you to hate me," he said, simply.

I didn't hate him. I shook my head. "I don't."

"Yeah, you do. I'm not used to people hating me. Especially beautiful girls," he said and flashed me a wicked grin.

He had called me beautiful. Did he really think that? Or was he feeling sorry for me because I was so socially inept?

"Harlow, do you realize that you're breathtaking? Just looking at you can become addictive."

Wow.

"That confused, flustered look on your face is all the answer I need. You don't have a clue how amazing you are. That's a shame," he said, reaching over and taking a strand of my hair and wrapping it around his finger. "It's a real shame."

I wasn't sure that I was breathing. My entire body had shut down. I couldn't move. Grant was touching me. And even though it was my hair, it felt so nice. I dropped my gaze to his hand and watched as his thumb gently ran over the hair he was holding.

"It's like silk," he said in a hushed voice. Like he didn't want anyone to hear him.

I just watched him. What was I supposed to say to him?

"Harlow," he said, leaning closer to me. I could feel his warm breath on my skin.

"Yes," I choked out, watching him closely as he moved toward me.

"I think about you. I dream about you," he said in a husky whisper against my ear. I shivered and felt my grip on my chicken loosen. God, please don't let me dump my food on myself.

"You're too sweet for me, but damned if I care," he said, then pressed a kiss to the skin under my ear. "I don't want you to hate me. I want you to forgive me for being with Nan. It's over."

The reminder of Nan was enough to snap me out of my trance, and I jumped up from the bed and walked across the room to stand far enough away that I felt safe.

I didn't look back at Grant. I kept my back to him and stared out the window. Maybe he would just leave. I felt my face grow hot. I had let him get so close. I had let him kiss my neck. What was I thinking?

"I shouldn't have said her name," he said in a defeated tone. He was perceptive. "Will you tell me what I can do to prove to you that I don't want Nan? That she was a moment of insanity and weakness? I was being a guy and she was there. I made a mistake."

He wanted me to forgive him about as much as I wanted to be able to forget Nan. I liked Grant. No . . . I fantasized about Grant. Since he'd cornered me at Rush and Blaire's wedding reception he had made it into my nightly fantasies. Even if he was someone I was afraid to trust. I liked looking at him.

I liked hearing his voice. I liked the way he smelled and the sound of his laugh. The way his mouth curled up on one side when he was amused. I also liked the tattoos I saw peeking out of the collar of his shirt. I wanted to know what they looked like.

"Can I have a chance? One to prove I'm not like Nan. I'm a pretty damn good friend. I just need you to give me a break."

I was typically a forgiving person. My grandmother had taught me to forgive. She had raised me to be a kind person and reminded me that everyone deserved a second chance. One day I might need a second chance myself.

I turned around and looked at Grant. He was still sitting on my bed. The dark blue T-shirt he was wearing fit his arms tightly and outlined the ripples on his chest. It also highlighted the color of his eyes. How was someone supposed to not trust him? "I'd like to be your friend," I said. I wasn't sure what else to say.

That crooked grin appeared. "You would? You're going to forgive me?"

I nodded and made myself take a step back toward the bed. "Yes. But don't . . . don't . . . do that again." I said, reaching up and touching the skin that still tingled from his lips.

Grant let out a defeated sigh and nodded. "That's gonna be hard, but I won't. Not until you ask me." He stopped and patted the spot where I had been sitting. I walked over and sat back down. Grant leaned forward. "But Harlow," he said.

His sexy male scent made me want to inhale deeply. "Yes?" I asked, hoping he wasn't about to touch me again. I seemed to forget myself when he did.

"You will ask me," he replied.

I opened my mouth to argue, but before I could he stuck a piece of honey chicken in my mouth. "Don't say it. I'll just get to say I told you so when you ask me. And I really hate to gloat. Especially to a girl I want to make smile, not slap me."

I managed to chew the chicken before the laughter bubbled up and escaped. He really was adorable. What he didn't realize was I could never give in. It wasn't fair to him. He didn't know the truth and I didn't want him to know. It changed how people looked at me. I couldn't stand the idea of Grant looking at me the way others had.

# Grant

**Present day**

I hadn't seen her since the night I got the call about Jace. The night I'd . . . the night I'd taken her virginity. *She'd been a virgin.* I hadn't expected that. It had been a first for me, too. I had never slept with a virgin before. Something about it affected me deeper than I was comfortable with. Even though I knew I wasn't ready for commitment in any form, I had wanted to stake a claim. I often wondered if that would have sent me running the next day, even if I hadn't gotten the call from Tripp.

And finally, here she was. No longer kept from me by her father, or whoever else had made sure I didn't get near her.

"Last night. It was you," she said, simply.

I took in her pajamas and felt like cursing and slamming my fist through the wall. I wasn't a violent guy. I never lost my cool, but right now I was close to it. Harlow was here. She'd heard me and Nan. *Holy hell!*

"You haven't called. I didn't realize." She stopped talking and shook her head. I couldn't find the right words. There weren't any. I had no explanation for this that she would understand. I watched as she put the milk back in the fridge and closed the door. She kept her head down and didn't look up again before walking around the counter and toward the door. I had to say something. I had to explain myself. I had fucking called. They never let me talk to her when I called the house. She never answered my damn calls when I called her phone. But, fuck, she didn't deserve this. Not when she'd trusted me with something as precious as her innocence.

"I guess it's me who gets to say I told you so this time," she said in a quiet voice before walking past me. The weight on my chest felt like someone had set a thousand bricks on it. I clenched my hands into fists and closed my eyes. What had I done? And why? Why was I letting Nan fuck up my life?

Why the hell had I drunk so much damn whiskey last night? I would have never come here had I been sober. And Harlow . . . Harlow . . . why was Harlow here? I turned and looked back toward the staircase. A door clicked closed. There was no slamming or yelling with Harlow. She wasn't that way. Any other woman would have cursed me and possibly slapped me then stormed up the stairs and slammed her door. But not Harlow. That made this even worse. If that was possible.

**Two months and three and a half weeks ago . . .**

Harlow stepped out of the house, looking unsure of herself. It had taken me twenty minutes to convince her to swim with me. She had made up all kinds of excuses. But I was pretty damn persuasive when I wanted to be. The oversized Slacker Demon concert T-shirt she was wearing covered up whatever swimsuit she'd finally put on. I had been waiting on her for half an hour. I was almost ready to go up to her room and pull her out here myself. I had just gotten back to L.A. a few hours ago. Being in Rosemary was hard when all I could think about was Harlow's sweet smile. I was anxious to be near her.

"About time. I thought you were gonna make me swim alone," I said, standing up from the lounger I had been reclining on while waiting.

Harlow blushed. "I'm sorry it took me so long."

As if she needed to apologize. There was no way a man could be even remotely annoyed with her. It was impossible. She was too damn sweet and innocently sexy, which was screwing with my head. There was no way she was that innocent. She was in college. She had to have dated before. In high school the guys would have been all over her.

"You're here now. Let's swim. It's warm out here today."

Harlow reached for the hem of her shirt and I considered diving in and not watching her take it off. It would be the polite thing to do, but hell if I could convince my eyes that looking away was the best idea. They were zoned in on her every move.

We had been . . . I wasn't sure what we had been doing. This was the strangest relationship—if you could call it that—I had ever been in. Harlow was letting me get closer every day but she still kept up her barriers. I hadn't managed to get my lips near her skin again.

My eyes drank in her long legs as the T-shirt slowly lifted, revealing a simple high-necked one-piece white bathing suit. I couldn't remember the last time I'd seen a girl my age in a one-piece swimsuit. But it was white. Holy fuck. I felt myself harden as my eyes traveled up from her legs to the nipple I could clearly see pebbled beneath the fabric.

I turned and dove into the water before I scared the hell out of her. I swam the length of the pool before coming up for air and turning to look at her. She was walking down into the pool through the sloping entrance. Damn, she was perfect. She lifted her eyes and smiled at me. It was a good thing my reaction to her was hidden under the water.

Once she was far enough in that the water touched her shoulders, she seemed to relax. Having her body on display made her nervous. It had been all over her face. I couldn't figure out why. It was like throwing me a challenge. I wanted her body completely on display for me. And I wanted her to like it. To want it.

"Come on, pretty girl. Come swim with the big boys," I teased. Her mouth puckered up in a frown. She didn't like me calling her pretty girl. Her reaction to it only made me want to do it more.

"I don't trust the big boys," she replied. Her head tilted to the side and she raised one eyebrow.

Chuckling to myself, I couldn't remember a time in my life that one female had entertained me so much. "Are you scared?"

Her eyebrows snapped together this time and I laughed harder. If you wanted Harlow to do something, then taunting her was the way to go. She didn't back down from a dare or a threat. There was a silent toughness in her that you didn't know existed until you spent time with her. "My pretty girl is getting all fired up. Come get me."

Harlow let out a small growl of frustration. "Stop calling me that."

"No," was my only reply.

"You drive me crazy."

I closed some of the space between us. "I drive most girls crazy, babe. It's what I do. And they like it."

A grin tugged at her lips but she was trying very hard to hold her frown. "I can't imagine why they would like it."

I stopped when I got a couple of inches from her body. "Same reason you like it. I'm so damn sexy, you can't stay away."

Harlow let out a laugh this time. "Is that so? If I recall, it's you who keeps showing up at my house. I'm not the one unable to stay away."

She had a point. I had just flown all the way back here from Florida just to see her. I reached out and rested my hand on her hip. Her whole body went rigid under my touch. "Okay, so maybe I can't seem to stay away, but you keep letting me in the house, pretty girl."

Harlow sighed. "Guess you got me there."

"So, see, I'm sexy and irresistible."

Harlow started to say something then stopped.

"You decide not to argue with me?" I asked, stepping close enough to her that our bodies were almost touching. One move and her breasts would brush up against my chest.

"What are you doing?" she asked. Her breathing was fast, and the nervous look in her eyes reminded me of a frightened deer.

"Just getting closer. You make me want to get closer."

Harlow took a deep breath and she glanced down at our bodies before looking back up at me. "I don't think friends do this," she said.

I pulled her up against my body, holding her hips firmly in both my hands. "They don't. But I don't think about my friends the way I think about you, either. Tell me you aren't attracted to me. Tell me you don't think about touching me or getting close to me."

If she said she didn't, I would back away. It would be hard, but I'd back away. I would give her the room she needed. I just wanted to hear her say she didn't want me, because I damn well wanted her.

"I'm not sure . . . I don't think . . . what I want is irrelevant. You and Nan . . ."

"Me and Nan are over. There is no me and Nan. But there is a me and you. Even if you don't want to admit it, it's there."

"I'm nothing like Nan."

"You think I don't know that? Damn, girl, if you were like Nan I wouldn't be here. I ended things with Nan because she's poison. You're everything she isn't."

Harlow's body began to slowly ease under my touch. I moved my thumbs against her waist in small circles, gently. "Most guys like me because of my dad. I keep my distance. I don't want to be a status symbol."

A sharp pain shot through my chest at her vulnerable words. Damn. Rush had lived with this same problem, but he hadn't been a girl. He'd been a guy who didn't care. He hadn't been looking for someone to want him just for him. Not until Blaire. Thinking about a guy using sweet Harlow just to get near her father pissed me off. If I could hunt down every bastard that had hurt her I would.

I lifted my hand and tilted her chin up so that she was looking me directly in the eyes. I wanted her to see I was serious. I wanted her to believe me. "Never would I use you to get near your dad. I've known Kiro all my life. Rush is my best friend. I'm not starstruck by the members or lifestyle of Slacker Demon. This is all about you. I want you. Just you, Harlow. Just you."

Tears prickled her big hazel eyes and she blinked rapidly. Had no one ever told her that?

"Will you kiss me now?" she whispered.

Damn. I felt like I was in junior high school again with my first crush. Five simple words from her and she had my hands trembling. I never expected her to ask me that. I wasn't giving her time to change her mind, either. Covering her soft lips with mine was like nirvana. She tasted so damn sweet. It was one of the reasons I'd started calling her sweet girl.

I licked her bottom lip because I couldn't get enough of her before exploring her mouth. Taking in her heat. Feeling her press her body against mine and her hands tangle in my hair. I was keeping her. I would do whatever I had to do to keep her. Hell, I'd move to L.A. if I had to. I wasn't letting her go. For the first time in my life I felt home.

"I told you so," I whispered against her lips before claiming her mouth again.

# Harlow

He had only called once after his friend had drowned. He'd been drunk and hadn't made much sense. I had hoped he would call again the next day, but he hadn't. I knew he was grieving and I decided it was a sign from God that he was fixing things. I had messed it up and allowed Grant to get close to me, and I hadn't told him. I was lucky he never really cared for me. I had thought he did, and for a moment I let myself live in that fantasy.

I knew better now. The sweet words he'd spoken had all been a ploy, and they had all worked on me. I had taken them hook, line, and sinker. If I could take back that night, I would. I wasn't going to romanticize it anymore. I had given him a part of myself I couldn't get back. He had taken my virginity and run. For once I had let myself pretend.

I sat on the bed and stared out the window at the gulf outside. This was going to be an even tougher nine months than I'd first imagined. Not only did I have to deal with Nan, but I had to deal with Grant and Nan. I wouldn't let it hurt me. I was stronger than that. Grant had taken my virginity but I had

23

already been robbed of my innocence. Loving Jeremiah Duke had done that to me. I'd thought he loved me; I had thought he was my forever. He was so attentive and sweet. He carried my books at school and treated me with such care. I had told him the truth and he had pretended it didn't matter.

Then I'd found him behind the bleachers after his football practice with Nikki Sharp's cheerleading skirt pulled up and his shorts pulled down as he screwed her up against the cement wall. That had been it for me. I realized then that I was just Kiro's daughter, and I was broken. I was only wanted for my social status. Nothing about me was special. That's all guys saw when they looked at me.

Except Grant.

He had been different. I hadn't been Kiro's daughter to him. I'd just been a challenge. Once he got the goods, he was done. My grandmama had always warned me about guys like him. She'd be so let down if she could see me now. I shook my head. I couldn't think about that. It only made me feel worse. I was a survivor and I didn't dwell on things. Feeling sorry for myself never got me anywhere. It wasn't something I did. Wherever I was and whatever situation I was put in, I survived. I was good at it. Grandmama always said, "Girl, you better hold that head up high and don't let 'em see you fall. You show 'em the steel in that spine. I ain't raisin' a spoiled princess. I'm raisin' a woman. A hard-working, self-sufficient, 'don't need no man' woman. You hear me?" Never once did she act like there was anything wrong with me. She believed I was whole. I was fine. And at times I believed it, too.

Standing back up, I went to take a shower. I would get ready and go to the club and play tennis. They had a tennis pro there whom I could work with. Then I would play a round of golf. I would fill my days with things I could do without friends. Maybe even lie out at the club's pool. I was going to make it through this.

**Two months and three weeks ago . . .**

The morning after Grant had kissed me in the pool, he was gone. The way he'd acted after kissing me had been strange. I wasn't sure what was wrong or if he had just regretted it and didn't know how to get away from me. Waking up the next morning without Grant there had answered that question.

Dad was also gone. He hadn't come home from his latest party binge, but then I wasn't surprised by that. Grant's running off had hurt me. I hated that I felt anything for him. Kissing him had been a mistake. I wasn't his type. I never wanted to be his type. Nan was not someone a sane person would desire to be with.

Locking myself up in my room to read didn't sound as appealing as it had before Grant. Instead, I threw myself into tennis and swimming. I pushed all thoughts of Grant's face out of my mind the best that I could. Someone should've put a warning label on his lips: *Beware, don't touch.* They were hard to forget.

Three days after Grant had disappeared, I was outside swimming. Today I had successfully managed to push all thoughts of Grant to the back of my mind. So when my head broke the water to find Grant Carter standing there, looking down at me, I wasn't sure if I was imagining things or if he was really there.

I pushed my wet hair back and wiped the water from my eyes. Then I opened them again, and there he stood. Still there.

"Hey," he said with his sexy grin. I wanted to hurl something at him to make that smile go away. It needed a warning label, too.

I wasn't in the mood to talk to him. "Nan isn't here," I replied. She hadn't been back since she'd left for Rosemary the last time. I was sure that was where Grant had run off to as well. He had gone to find her. Like he always did.

"Yeah, I know," he replied.

I really should've gone back to swimming and ignored him. It was the smart thing to do. But then he could possibly take that as an invitation to join me. "What do you need?" I asked, in the most annoyed tone I could muster.

"I came to see you. It seems once a guy kisses you, you're hard to forget," he replied.

Not what I had been expecting. I swallowed the nervous knot in my throat. I would cave and forgive him too easily if he started saying things like that. Where had my backbone gone? I used to be stronger than this.

"You're mad because I left," he said.

I thought about retorting and changed my mind. That would only give him more power. He didn't need to know he affected me at all.

"It was a jackass thing to do. But you scared me. I like to flirt with beautiful girls, but I don't handle it well when one simple kiss makes my fucking head spin. You make me want things and feel a certain way. I'm not ready for that."

I was expecting a lame *I'm sorry*; not that. "Oh," was the only thing I could come up with. What did it mean, exactly, that our kiss made his head spin? Was that a good thing? It sounded like it . . . maybe.

Grant ran a hand through his long, unruly hair and let out a frustrated sigh. "I shouldn't have left you without an explanation. It was unfair and I was only thinking of myself. I'm good at that. I just . . . what can I do to get you to forgive me?"

He still wasn't asking for forgiveness. He was asking how to get forgiveness. Had anyone ever asked me how to get forgiveness before? How . . . unique.

Warning bells were going off in my head loudly, but somehow I ignored that. Because my heart wanted to forgive him. I didn't want to push him away. No one ever took this much time to get to know me. Being lonely was something I had grown used to. Having someone here who wanted to get to know me bad enough to admit he was wrong, someone who cared to ask me how he could fix it, meant more than he realized.

"Don't do it again," I replied.

Grant's eyes went wide and then a slow smile slid across his handsome face. "I won't."

I stepped back as he started tugging his shirt over his head. He threw it aside and slipped off his shoes, and then his eyes lifted to meet mine. "I'm not leaving this time. When you get tired of me, you'll have to force me out."

I couldn't keep the silly smile off my face.

**Two months and two weeks ago . . .**

When the door to my room clicked behind us, I knew this was it. For a week, we had been kissing and touching. It was hard for us to keep our hands off each other. Grant made me feel things I didn't know were possible. He showed me what a real orgasm was. He had also taught me that screaming out in pleasure was okay. He liked it when I was loud. It always made him more frantic. His breathing would accelerate and his eyes would almost glow from excitement.

But tonight, I wanted more. I wasn't going to stop things when they got too far. I wasn't going to make him keep my shirt on. I was going to let us do what we both wanted. I was twenty years old. It was time I became a real woman and had sex. I was holding on to my virginity like some grand prize, and I wanted to experience a total connection with another human being. I wanted to know what it felt like to have Grant inside me. To get as close to each other as possible. I wanted this experience.

Grant's arms wrapped around me from behind as his mouth touched my neck and began taking small nibbles. That always made my knees a little weak. "You taste too damn good," he whispered in my ear, making me tremble. "I want your shirt off. I've been thinking about pulling one of your nipples into my mouth all week."

His hands found my hem and pulled my shirt up over my head, then he unsnapped my bra. He pulled it from my body and froze. I knew he would see it. I was prepared for that. His hand reached out and ran along the line across my chest that was so faint now, it wasn't even very noticeable.

"What is this?" he asked.

"I was a preemie. I was born ten weeks too early. I had some surgeries before I was in the clear." I didn't want to explain anymore. He didn't need to know the truth. That was enough. He lowered his mouth to my chest and instead of kissing my breasts he kissed the scar. I closed my eyes because it made me feel guilty for not being completely honest. Then both his large, tanned hands covered my breasts and I sighed from the pleasure of it.

"Does that feel good, pretty girl?"

I managed a nod as he began to kiss my neck and squeeze my nipples gently.

"That's it, baby, arch that back for me."

I hadn't even realized I was doing it but I was. I couldn't get close enough to his touch. The way he made me feel was intoxicating. I craved it. Grant had opened up this world to me with so much pleasure and excitement that I hadn't realized existed.

"Lie down on your back. I want to kiss these needy little nipples."

I didn't argue. I wanted it, too. I climbed on the bed and lay back just in time to see Grant pull his shirt over his head. See the tattoo on his shoulder that came down over his right pec. I wasn't sure what it was, but it was sexy. It looked like some sort of tribal print. Then some Chinese symbols were on his chest just above his pecs. I planned on asking him about them, but not now.

He reached for his jeans and unbuttoned them. I was fascinated with his lower abdomen. All those tight ripples in his stomach, the way his hipbones stuck out, and the small patch of hair that started low, just under the band of his underwear. I wanted to see exactly what it looked like under there, but until tonight I hadn't gotten a chance. Grant always got my panties off but he said he needed to keep his pants on if he was going to keep his head straight. I didn't push. But I wanted to see.

I lay there as he crawled over me and stared down at me with a sexy, hungry look in his eyes. He didn't break his gaze as he lowered his mouth to my breast and pulled a nipple into his mouth. I watched him. It made my stomach quiver and I had to squeeze my legs together to ease the ache between them.

He let it pop out of his mouth, then stuck his tongue out and flicked it with a grin before moving over and giving the other one the same attention.

I grabbed handfuls of the covers underneath me to keep from crying out. It felt so good. The warmth of his mouth anywhere on my body was amazing, but when he found the sensitive areas it made it even more incredible.

When that nipple popped free of his mouth he started kissing down my stomach, and I knew his next step would be to pull my shorts off. He would use his mouth to send me flying off into bliss. I wanted more than that tonight.

"Take off your pants," I said.

He froze and his eyes lifted back to me as he pressed a kiss just below my belly button. "You know the rules. I can't do that. I don't trust myself."

I swallowed against the nervous knot in my throat. "I want . . . I want you to take your pants off. I'm not worried about keeping you from doing anything . . ." I wasn't sure how you told a guy you were ready. I hadn't ever been in that position before.

Grant frowned for a moment, then his eyes flashed with that bright, excited gleam he would get when I came down from the highs he sent me on. "Are you telling me I can finally feel just how fucking amazing you are?"

I had been prepared for him to say fuck me or screw me

but this . . . this was better. It was real. Calling it anything more or making it romantic would cheapen it somehow. This was about mutual attraction, and I got that. I didn't need pretty words that he didn't mean. I needed honesty, and he seemed to get that.

Grant moved over me and placed a hand on each side of my head as he looked down into my eyes. "We don't have to do this. I'm not asking for it. If you aren't ready, I'm good with that. I'll wait."

Because of that reason alone, I was ready. He meant what he was saying. He didn't want to push me. "I want this . . . I want you."

"Fuck," Grant growled and pushed himself off the bed. He reached into his pocket and pulled out a condom. I wasn't sure what I thought about that but I was glad he was prepared, even if it bothered me a little bit. He tossed it on the bed. Then, finally, I got to see him unzip his jeans. He let them fall to the floor along with the white boxer briefs he was wearing. I gasped. I had felt it through his jeans many times; once I had rubbed against it until I'd gotten off. But never had I imagined it was so . . . big. I wasn't sure it was going to fit.

He didn't leave me time to get too worried about it. He reached up and pulled off my shorts and panties with one firm tug, then he was back on the bed. His hands took both my knees and moved my legs apart. I hadn't been ready for him to just go at it. I needed to be eased into this . . .

Grant began kissing the inside of my leg, and he slowly made his way to where I wanted his mouth the most. Once his kiss pressed the top of my mound and I felt his tongue take a long slow trail down to my core, I was ready. My hands clenched the covers as I cried out in relief as he pulled my clit into his mouth.

The first time he'd done this, I'd been embarrassed until he had me crying out and panting from the highest level of pleasure. But he hadn't let up—he'd done it again. When he'd left me that night I'd been exhausted and unable to move.

I had no one to compare him to, but I was positive that Grant was an expert at this. I didn't want to dwell on that, either. But the fact was he knew what he was doing. He could make me lose control, and I never lost control.

I felt the familiar building and tightening inside me and my body got excited. It knew how good it felt to reach that height that Grant took me to so easily. Then he stopped and I wanted to scream in protest. I was almost there.

He moved up my body, pressing kisses on my warm, sensitive skin as he worked his way up to my neck.

"I'm gonna put that condom on now," he whispered as he moved over to grab the small packet I'd forgotten about. He ripped it open and I took in the sight of him rolling the protective covering over his large length.

"You look scared," he said, not moving back to me. I lifted my eyes to look up at him.

"Will it fit?" I asked.

A crooked grin tugged at his lips. "Yes, sweet girl. It will."

I wasn't so sure. He seemed optimistic.

Grant went back to kissing my neck and nibbling my ear as his body lowered between my open legs. I was going to do this. I wanted it.

"You seem tense. Have you had a bad experience?" Grant asked with a frown, puckering his brow. He looked upset.

I shook my head. No, I hadn't had a bad experience. I had no experience. Didn't he know that? I mean, we hadn't talked about it but surely he had figured it out by now.

"It's just, I know what to expect, I think . . . from what I've heard."

His entire body went rigid as he held himself over me. His frown transformed into a look of surprise. "What are you saying? Of course you've . . ."

He didn't know. I guess he hadn't figured it out after all. "This is my first time."

Grant's eyes snapped closed and he let out a muttered curse. Did he not like to do it with virgins? Was that a bad thing? I wanted to put some distance between us. For the first time, I felt vulnerable.

He opened his eyes and stared down at me. The tenderness in them took me off guard. He tucked his head into the curve of my neck and shoulder and drew a deep breath. I waited silently.

"You chose me" was all he said. His warm breath against my skin made me shiver, and his body mimicked mine. He pulled back and looked at me. "I will make this good for you. I swear."

I never doubted that he would. I knew it was going to hurt me at first. I wasn't an idiot about how this worked. I also knew I probably wouldn't reach an orgasm this time, but that wasn't what this was about. I wanted Grant inside me. I wanted to feel closer to him than I had ever been to anyone. That was all I wanted from this.

Grant pressed his lips to mine gently, then lowered his body until I felt the head of his cock pressing against me. It excited me as much as it scared me. I lifted my hips to reassure him and he slid inside me. When he reached the barrier his eyes locked on mine as he rocked his hips in one swift thrust. I didn't cry from the pain—it was only a burn. He had slid completely inside me and gone still.

"You're so fucking tight," he said in a hoarse groan. "Damn. It feels like," he panted and ducked his head and took a deep breath, "a hot satin glove squeezing me just right. God, baby."

I wasn't sure what all that meant, but the way he was panting above me sounded like this felt good to him. It was more than I had expected. I was full. Grant was inside me and I felt complete. I wanted him here.

"I gotta move, but damn, I'm afraid to," he said as he slowly pulled out of me then sank back inside me. A low sound came from his chest, which sent pleasure coursing through me. Just seeing him in this much pleasure from being inside me was a major turn-on. I spread my knees and he sank deeper into me and let out a curse that sounded like it had been torn from his chest.

My clit throbbed from just hearing his voice. I was climbing toward that release I recognized and it made me want to beg him to move more. Move harder. Each time he filled me he rubbed against my clit and massaged something inside me. I wasn't sure what it was but it felt so good.

"Fucking amazing," he groaned before covering my mouth in a ravenous kiss. He had never kissed me like this before. He was losing control the same way I did when he kissed between my legs. I was reaching that point with him. Seeing him react this way was making my body respond in ways I didn't know it could.

"It feels good now," I assured him.

He tensed and then moved to lower his head back to the corner of my neck and shoulder. "The pain is completely gone?" he asked with a low, strangled moan.

"Yes," I replied. The little sting that was still there was smothered by the pleasure.

He lifted himself up and his gaze locked with mine. His neck muscles flexed and stuck out as his jaw went rigid, like he was holding onto something as hard as he could. "This is . . . this is more than . . . ," he closed his eyes and a pained look came over his face. "I can't hold out much longer. I'm so close."

His words were all I needed to send me spiraling off to that place I knew he was sending me. I heard him shout out my name as I screamed his and lifted my hips to meet his last thrust. I wrapped my legs around his waist to keep him there. I wanted to feel each spasm of ecstasy with him inside me. I didn't want him to move.

I let each cry free as I clung to him.

"Never been that fucking amazing. You've ruined me. Fucking ruined me. I can't not have this," he said in my ear as he breathed heavily and his body jerked against me.

I agreed. I wanted this. I never imagined that this was what I was missing. I wasn't about to let this go. I needed more. My fear of the truth was pushed aside. I couldn't stop this. Not now.

# Grant

**Present day**

If I went upstairs after her, there was a chance that Nan would get out of bed and catch me or overhear us. I wasn't scared of Nan, but I was scared of what she'd do to Harlow. I was positive Harlow wasn't here by choice. Nan knew she was here last night when she brought me back. She was playing a game here. There was an ulterior motive, but then there always was with Nan. And I'd walked right fucking into it. Literally.

Kiro wasn't a fan of Nan and he adored Harlow. I couldn't imagine why he would send Harlow down here to live with Nan. He owned this house, so I was sure that was the only reason Nan had let Harlow live here. Kiro hadn't given her an option. There was no guessing there.

"You're still here? Why?" Nan asked as she walked past me in nothing but a pair of panties that did nothing to cover her ass and a tiny tank top. Once, that had heated my blood. Her body would heat any man's blood. But not anymore. I was over that. Sex with her was empty. So incredibly empty.

"I was gonna get coffee before I left but I can leave without it," I said, turning to head to the stairs.

"You can have some damn coffee if you want it. Then leave. I have things to do today," she called out behind me.

I wasn't staying here. I'd get Harlow alone, but not here. "No thanks. You're awake now. It's time to leave," I replied.

This was the last time. She thought I was a sex toy she could pull out and play with, and the fact was I had been. But I'd been closing my eyes and pretending like she was someone else. It never felt as good, but it helped me deal.

The guilt had been eating me alive. Leaving Harlow only hours after I had been with her to race home on Slacker Demon's private jet and face the loss of a friend had broken me. Life was short. It had never been real to me before, but watching Jace lowered into the cold, hard ground had been a wake-up call. How long did we have? Seeing Bethy buckled over, sobbing at his loss, made me realize that kind of pain would be unbearable. She would have to live the rest of her life without him. That was scary as hell.

I had never loved anyone the way she had loved Jace. But I was close . . . I had been falling but then I stepped back. I couldn't be that open. I couldn't do that. What if I let myself be completely owned by Harlow? I knew now how easy it would be. She was the one for me. If I let her, she would be the one to own my soul. I couldn't do it.

Each heart-wrenching sob that had torn from Bethy had been like a bucket of ice water poured over me. I had watched Rush as he held his wife, Blaire, in his arms, and she had cried silently against him. And I'd seen it there on his face. He had given his soul. He was thinking the same thing, but it was too late for him.

He was vulnerable. If he lost her he wouldn't be able to survive it. She would take every ounce of life in him with her. He couldn't breathe without her. I'd left that day and drank until the idea of Harlow was numb. The sweet taste of her mouth was a blur, and the way she'd felt when I'd been inside her was a memory.

Harlow scared me. What I felt for her scared me. I had fought going back to her. I had been tormented with the memories of how her smile made my chest swell, and the way she made those innocent little sighs of pleasure. Then that night . . . that one incredible, mind-blowing night. I was afraid I would never be able to wash it away and move on. That was a power I had never allowed anyone to have over me. When Harlow didn't respond to my calls and her dad warned me to stay away, I finally forced myself to push those memories to the back of my mind. Whiskey helped. When I didn't have whiskey she was hard to forget. Even with whiskey, I remembered her—it just hurt less.

My need to see her had started to control me, and I had called Dean Finlay to get some help. He had told me that Kiro would have me arrested if I stepped foot on their property. He wasn't happy with how I had used Harlow. Kiro believed I had slept with Harlow while I was still sleeping with Nan. I tried to explain and defend myself, but Dean had hung up on me.

So I'd drunk even more, because when I was sober the need for her returned. Before, I had done it to deal with Nan's shit. But now I needed it more. I needed to forget what I'd done to someone so innocent and undeserving. I'd done this for two months. It helped me deal with the loss of Jace, and the taste of something I'd had but destroyed.

After all that . . . Kiro had sent Harlow here. To sit right under my nose without his security and protection. It was confusing as hell.

I reached Nan's room and the sick feeling in my stomach returned. This felt dirty. Sex for fun had never felt dirty but this . . . it felt fucking disgusting. I hated myself. I grabbed my jeans and jerked them on and slipped my T-shirt over my head before grabbing my boots and shoving my feet into them.

I didn't tell Nan bye. She didn't care and I didn't want to. I just got the hell away from there. I needed to get clean. I wanted to wash her off me. Then I was going to call Harlow. I had to find a way to explain. I just hoped she'd let me.

The sporty little black Audi sitting in the driveway right beside my truck had been a kick in the gut. Why hadn't I noticed it last night? I should have known someone was here. Too much damn whiskey. That's why I didn't notice.

Jerking the keys out of my pocket, I slammed my car door, furious with myself, and cranked the engine. I wouldn't be drinking today. Or any damn day from here on out. I couldn't do that anymore. I had to find a way to deal with Harlow being here, and get her to understand why I had backed away.

I just hoped she would understand. I didn't want her to be hurt. But as much as I wanted her, the fear of being that vulnerable to one person was stronger. She had trusted me and I had betrayed her. I wouldn't forgive myself for that.

I needed to talk to Rush. He was the only one I could talk to. We might not have been brothers by blood, but he was my brother. He had been since I was a kid. He was the only person in my life I'd ever let get that close. Not even my father truly knew me. He had never really tried. And my mom . . . she was a whole other story.

I called Rush's number before pulling out of Nan's driveway.

"Yeah," he said. The sound of a baby's laughter came through on the other line.

"I need to talk. You keeping Nate today?" I asked. Rush spent more time with his son, Nate, than any dad I knew. I would say it was because he was making sure he gave his kid something neither he nor I'd had, but I knew better. He adored that kid. He adored his wife. Getting him away from them wasn't easy.

"Blaire's here. We were headed out to the beach, but if this is important you know she won't mind me leaving for an hour or so." He had picked up on the urgency in my voice.

"If she doesn't mind. I really need to talk."

"Let me finish putting sunblock on the little man and help her get set up outside. Then I'll head over to your place."

"I'm headed to the club. Meet me there. And thanks," I said.

"Only for you," he replied, and I understood. He didn't make time for anyone outside of Nate and Blaire except for me. It was our bond.

"Tell Blaire thanks for me, too."

"Okay. See you in a few."

I hung up the phone and threw it over to the passenger's seat and headed to the club.

# Harlow

Finding the club was easy. Rosemary Beach was a small coastal town; it couldn't even be called a city. It was where the elite lived and vacationed. After driving through it and seeing the houses up and down the gulf front, I understood why Nan wanted to live here.

Pulling up to the front gate of the club, I flashed my member's pass that Daddy had given to me at the gatekeeper. He opened the large iron gates for me to enter and I followed the signs toward valet parking. I didn't want to figure out where the parking lot was, and I could ask the valet how to get to the tennis courts.

A young guy in a white polo and white shorts walked toward my car when I pulled up to the valet. I reached into the backseat and grabbed my racquet before he opened my door.

"Good morning, Miss," he said with a friendly smile. His long blond hair fell over one eye and he tucked it back behind his ear. I imagined that he was a surfer. He looked like one.

"Good morning," I replied, pulling my bag over my shoulder. "I'm new here. Can you tell me where I can find the tennis courts?"

He nodded. "Go into the main entrance here. Take the first

left and head to the double doors leading out onto the back veranda. Go down the stairs then take a right. You'll see the courts straight ahead."

That sounded easy enough. "Thank you," I replied, handing the young guy my keys.

"Can I see your card, Miss? I need to register your car into the system."

I reached inside the car and got the card off my dashboard and handed it to him.

He quickly read it then ran it through a card reader before handing it back to me. "Just let us know when you're ready for it, Miss Manning," he replied.

"Thank you." I thought about telling him he could call me Harlow but there was no point. He would probably get in trouble with management if he were ever caught calling me by my first name.

I headed inside. The fact that I knew I wasn't going to run into Nan here was the most relief I'd had all morning. A man dressed like the guy outside opened the door for me, and I followed the valet's directions to the tennis courts.

I passed a restaurant on my way and decided I would come back for lunch. It looked nice and the food smelled amazing from out here. A girl in white shorts and a white polo stopped in front of me. A slow smile touched her face. Her brown hair was pulled up high in a ponytail, and it was obvious she was an employee—her outfit was the same as those of the men who'd helped me, only more fitted. But she looked familiar.

"Harlow?" she asked.

I recognized her. I had met her at Rush and Blaire's wedding. "Yes," I replied, frustrated because I couldn't remember her name. Grant had messed with my head that day and I couldn't remember much more than my conversation with him.

"I'm Bethy. Blaire's friend. We met at the wedding," she said.

I felt my face heat up. I hated not remembering people. It was part of my socially inept thing. "I remember," I replied with a smile. "It's nice to see you again." I hoped that was the correct thing to say and that I didn't sound like an idiot, because I sure felt like one.

Bethy's expression was friendly, but there was a sadness in her eyes. "I understand. You met a lot of people that day. I didn't know you were in town."

I liked this girl. She was making me feel comfortable. That was rare. "I'm here while my dad's on tour. He sent me to live with Nan."

Bethy's eyes went wide and she let out a low whistle. "Damn. I thought you were the daughter he liked."

She obviously was very close to Blaire and knew exactly what our family situation was like. "He bought Nan the house here, but in return I get to live in it, too, when he's on tour. He doesn't like leaving me alone in L.A.," I explained, trying not to sound too defensive about Dad.

Bethy let out a long sigh. "Personally, I'd brave L.A. if I were you."

I felt like laughing but I didn't. I bit my lip to keep it in.

"You know I'm right. The bitch hates you," Bethy said. "She hates Blaire, too, so the two of you should team up and join forces."

"I really like Blaire. I'm so glad Rush found her."

Bethy studied me a moment. "I guess you and Rush have

a lot in common. You two were practically raised by Slacker Demon."

There was also my brother Mase. No one ever mentioned him. He lived with his mother on a ranch in Texas. Dad had gone to see him several times that I knew of, but he rarely came to L.A. He liked his life in Texas. He was also very close to his stepfather. "Yeah. We've seen a lot," I replied, deciding not to mention Mase. That would only lead to questions I wasn't sure how to answer. Dad hadn't seen Mase in over a year but Mase called me at least once a month to check in with me and see how I was. It gave me a chance to ask him about his life. My grandmama used to make sure I saw Mase several times a year. I hadn't seen him since she passed away. I never told Dad about it because I worried that he would be hurt that Mase didn't reach out to him that way.

"Well, I'm glad you're in Rosemary, although I wish you had better accommodations. You need help finding anything around here?" she asked, then looked down at my tennis skirt and the racquet over my arm and smiled. "You're headed to the tennis courts. Follow me. I need to make sure you don't get molested by Nelton, our sleazy tennis pro. We have a much nicer pro, Adam. That's who you need."

Good to know. Stay away from Nelton. She spun around and we headed toward the doors. Her ponytail swished back and forth as she went, but there was no bounce to her step. Even though I didn't know her very well, that seemed odd.

We headed out the door and she waved at several people. Most of them members. It was interesting that she was on friendly terms with members yet she worked here. I wasn't used to that sort of country club. I liked it. Very much.

"So you play tennis a lot?" Bethy asked, glancing back at me.

"At Dad's place they have a court. I use it for exercise and just to have something to do. Gives me time to think."

"And here you're going to use it to get away from Nan. Good idea," Bethy replied.

This time I did smile.

A tall, blond man with a dark tan and green eyes saw us walking his way and his eyes began to travel down my body. I didn't like it at all. The visor he was wearing was turned around backward and he was dressed in an all-white tennis outfit.

"Not for you, Nelton. Stick to your cougars. I'm looking for Adam," Bethy told the man, and I found myself moving closer to her as we passed him.

"Why don't you let her decide who she wants? I got a free hour for that one," he replied.

"Yuck, ew, go away," Bethy snapped, and kept walking.

I was really thankful for Bethy right then.

"Sorry. Nelton thinks he's God's gift to women. If he weren't so creepy he'd be attractive but he's just . . . ugh. The older women love him, though. Adam is new. Woods, the owner of Kerrington Club, hired Adam two weeks ago—or maybe I should say Della, Woods's fiancée, hired Adam two weeks ago. She wasn't a fan of Nelton and wanted another option out here."

I didn't know Della but I liked her for that reason alone.

"Adam," Bethy called out, and I looked out on the court to see a tall, muscular man turn around. His hair was red. Maybe more of a strawberry blond from being out in the sun so much. He had a white sweatband around his head, and he was also wearing the white tennis outfit that Nelton had been wearing. I noticed the words "Kerrington Club" stitched on his shirt in small, scripted letters and "Tennis Pro" under it.

Adam came jogging over to us with a smile on his face. As he got closer, his clear blue eyes came into focus. They were startling and very pale. He wasn't as tan as Nelson—he was more on the fair side. He even had freckles on his muscular arms. He would be what my grandmama called a ginger.

"Hey, Bethy, what's up?" he asked, smiling at Bethy and glancing over at me with a grin then back to Bethy.

"I have a new member. She's a friend of Rush's and, unfortunately, Nan's half-sister. We won't hold that against her. Like Rush, she's nothing like Nan. Anyway, she wants to play. Set her up and schedule her; she's gonna need some place to escape while she's living with the wicked bitch. Anyway, Harlow, this is Adam. Adam, meet Harlow."

Bethy really hated Nan.

"Nice to meet you, Harlow," he said, holding out his hand. I slipped mine in his and shook it. It was brief. Nothing awkward or uncomfortable. I didn't like shaking hands or touching people I had just met.

"I have a couple of openings in my schedule I need to fill. Nelton stays pretty booked and he gets most of the regulars," Adam informed us. His teeth were perfectly straight and very white. I had a thing for pretty teeth.

"Okay then. My job is done," Bethy said, then turned to me. "You're safe with Adam. He's not a creeper. Enjoy your day."

"Thank you for your help," I replied.

Bethy flashed a smile, but again the sadness in her eyes was there. "No problem. Blaire has sung your praises. I wanted to make sure I took care of you for her."

I nodded and Bethy waved back at Adam before heading back to where we came from.

"Why don't we look at my schedule over here on the Mac and set up your daily sessions? That is, if you're coming every day."

"Yes. I'm going to need something to do," I assured him. Adam was easy to be around, and the idea of having something to look forward to and someone to talk to, even if it was about tennis, sounded appealing. Besides, he was attractive and his smile made his eyes twinkle. I liked that. I liked it a lot.

# Grant

Harlow wasn't answering my calls, dammit. Just like before. She was shutting me out. The look on her face this morning had been so painful. She hadn't answered my calls and she believed I had been fucking Nan all along. It was why she was shutting me out . . . right? I had caved and started sleeping with Nan again when I realized Harlow wasn't letting me into her stone fortress. I had tried to wipe her from my mind. It hadn't worked. But I was fucking trying. The hurt, betrayed look in her eyes was eating me alive. What was she thinking? Had I gotten all this wrong?

I needed to talk to her.

I stalked into the club and almost ran over Bethy. I hadn't seen much of her over the past few months. She'd stayed to herself and kept busy with work.

"Hey," I said as she stopped and looked up at me with a forced smile.

"Hi" was her only response.

"What's up?" It was an empty question but I didn't know what else to say. Out of all of us, she'd suffered the loss of Jace the most.

She shrugged. "Headed to work. Just got Harlow signed up

with Adam, the new tennis pro, so now my good deed for the day is done."

Harlow.

"Harlow's on the tennis courts?" I asked, trying not to take off running in that direction.

Bethy nodded. "Yep. Hiding from Nan for the day. I feel sorry for the poor girl. But then you wouldn't understand anyone's dislike of Nan," she replied and rolled her eyes before stepping around me and walking out the door.

I wanted to defend myself but I was too focused on getting to Harlow.

When I stepped onto the brick sidewalk toward the courts, I noticed Nelton with Thad's mother. I was pretty sure Thad's mom wasn't one of Nelton's groupies. She was a nice lady. I couldn't imagine her sleeping around on her husband. Besides, she wouldn't do anything to let Thad down. The boy was spoiled and lucky as hell.

I walked past them and my gaze immediately singled out Harlow. She had a pinched, determined frown on her face as she hit every ball Adam sent her way. She also looked like a fucking dream in that skirt.

"That's it, girl," Adam called out in appreciation. I didn't like his tone of voice. He seemed too happy for her. Too . . . interested.

"We're gonna take it up a notch. Think you can handle it?" he asked.

"Bring it on." She stopped when her eyes found me. I could see the series of emotions before she closed them off and turned her eyes back toward Adam. "Give me a minute."

Adam had turned and was looking my way. I could feel his

gaze on me but I wasn't taking my eyes off her in case she got away.

She reached for her towel and wiped the sweat from her face and neck then grabbed her water bottle and took a long swig. I waited patiently, enjoying the way she moved. I had never seen anyone quite as poised as Harlow. She had this graceful, polished way of doing things. Even when she was out here sweating, she reminded me of some sort of royalty.

Her shoulders lifted and fell as she took a deep breath, then she turned to walk toward me. There was a determined gleam in her eyes. It did nothing to deter me. If anything, I wanted to grab her and kiss her until we both forgot the past two months.

"What do you need?" she asked, keeping a good foot of distance between us. The uptight, cold, sexy-as-hell tone to her voice was one I was familiar with. This had been the Harlow before I'd brought her Chinese food and convinced her to trust me.

"We need to talk. There's a lot I need to explain," I said.

Harlow cocked an eyebrow. "I'm not deaf or blind. No need to explain. I understand completely."

Dammit. "Harlow, last night is not what you think. You wouldn't talk to me. I called and you shut me out. What was I supposed to do? I was . . . Hell, I've been trying to forget you. To forget us. Because that's what you were forcing me to do. And last night I was so fucking trashed I didn't know my name."

Harlow straightened her shoulders, and she stared at me as a slow, angry rage lit her big, heartbreaking eyes. It didn't look promising. "I'm not an idiot. I know that you never called me except for that one time, and then you were too drunk to know your own name. Don't patronize me to make yourself feel better. I'm a big girl, and thanks to you I'm not nearly as naïve as I once was. I've learned a few hard lessons." She swallowed hard and shook her head. "No. We have nothing to talk about, Grant. Talking time is over. Please, go to Nan. Enjoy her all you want. I'm not your concern, nor will I ever be." She turned and started to walk back onto the court.

I reached out and grabbed her arm to stop her. I had to say something. I had to get her to listen to me. This whole time I thought Kiro had told her I was sleeping with Nan. I wasn't sure where Kiro got his info or if he was just assuming it, but from what Dean had told me that was why Harlow was ignoring my calls.

"If you didn't know about me and Nan before, then why have you been ignoring my calls?"

Harlow stopped and didn't try to jerk her arm free from my grasp. She stood there, so calm. The females I knew did not deal with their emotions like this. They were loud. They yelled, screamed, and threw shit. Harlow was so unemotional.

"You called once. You were drunk. You never called again. Now please let go of my arm. I have forty minutes left with Adam and I'd like to use my time properly."

"I did fucking call you. A million times! You wouldn't answer. I called the house and got threatened by your dad. Even Dean warned me off. I thought that was what you wanted. I need to explain."

She spun around and the fire behind her eyes startled me. "No, Grant, you don't. I'm a real smart girl and I'd know if I missed a call. You didn't call." She jerked her arm free and headed for her side of the court.

This was not the way I had imagined this going. And I didn't have a fucking clue how to get her to listen to me. She was so careful to protect herself. Walls had been erected between us and it felt as if they were made of steel.

"If that is all, Mr. Carter, we need to proceed with our session," Adam said in a businesslike tone.

I didn't want to do this here anyway. Not with an audience. Instead of answering, I just walked away. I didn't know what else to do. I needed to regroup and plan what to do next. I also needed advice. Forget waiting on Rush. I was going to see Blaire.

# Harlow

Adam acted as if nothing had happened. Even after I started missing every ball he sent my way. I couldn't concentrate. Grant's words were replaying over and over in my head. He was so determined to make me believe he had called me. Yet he didn't think about the fact that his comment about sleeping with Nan was like sticking a blade through my chest. I just stopped trying. Adam stopped hitting and we stood there, staring at each other.

"I'm sorry. I don't think I'm going to be able to finish today," I told him. He didn't need any more explanation; I knew he'd heard us. We weren't exactly whispering.

"I'm free for another hour and twenty minutes. Want to grab a cup of coffee?" he asked, surprising me.

I wasn't sure if that's what I wanted. I didn't really have a lot of friends. My books were my friends.

"I won't ask about what happened if you don't want me to. I just thought coffee sounded good, and I'd like some company," he said when I didn't respond.

I needed to do this. It was time I got a life. Dad had sent me here and made it impossible for me to hide in my bedroom. Staying at home meant being near Nan. "I'd like that," I replied.

Adam seemed relieved when he shot me a smile. "Good. I thought I might have to beg."

I wasn't sure what he meant by that or if he was teasing me. I waited while he used his towel to dry the small amount of sweat he'd worked up and take a long drink from his water.

When he turned back to me I decided that I liked Adam. He was attractive and he was nice. And he hadn't slept with Nan . . . or at least I didn't think so.

"Before we have coffee together, do you have any relationship at all with Nan?" I asked. I knew this was ridiculous but I was protecting myself. If he had then I was better off not spending any time with him off this court.

Adam laughed. I guess I sounded like a child asking something like that. But I didn't care. "No. Nan is the kind of girl I keep my distance from. She's also messing around with August Schweep. He's the club's new golf pro."

Awesome. Grant was sleeping with her while she was sleeping with the golf pro. Ew. Just ew. "He's not the only person she's messing around with."

Adam's eyebrows shot up. "Like I said. Not my type."

Yes, we could be friends.

"Good. Not that coffee means anything. I just prefer not to waste my time with people who have had any relationship with Nan."

"Hate her that much?" he asked.

I shook my head. "No. It's just a big red flag that the person lacks something."

"Really? What would that be?"

"Integrity," I replied before snapping my mouth shut. I shouldn't have said that.

Adam, however, burst into laughter again.

⌗

We walked into a small café area just inside the doors on the large wraparound porch. My eyes immediately found Rush standing at what looked like the entrance to a larger dining room or restaurant. He glanced from me to Adam and raised his eyebrows slightly, then nodded a hello before turning his attention back to a guy whom I recognized from the wedding.

"Is it okay if we get coffee in here? The dining room is packed this time of day. Or would you rather go in there and get something to eat?"

It was lunchtime but the idea of walking in there while it was full of people didn't sound appealing.

"Can we get a sandwich in here?" I asked

"Sure can." He pulled out a chair for me. "Have a seat and I'll grab a menu. They don't normally bring them in here."

I started to tell him not to bother, that coffee was fine, but he had already headed for the door. I didn't look to see if Rush said anything to him. I kept my attention focused on the windows overlooking the courts. Letting myself think about this too deeply would make me nervous. There was no reason to be nervous. Adam was a nice guy. He played tennis. We already had something in common.

"I like Adam." Rush's voice startled me, and I turned around to see he'd walked over to my table.

"Me, too," I replied, wondering if he knew much about me and Grant or anything at all.

"Nan treating you okay?"

He would be worried about that. Rush knew more than

anyone how bad it was between us. "Haven't seen her yet. I'm avoiding her."

Rush smirked. "Not a bad idea."

"How's Blaire and the Nate?" I asked.

A glow touched his face and his smirk transformed into a smile. The genuine kind that you knew went deep. "They're perfect."

He never was a man of many words. "I'd like to come see them."

"Blaire would like that. As soon as I tell her you're here, she'll be hunting you down."

That made me smile. I really liked Blaire. She was the kind of person you couldn't help but be drawn to. "Good. I look forward to her finding me."

Rush glanced up and then back down at me. "I'll let you enjoy your lunch. Don't let Nan take control. Stiffen your spine."

He didn't say any more; he just walked off. I turned to see Adam walking back into the room. He and Rush greeted each other in passing. Adam set the menu in front of me before sitting down across from me and glancing back at the door.

When he turned back to me he looked like he was thinking about something. I decided to wait and let him build up the courage to ask me. Opening my menu, I studied the selections of salads and sandwiches.

"So you're friends with Rush but not Grant. Aren't they close or brothers or something?"

Ah. He was finally going to ask about the scene Grant and I had caused earlier. I wasn't ready to give him details. We'd just met, and what had happened with Grant was too personal.

"Rush is a friend. He has been since we were kids. Grant is someone I met a few months ago and made the mistake of trusting. That's about it."

Adam nodded and then turned his attention to his menu. He was going to be satisfied with that explanation. Good. I wasn't going to tell him more.

# Grant

I had started for my truck when I noticed Rush's Range Rover. He was here. I turned around and headed back inside while calling him to find out exactly where he was.

"Yeah," Rush said.

"I see your truck. Where are you?"

"Inside. Are you outside?"

"Yeah."

"Wait out there. I'll come outside."

Then he hung up. What the hell? He had been in the dining room. I could hear familiar sounds in the background. Why was he leaving to come see me? Unless . . . Harlow was in there. What did he think I was going to do? Make a scene? Hell, I'd already done that on the tennis court. I needed a game plan. Not another train wreck.

I waited on him. He was there fast. Rush walked out the door and glanced over at me with a concerned look on his face.

"Did I beat you here?" he asked, as if he weren't at all suspicious.

I decided to ease his mind. "I know Harlow's in town. I know she's living with Nan and we've already had our first encounter . . . and second, actually."

Rush let out a relieved sigh. "Good. After your last drunk-ass rant I was worried this was going to be an issue."

"My only issue is she won't let me explain. She hates me. I need advice, man. I fucked up. That's why I wanted to talk to you. But I think . . . I think I may need to talk to Blaire."

Rush's eyebrows drew together. "How'd you fuck up? Kiro was keeping her from you. That was it. Harlow is a sweet girl. I can't imagine her hating anyone."

"There's more to it than that," I said, running my hand through my hair. I didn't want to tell Rush that I'd been sleeping with Nan again. She was his sister, and even though she was selfish and mean as a snake, he loved her. I wasn't sure how he'd react to me using her.

"What more is there?"

I thought about that. I wished he would just let me talk to Blaire. I didn't need help from him.

"Tell me you didn't screw around with Nan," he said with an exasperated sigh.

He knew. He always figured shit out. "Yeah, some."

Rush shook his head and let out a hard laugh. "You're fucked. I said Harlow doesn't hate people, but Nan is as close as it gets for her. You need to let the Harlow thing go and move on. Ain't no way you're fixing that shit."

I wanted her to understand. I wanted her forgiveness, and I wanted her to know I cherished what she had given me. No one or nothing would ever be that special for me again. I would never forget it. Maybe it was best for both of us if that was all she was willing to do. That night when I had been inside of her, I had been shown something much deeper than I ever imagined. It scared the hell out of me.

To love someone the way Rush loved Blaire . . . that was intense. It was controlling and it had the power to destroy you. I had seen so much heartache and pain in my life. My father had been in love more than once, and each time it had ended painfully, not only for him but for me. Love forever wasn't something I believed in. Harlow was dangerous for me. She was the first person I had ever allowed myself to picture forever with. What if she stopped loving me one day . . . or what if I lost her? I saw the vacant look in Bethy's eyes. The pain deep inside her. She had to wake up every day and live with it.

"I just want her to listen to me. I don't want anything else. I want her to know . . . that . . . that she was special. That night was special. That's all. Nothing else. I'm not asking for a second chance. I can't do that. I just want her forgiveness. And I can't live with myself if she believes I took her innocence as a game. It was never a game."

Rush stood there staring at me as if I were speaking a different language. I was rambling. I wasn't making sense. At least not to him. I needed to talk to Blaire, dammit.

"You just want her to know that your fucking her meant something? Is that what I'm understanding? You don't want anything else?"

I flinched at his description but nodded.

"Can I ask why?"

The image of Bethy doubled over wailing as they lowered Jace's body into the ground was etched in my brain. "I can't love someone the way you love Blaire."

Rush cocked one of his eyebrows. "Why is that?"

"Because it scares the hell out of me. I'm not going to be that vulnerable. I don't want to be."

Rush didn't look as if he understood, but he finally nod-ded his head toward his Rover. "I'm headed home. If you want Blaire's advice then meet me there and you can tell her this crazy shit. But she isn't going to take your side in this. I'm warning you now."

I didn't expect her to. "I know."

"When you tell her you slept with Nan after taking Har-low's virginity then I'd duck, because the gun will come out, and this time I'm pretty damn sure she'll pull the trigger," he said with an amused grin before walking out toward his truck without looking back at me.

He was right. Blaire was going to chew my ass out. But once she got over it she'd help me, if only because she would understand that Harlow deserved it.

⌗

Thirty minutes later, Blaire was glaring at me. Her face had gone from horrified to completely pissed off. Nate had luckily crawled into her lap, otherwise I was pretty sure she'd have taken a swing at me.

"You want me to take him, baby?" Rush asked, walking into the living room.

"No. Leave him in her arms. I'm safer that way," I replied.

Rush chuckled and walked over to sit beside her. Nate went to Rush with a happy laugh and I watched my badass best friend become complete sappy mush as Nate laid a loud smacking kiss on Rush's face. Yeah . . . that kind of love. I couldn't do that. What if something happened to Nate? How could Rush wake up every morning?

"I'm not like Rush. I can't do this. This . . . life. I can't love someone so completely that they hold my heart in their hands. I'm not that strong. I've had bad experiences with that kind of trust. But I care about Harlow. I let it get far with her. I let her in enough to care that I've hurt her. I don't want her to be hurt. Help me, please."

Blaire's angry glare softened some, and she leaned forward, not taking her eyes off me. "Why? Tell me why, Grant. What is it about what I have with Rush that you can't take?"

I wasn't dredging up my past and talking about my childhood like that was a good excuse. And none of us wanted to bring up Jace. That was still too fresh. "I'm not ready for that. I would eventually hurt Harlow, and I can't do that. I just want to get her to listen to my explanation and walk away from this as friends. She's sweet and special and I can't stand the idea of her thinking I used her." Friends. That word sounded flat. If Harlow forgave me, could I live with just being friends? How was I supposed to look at her and not remember how good she felt in my arms? Was I asking for something impossible? I didn't want to leave Rosemary. Hell, I couldn't leave Rosemary. Someone needed to make sure Harlow survived with Nan.

Blaire tucked a strand of her long white-blond hair behind her ear and pierced me with her steady gaze. "You don't want her but you want her to know that what y'all did was special to you. I can understand that. It's typical you. You don't like hurting people."

"Can you tell me what to do? She hates me right now."

Nate reached over and tugged at Blaire's hair and giggled happily.

"Don't pull Momma's hair. We've gone over this, dude," Rush said, saving Blaire from another hard tug.

Blaire thanked Rush and pressed a kiss to Nate's head then turned back to me.

"Let me talk to her. Then I'll let you know when you can talk to her. Until then, stay out of Nan's bed, especially now that Harlow's living there."

"Not going there again. I'm hanging up the whiskey, too."

"Good, I'm tired of picking up your sorry ass from the bar," Rush said.

"Language," Blaire reminded Rush.

"Sorry," he replied quickly.

Blaire sighed. "Nate's first word is going to be a four-letter one, I just know it."

"'Ass' only has three letters," I replied.

"The gun, man. Remember the gun. My woman comes armed," Rush warned.

Blaire stood up and let out a frustrated growl. "You two. I swear," she said, reaching for Nate. "I need to go feed this guy and then it's his naptime. I'll call you, Grant."

I watched her walk out of the room.

"Eyes off my wife's ass," Rush warned.

It was the first time I'd felt like laughing all day.

# Harlow

Lunch had been painless.

But I wasn't sure I was doing it again anytime soon. I just wasn't ready to trust anyone right now. This was temporary, and as appealing as having a friend sounded, I didn't see Adam wanting friendship. He would eventually want more.

I left the club and headed to my car. I wasn't in the mood for golf. I just wanted to read and escape this mess Dad had left me in. I needed to get out of Rosemary and find some public park where I could sit under a tree and read. I had two books on my e-reader I couldn't wait to read.

Then I spotted him. Long dark hair with just enough curl to make it look messy pulled back in a ponytail. Cowboy hat perched on his head. Blue plaid shirt pulled tightly against his broad shoulders and back as he leaned against my car with his arms crossed over his chest. Excitement bubbled up inside me, even as I wondered why he was here. I started running.

The sound of my footsteps caught his attention and he turned toward me. A slow, easy grin spread across his handsome face. I saw so much of our father in him. I often wondered if this was what Daddy would have looked like if he hadn't let sex, drugs, and rock and roll take over his life. Mase was healthy and strong.

I threw my arms around him as he opened his. "What are you doing here?" I asked, holding on to him tightly. Tears stung my eyes. I hadn't realized how alone I'd felt until this moment. Just having Mase here. Someone who loved me. It was a relief.

"Heard our dear ol' dad threw you to the wolves and wanted to make sure you were okay," he drawled in his Texas twang that always made me smile.

I couldn't respond just yet. If he saw the emotion in my eyes or heard it in my voice he would pack me up and take me to Texas. I swallowed the lump in my throat.

"It isn't so bad. I've had a good day."

Mase grunted and pulled back to look down at me. "From what Dad's told me, she's a raging bitch. The next thing I hear he sends you off to live with her. I'm finding it all a little hard to swallow."

"She hates me. She'll hate you, too, just because she can. But Rush and his wife, Blaire, are here. You'll like her. She's very nice. I'm not completely alone."

Mase frowned and the dimple in his left cheek disappeared. "Rush got married? Damn, I'm behind on family shit."

"Yeah. He has a baby, too. Nate. He's adorable, but then Rush is, well . . . Rush and Blaire are stunning."

"Well, I'll be damned. The heartthrob got married. Haven't seen him in forever, but didn't expect that."

"People change. Rush has changed."

Mase nodded. "Yeah, they do."

Reading no longer sounded appealing. I wanted to spend time with Mase. "How long are you here?"

Mase cocked an eyebrow and rubbed his stubbled chin. "As long as you need me, little sister."

I needed him for nine months, but I wasn't going to tell him that.

"Where are you staying?"

Mase let out a chuckle. "I'm staying at that big, nice house my father paid for."

My jaw dropped. Surely he knew Nan lived there. She wouldn't just let him move in. "But Nan won't . . ." I trailed off.

Mase winked and leaned closer to me. "I called Kiro. He knows I'm here. And he said if the bitch gave me problems to have her call him. He'd handle it." He smirked. "Not that I needed him to handle her. I'll move my shit in there and pick my own room. Ain't one damn thing she can do to stop me."

I thought about her reaction and knew this wasn't going to be good. "She's going to go crazy. She *is* crazy."

Mase threw his arm over my shoulders. "Good. I need some entertainment. Now, why don't you show me how to get to this house and you can help me settle in. Then we're going to find ourselves a decent bar to get a couple beers and play some pool. One with no damn polo shirts and luxury cars." He looked around the parking lot with a disgusted expression.

He might be the only son of the most infamous rocker in the world, but he was a country boy. His big black Dodge truck had mud on the tires and dirty work boots in the back. He wasn't one for pretenses.

"Okay. Want me to drive and you follow?"

"Yeah. We need to get your car to the house before we head out tonight."

I opened my door and glanced back to see him walk over to his truck and climb in.

My brother was here. He was moving in with us. All three of Kiro's kids living in one house. This was going to be . . . a disaster.

# Grant

"I need you to come here now! Right fucking now!" Nan screamed into the phone. I held it away from my head to keep her from breaking my eardrums.

"Stop yelling in my damn ear," I barked.

"He won't leave! I need help. I can't get my sorry-ass father on the phone. I need you. Please. Help me!"

"Who?"

"Just get here!" She screeched and hung up the phone.

Shit. I didn't want to go anywhere near Nan. But Harlow . . . if "he" was upsetting Nan this much, could this person hurt Harlow? Had Nan brought someone home she didn't know? Was he dangerous? Fuck! I ran and grabbed my truck keys and headed outside. I'd go over there, but this wasn't for Nan. I was doing this for Harlow.

⊞

A black Dodge truck with an extended cab that looked like it had been mud-riding was parked beside Harlow's car. Who the hell did Nan bring home this time? The idea of Harlow being in danger made the anger inside me start to boil. Fucking Nan wasn't safe enough for Harlow. She needed a safe place to live, and Nan made dumbass choices like this Dodge truck.

I stalked up the steps and opened the door without knocking. Nan's high-pitched screaming was easy to follow. I walked up the stairs to the first bedroom on the second floor.

"You are NOT living in my fucking house! Pack your damn bags and leave now! This is not the agreement I had with Kiro." Nan was red in the face when I walked into the room. Her wild eyes found mine and she lunged for me and wrapped her arms around me. "You came. Thank you, thank you. I need your help."

My eyes found Harlow's. They were wide with a mix of emotions. The only one that mattered to me was the hurt. I took Nan's arms off my body and moved her away from me without looking away from Harlow. I didn't want her to think I was here for Nan.

"You called your boyfriend? That's pretty damn funny." The deep drawl caught my attention. I shifted my gaze to the guy standing beside Harlow. His tone sounded relaxed, but the way he was standing slightly in front of Harlow and the stiff posture told me he felt as if he was protecting her.

"Who are you?" I asked, stepping past Nan and closer to Harlow. I didn't know who this guy was trying to protect, but damned if I was gonna let him get any closer to Harlow.

"He thinks he's moving into this room! Tell him he's not," Nan demanded.

He thought what?

I watched Harlow take a step toward him and wrap her small hand around the guy's bicep. I didn't like that. Not at all. I glared at her hand on his arm then I moved my gaze to hers. Was he hers? Had she moved on? "Who is he, Harlow?" I asked. I needed to hear her tell me this.

Harlow looked up at the guy then back at me. I could see the indecision on her face. She didn't trust me. I fucking hated that. I'd worked so hard to get her to trust me. Now she was holding on to this other guy like he was part of the damn cavalry.

"I don't believe this? You come over here and you ask *her* who he is? What the hell is wrong with you? He's in my house and I want him out. Now." Nan grabbed my arm and jerked it, trying to get my attention. I just ignored her. I kept my focus on Harlow.

"Grant, this is my brother, Mase Colt-Manning. Mase, this is Grant Carter. He's Rush's best friend and Nan's boyfriend."

All I heard was "my brother" and my entire body relaxed. He was her brother. The tightness in my chest was gone and I could breathe again. Nothing else she said mattered. Mase Colt-Manning. The only son of Kiro Manning. I wondered if I had just breathed that sigh of relief too loudly.

Mase took a step toward me and held out his hand. "Nice to meet you," he said in his thick Texas accent.

I shook his hand. His grip was more like a warning than a greeting. "You, too," I replied. The silent threat in his eyes wasn't unmissed. He had noticed my attention to Harlow. The message he was getting in this room was wrong, and I wanted to fucking correct it but not for his sake. For Harlow's.

"For fucking real? You're shaking his hand? He's moving into my house! Uninvited!" Nan screeched.

I stepped back and looked at Nan for the first time since

I'd walked into the room. "It's Kiro's house, Nan. If he wants to move another one of his kids in, he can. I don't see how you can stop it."

Nan's face went from red to bright red as she stamped her foot and let out a loud noise that sounded like a five-year-old's temper tantrum.

"Not that it's my business, but how do you put up with that?" Mase asked.

"I don't. She isn't my girlfriend. Harlow has misunderstood some things that she won't let me clarify," I replied, looking over at her. She ducked her head and stared down at her feet.

"I see," Mase replied, and I had an idea that he did see. A lot more than Harlow did. He was a guy and it was all over my face. I just wanted her to forgive me, and I had no use for Nan. Not anymore.

"Leave," Nan demanded, pointing to the door. The angry gleam in her eyes was directed at me. "Now. Get out of my fucking house. You *are* someone I can throw out. So just go. I shouldn't have called you."

"I'd tell you to stay, but Harlow and I got plans. I'm sure we'll see each other around," Mase said. "You can leave my room now, Nan."

The infuriated scowl on her face as she turned and stalked out of the room almost made me laugh. Mase wasn't going to let her get away with anything. Was that why he was here? Was he here for Harlow? The way he kept his body slightly in front of her as if he was ready to pounce on anyone who got too close told me that it was exactly why he was here.

"Thanks," I replied before turning to leave.

"You're welcome, but what are you thanking me for?" he asked.

I glanced back but I didn't look at him. My eyes went straight to Harlow. "For coming to protect her. I can sleep easier at night knowing she has you." I didn't wait for him to ask any more questions. I just walked out.

# Harlow

I couldn't look at Mase. His eyes were on me, though. I could feel his curiosity. It was filling up the room. What had that been about? Grant had come barreling into the room like he was ready to save Nan. Then he had basically thrown her from him. I almost felt sorry for her. He'd had her screaming in orgasm last night but today he wouldn't even touch her.

"Explain that shit, please, 'cause, Sis, I'm seriously trying to figure all this out." Mase said as he sat down on the king-size bed behind him.

"I don't know what you mean," I said, still not looking at him.

Mase chuckled. "The hell you do. Spill it. Or I'll ask him."

No. I couldn't let him talk to Grant. I wasn't even sure what he thought he knew. "I don't know exactly. Grant and Nan sleep together but it appears to be all they do. He was here last night."

"He sleeps with her? Really? With you in the house?"

I shrugged. "He didn't know I was here last night."

Mase didn't reply right away. I had no idea what he was thinking but for the first time since he'd gotten here I wanted to be alone for a few minutes.

"You know he likes you, right?" Mase finally said.

I shook my head. "No, he doesn't. He wants me to forgive him for . . ." I stopped. I couldn't tell Mase the truth. It was very likely Mase would go after Grant with one of the big guns he used for hunting.

"For what?" Mase asked, standing back up, his body tensed. Crap. I had to fix this.

"He and I became friends a couple of months ago. I started to like him. We kissed. Then his friend drowned and he came back here. He didn't call me again. I thought maybe he was just mourning his friend and needed time. Then I found out he was sleeping with Nan."

Mase gave an unhappy grunt and crossed his arms over his chest. "That's all he did? Kiss you? Did he make you any promises?"

I shook my head because lying to Mase was the only way I could keep Grant alive.

"If it makes you feel better, he's beating himself up over hurting you. He doesn't want Nan. My guess is he wants you and knows he's fucked up. My advice is stay the fuck away from him. Guys that weak aren't the ones worth sticking around for. When a guy gets the attention of someone like you, he's sup-posed to understand his luck. Not toss it away. He doesn't get it. Find a man that understands your worth."

I smiled and finally looked over at him. "Is that big brother advice?" I asked.

"The best. I'm full of it. Now, go, get on your jeans and pull on those cowboy boots I sent you for Christmas. We're going to hang out with the common folk," he replied with a wink.

I walked over and hugged him. "Thank you," I whispered.

"Don't thank me for taking care of you."

❖

The bar Mase found was a good twenty-minute drive outside Rosemary. The bright neon lights in the windows and several trucks in the parking lot had been all the incentive Mase needed to pull in.

"Mud on the tires means there's good beer here," he explained, opening his door. I rolled my eyes and opened my door to jump down out of the truck.

We walked toward the door and Mase stopped, then looked back at me. "Try not to look appealing. I just want to play pool and have a beer. Spend some time with my sis, not beat a stupid shit up for coming on to you."

I laughed, then nodded. What did he think I was going to do? Go in there and bat my eyelashes at everyone who looked my way.

He pulled open the door to the bar and we walked inside. The smell of cigarette smoke filled the air. This was a familiar scent for me. Mase took a deep breath and grinned at me. "I can smell the beer from here. The tap is good," he said with a goofy grin before heading over to the bar. I followed quickly behind him. I glanced around the large room while Mase ordered us both a beer. I didn't point out I was underage. I just let him do it.

The pool tables were full and I searched for a booth that was empty. I tried not to make eye contact with anyone. But my eyes found a familiar face. She wasn't looking at me. She was staring at the drink on the table. I watched as a man walked up and spoke to her and she replied without looking at him. The guy shook his head and walked off. The sadness in her profile and the slump of her shoulders broke my heart.

I turned back to Mase. "I see someone I know. Can you let me talk to her alone? I'll be back in a few minutes. She just looks like she needs a friend."

Mase glanced out over the crowd and I knew when his eyes found Bethy. He nodded. "Sure. I'll just be right over here."

"Okay," I replied, then made my way over to Bethy. She didn't look up until I slid into the seat across from her.

The confusion in her eyes turned to surprise. "Harlow?" she asked, then glanced around in case I was with someone else she knew. I could see the moment of panic. She didn't want anyone to know she was here drinking away her pain.

"I'm here with my brother. No one else," I assured her, and she looked back at me, relieved.

"Oh," she simply replied.

I wasn't good at this. I had dealt with loss. I had lost my mother, whom I barely remembered, and then my grand-mama, but never someone I was in love with. Never someone so young with a life ahead of him. "You want to talk about it?" I asked.

Bethy frowned and glanced down at her glass. "I don't know. Not really."

I had never been loved or been in love so I wasn't sure how that felt. How vulnerable it made you. I just knew the hurt I had endured from trusting someone who betrayed me. That had been painful, but it didn't hold a candle to this.

"Some days I think I'll wake up and this will have been a nightmare," she said, still staring down at her glass as if it held all the answers.

I decided the best thing for me to do was stay quiet and let her talk. I was a good listener. I could help her that way.

"But then I wake up and he's gone. He's not beside me. He isn't smiling at me with those pretty eyes of his. I don't have him to snuggle up to and plan forever with. He was my safe place. I'd never had a safe place before. But Jace had been my safe place. He had taken care of me . . . and I . . . I didn't deserve him."

I started to tell her that wasn't true, but she kept talking.

"He never knew the truth about me. He never knew my secrets. I wanted to tell him everything. But I knew once I did I could lose him, and I couldn't lose him. Then . . . then Tripp would come home for a visit and I would spiral out of control. The memories, the lies—it all was too much. That night I'd been drinking because I had finally convinced myself to tell Jace the truth. He deserved to know who it was that he loved. And because I was a coward, I drank. And then . . . I killed him."

I reached across the table and grabbed her hand. "You didn't kill him," I assured her. I knew that much. Jace had drowned.

She lifted her eyes to me and the tears pooling in them rolled slowly down her face. "He was out there saving me. I had walked out into the water and almost drowned. It should have been me," she gulped. "It should have been me. He should have let me go and saved himself, but he wouldn't do it. He saved me and it should have been me. I was the liar. I was the unworthy one."

It wasn't my business. I didn't know her secrets and I didn't want to know. But what I did know was Jace would have saved her regardless. Love didn't just go away because of lies. I loved my dad, and he was very far from perfect.

"He would have saved you even if you had told him these secrets. Love doesn't just go away. He might have been hurt. He might have even been unable to trust you again. But he would have come after you, because that's what love does to a person."

Bethy let out a small sob and covered her mouth. "He deserved life. A full, happy one," she said once she dropped her hand. "I took that from him."

I couldn't help her forgive herself. It would take time.

"But you made a mistake. Jace protected you. Someday you'll be able to stop blaming yourself. Until then, try to think about all the good things. Don't dwell on the bad things."

"But Tripp is in town now. He reminds me. Just seeing him from a distance reminds me."

I had no idea who Tripp was and why she kept bringing him up. Again, not my business. He was obviously a part of the past that tormented her. "I'm sure a lot of things will remind you of him and the past. In time, it will get easier."

Bethy closed her eyes tightly. "I hope so," she whispered.

I didn't want to leave her here alone. "Why are you here by yourself?" I asked.

She frowned. "I like it. I don't want to see people. But I think I'm ready to go home tonight."

I squeezed her hand and pulled my hand back to my side of the table.

"If you ever need someone to listen who isn't attached to the situation then I'm here," I told her as I scooted to stand up.

Bethy gave me a weak smile. "Thanks, Harlow. That means a lot."

# Grant

Rosemary wasn't a big town. It was a small strip of beach. So how was it that Harlow had managed to completely avoid me for three days? I had done everything I could think of to run into her. I knew she had Mase here but I still wanted to get her alone so I could talk to her. I needed to find my peace with her.

I stood outside the club, waiting on her to pull up. She had tennis in ten minutes. I had cheated by having Woods call Adam and ask her court time then had him change it for an hour later. He hadn't been happy about it but he had also wanted me out of his office so he had agreed as long as I left him alone for the rest of the day.

I watched as Harlow pulled her car up to the valet and climbed out in a short white tennis skirt that didn't help my focus. Tennis skirts weren't meant to be that damn sexy.

I walked over to open the door for her before one of the staff could. She lifted her eyes and stopped walking when she saw me standing there. I could see the questions in her eyes and I wanted to answer every damn one of them. She just needed to listen.

When she started walking again she kept her head down

and attempted to go inside without acknowledging me. I gently wrapped my hand around her arm. "Your court time was postponed an hour today. I need to talk to you. If you will let me talk. I will leave you alone if that's what you want. I just need you to listen to me first."

Harlow's spine was stiff as I spoke quietly in her ear. She didn't move or respond right away. Finally, she simply nodded.

"Thank you," I replied. "We need privacy. Will you come to my truck?"

Harlow let out a defeated sigh. "Yes, I guess I will."

She wasn't happy about it but she was doing it. I needed to celebrate the small victories.

We walked in silence to the parking lot and I unlocked my truck and opened her door then walked around and climbed in on my side.

"Talk. I'm listening," she said without looking at me. Her eyes were fixed straight ahead.

"What we did . . . what happened meant something to me."

Harlow didn't even flinch.

"When I got the call about Jace I rushed back in a state of shock. Then . . . then I watched as Bethy completely crumbled. At the funeral, she was bent over in so much pain from her loss that it terrified me. She had planned forever with Jace. She had loved him with everything she had and he had been taken from her. She couldn't get him back."

Harlow was still staring straight ahead, although I could see the worried frown on her face.

"And all I could think was what if I loved someone that much and I lost them? How could I live? I glanced over at Rush and Blaire. He was holding her while she wept and I

wondered how he would even be able to wake up every morning if he lost her. Or if he lost Nate." I paused and took a deep
breath. I was more open than I'd been with anyone about this.
I hadn't even explained it this way to Blaire and Rush. I had
held myself back some. I was just laying it all out for Harlow.

"I decided I never wanted to be that vulnerable. I never
wanted to love someone that much. I never wanted to face
losing the one person that owns me. So, I got drunk. Because
I also realized I could easily fall in love with you. In just two
short weeks I had begun to care for you. I had feelings I hadn't
experienced before. Not like that, at least. It scared me. I knew
you would be the one to own me if I let you. I ran from it. I
drank too much whiskey and when Nan showed up I messed
up. I should have stayed away from her. But in my head she
was the one I thought I was in love with once. I hadn't been. I
realized that after only two weeks with you. I was in *lust* with
Nan. I liked being needed by someone, and Nan needed me.
That was all it ever was for us."

Harlow finally dropped her gaze to her lap as she twisted
her hands nervously.

"I never meant to hurt you. Hurting you is the last thing I
ever wanted to do. What you gave me I didn't deserve, but believe me when I tell you I'll cherish it forever. It meant more to
me than you know. But I shouldn't have taken your innocence
that night. I should have been a man and realized I didn't deserve it and walked away. But you made me weak. It's one of
the things about you that scares me. No one has ever made me
weak."

Finally, Harlow turned her head to look at me. Her hazel
eyes no longer looked hard. Instead, I saw understanding

there. She simply nodded. "Okay. You're forgiven." Then she opened the door and climbed out without another word.

I sat there and tried to let all the emotions that were churning inside me calm down. I didn't want her to take it so easily and walk away. But I couldn't give her more. That was it for us. I had explained it and she forgave me. So, we were over now? The ache that came with that reality hurt. I reached up and rubbed my chest and laid my head back on the seat and closed my eyes.

"What did I just do?" I muttered.

A loud knock on my window caused me to jump as I opened my eyes and sat up to see Mase standing there.

I rolled down my window as he pushed his sunglasses up and onto the top of his head.

"What was that about?" he asked.

"I needed to explain some things to her. I had hurt her and I needed to make sure she knew the truth."

"What was the truth?" Mase asked, his eyes narrowing as he studied me.

"That I wasn't ready for any kind of commitment and she was the kind of girl you committed yourself to."

Mase snarled. "Hell yeah, she is, and she's too good for you. Harlow won't ever settle for Nan's seconds. And dude, you're Nan's seconds." He moved his sunglasses back into place and sauntered off to that black truck of his that needed a damn car wash.

As pissed off as I was, he was right. I wasn't good enough for Harlow. I knew that, dammit. I didn't need reminding.

# Harlow

Tennis had been just what I needed to get my aggression out. I hadn't wanted to talk; I had just wanted to hit that stupid little ball for an hour. And I had hit every one of them that Adam had sent my way. When Adam dropped his racquet and threw the ball into the air, caught it, and tucked it into his pocket I knew our hour was up.

"You were killing it today. I was expecting you to bust a ball before it was over," Adam teased as I walked over to my water and towel. I wiped my face then took a long drink of water.

"Was that all about the love of the game, or were you picturing someone's head on that ball?"

I forced a smile. "Just one of those days. I feel better now," I told him.

"Good. Because I was wondering if you would like to have dinner with me tonight? Maybe a movie, too?"

I paused. Wait . . . was he asking me out on a date? I turned to look at him and the hopeful look in his eyes told me that was exactly what he was doing. Adam wanted to take me out.

My immediate reaction was no. I wasn't ready to do this, but I stopped myself before I could say something. That Grant had hurt me didn't mean everyone would. Besides, Grant had saved himself some trouble. He didn't know it, but he had. Adam wasn't in that danger. I wasn't going to want him the way I did Grant. Besides, was it fair that I protect myself from everyone? Did I want to be alone my whole life? No. I didn't. I didn't want to be living with my dad until I died. I deserved to know what living was like. I wanted to know I was loved. How would I ever find that if I didn't look for it or allow it to come to me?

"I'd like that," I said without thinking about it further.

The grin on Adam's face was immediate, and I had to smile myself. I was going on a date. A real one. Dad would be proud of me.

"Whew, I'd been preparing myself all day for you to turn me down, and I had to pump myself up to ask."

He had put himself out there. That made me feel special. More special than Grant had ever made me feel.

"I'm glad you asked," I told him honestly.

"Me, too," he replied, and threw his towel over his shoulder. "You leaving now?" he asked.

I nodded.

"Let me walk you to your car. My next appointment can wait a few minutes," he said, and opened the gate for me. I liked that, too.

He fell into step beside me. "I can pick you up at your place if that's okay," he said.

"Oh, yes, that would be good. I live at 43 Rosemary Beach Estates," I told him.

"Seven too early? Late?"

"Seven is perfect," I replied.

We walked around the building instead of through it but Adam didn't seem to be in a hurry.

"Things with Nan going okay?" he asked.

I shrugged. Not really. She hated Mase and she hated me more for being there, but I didn't care. "Tolerable," I replied.

We stepped into the parking lot and I remembered I'd valet parked.

"Harlow," Mase called from his truck. I glanced over at him then back at Adam.

"That's Mase, my brother. He's here visiting." I explained.

Adam's eyes widened slightly. "I'd heard that Kiro had a son, but I thought it was a rumor."

A nervous knot formed in my stomach. The mention of my dad threw me off. He had "heard" about Mase? Only diehard fans had heard of Mase. He stayed out of the news. I wasn't sure what to think.

Adam turned his grin back to me. "I'll see you tonight," he said.

I nodded and he turned to walk back the way we came before Mase got too close to us.

"Get in. I want lunch and I don't want it here. I need real food," he said as he stopped in front of me. I climbed into his truck.

"Tennis instructor?" he asked

I nodded, still thinking about Adam's comment about Mase.

"You like him? He's sure got the hots for you. The dude's tongue was almost hanging out."

"Where are we eating?" I asked, hoping to change the subject.

"Hooters. Now answer me, do you like the guy?"

I let out a frustrated sigh. Mase was like a dog with a bone. "He asked me out."

"That don't answer my question," he replied.

"Fine. I think I like him."

"You think?"

I growled and shot Mase a frustrated glare. "I don't know. He seems nice and sincere but I've been down this road before. Guys like me because of Dad. It gets old, and I've let myself get hurt this way before. I'm older and smarter and more careful now."

Mase frowned. He didn't understand this problem. He had women throw themselves at him because of him, not Dad. He was beautiful and no one really knew he was Kiro's son.

"You think that dude is interested in who your daddy is?"

I shrugged. "I don't know."

"Did you say yes?"

I nodded.

"Well you must think there's something to him then."

I did. Until he knew about Mase.

"He knew about you. When I said you were my brother, he already knew Kiro had a son. Only diehards know about you."

Understanding lit Mase's eyes as he turned onto the main road and headed out of town. "I see. Yeah, that's odd. But maybe he isn't really a fan; maybe he's just heard the Rosemary gossip. This town knows more about Slacker Demon than anywhere else since Dean's son grew up here. They feel like they have some sort of inside scoop. He's probably just heard rumors since he lives here."

I hadn't thought of that. He probably saw many of the band members as clients all the time. He could've heard something through the country club grapevine. Rosemary did have a close relationship with Slacker Demon. I let out a relieved sigh and leaned back against the seat. That made sense.

"Feel better now?" he asked.

"Yeah," I replied.

"Good. But if I'm wrong, you just say the word and I'll rearrange his face for you."

I just smiled. Not because I didn't believe him. Because I did. Mase was rough. He was Texas tough, and I'd learned a long time ago that was a whole other kind of tough. It was how a little boy grew up with an absent father. His stepdad was a Texan. He owned a ranch and wore boots and a hat all the time. He was big and tall and loud and I loved him. Even when I was a shy little girl, he always made sure I felt like family when I went to visit.

Out of the three of us, Mase had been the lucky one. He had a mom who adored him. A stepdad who treated him like his own. Maybe that was why he was the best of us. At least I wasn't the worst. Nan held that title. But then she'd been given the worst life, from what I could tell.

A small part of me felt sorry for her. But only a very small part.

# Grant

I walked into Rush's after only knocking once. I wasn't in the mood to wait. Blaire came walking down the stairs with Nate on her hip and a handful of her hair in his mouth.

"Grant?" she said, looking concerned. I hadn't barged in as if I owned the place since Blaire and Rush got married. It was no longer my brother's bachelor pad but their house.

"She let me talk and then she said okay and forgave me and left. Nothing else. No questions. Nothing. Then . . . then fucking Adam said he was taking her out tonight. I stopped by the café to get a bottle of water and he was talking to someone else and I overheard him. Adam! He's . . . he's . . . just . . ."

"He's a nice guy," Blaire finished for me as she tugged her hair from Nate's fists. Then she handed him to me. "Take him. But don't curse. I need to fix myself something to eat and you can talk while I do that."

Nate grinned up at me and I noticed one small tooth peeking through his bottom gums. "Look at you. You got a tooth, little man."

Nate continued smiling as he reached for my hair. The kid had a good grip and I had too much damn hair. "Whoa, dude. That needs to stay on my head." I reached into my pocket and grabbed my keys and handed them to him to distract him.

Blaire turned at the sound of him jingling them and reached to take them from him. "Those have germs. He puts everything in his mouth. He's teething." She walked into the kitchen and opened the freezer and took out some blue frozen-looking toy and handed it to him.

"It's gonna freeze his hands," I said, wondering what the heck she was doing.

"No, it's meant for teething. It will numb his gums."

This kid shit was more than I wanted to think about.

"Where's Rush?"

"He went running on the beach. He'll be back soon. He's been gone for an hour. Now, back to Harlow," she said, reaching into the fridge to retrieve food that didn't look appealing at all. "She forgave you and let you off the hook and you're pissed because she didn't put up a fight and is now going out with Adam."

Not exactly. She made it sound like I was being selfish.

"I just . . . wanted to talk about it more."

Blaire looked up at me from where she was slicing a tomato. "Really? That's what you wanted? Because most of the time when a guy is trying to give a girl the brush-off he wants no drama. Sounds like Harlow gave you the easy out."

"I wasn't brushing her off," I said defensively as Nate threw his frozen blue thing onto the floor and began clapping as if he had just done something fantastic.

Blaire smirked. "He wants you to pick it up. Be warned, this is his favorite game. He'll treat you like a dog. He will keep doing it as long as you fetch it."

I raised my eyebrows. "Well what the he— I mean, heck do I do then?"

She shrugged. "Be his favorite uncle and pick it up or be the party poopero and ignore his game."

Dammit. I reached down and got it and handed it to him and he beamed at me as if I was the most wonderful person in the world. The kid was cute. And at the moment I felt pretty damn special . . . until he threw it on the floor again and began clapping.

"He's a manipulator," I told her as I bent down to get it.

"Or you're a sucker," Rush said as he opened the back door and stepped inside. He smirked at me, then went over to Blaire to kiss her openly right there in front of me and the kid.

"I need help. Let her face go, you're gonna eat it off," I grumbled.

Rush went a little longer on the kiss just to be an ass, then shot a look over at me. "This about Harlow again?"

"Yes," Blaire said, pressing one last kiss to his lips before going back to the tomato.

"Dadadadada," Nate said happily, and Blaire and Rush both froze. Blaire dropped her knife on the bar and covered her mouth.

Rush stared at his son with an emotion I didn't understand.

"Dadadadada," Nate said again.

"Ohmygod he did say it," Blaire said as tears filled her eyes and she laughed out loud.

Rush walked around the bar and took Nate from me as if I wasn't even standing there. "Hey, buddy," he said with awe in his voice. Nate patted Rush's chest. "Dadadadadada," he said again.

Blaire made another happy cry sound and Rush grinned. "That's right, buddy. You can say it now, can't you?"

I looked over at Blaire and I realized this had to be Nate's first word. I was witnessing a special family moment and I needed to leave. This was their time with their son. I would talk to Blaire later.

Blaire ran around the counter and wrapped her arms around Rush's back. "Who is this, Nate?" she asked, and once again he happily answered.

I didn't say anything as I slipped out the door and headed for my truck. I quickly sent Rush a text.

"Tell Nate I said congrats on his first word. I'll talk to y'all later. That was a moment y'all needed to enjoy alone."

⌗

It was after eight and all I could think about was Harlow's fucking date. Why? I had let her go. I had told her I couldn't commit to her. No dating. No nothing. I just had one damn good memory to cherish. The best. Now I had to move on. If I was scared to be involved in more than a shallow relationship then I needed to embrace my fate. I just wasn't going to be shallow with Nan. That was too fucked up.

Harlow was looking for more. I was looking for less. So, I headed to the closest honky-tonk. I'd find a hot little number who just wanted a good time and take her home. I didn't want the strings of a girl from the club. They were all fucking looking for more than I wanted to give.

I was familiar with this place. It was go-to when I wanted to get out of Rosemary. They had good cover bands and cold beer. College girls were always in abundance from the local state school.

Walking in, I scanned the place until I saw several promising opportunities then made my way over to the bar. Lynette was bartending tonight. She was a looker for someone old enough to be my mom.

"Hey, handsome. Haven't seen you all week. Thought you might have left town again."

I flashed her a smile that I knew wouldn't make her blush. She was too hardcore, but I knew she still liked being flirted with. "Can't leave you for too long," I replied.

"Bullshit." She grinned and set a tall mug in front of me. "That's the best we got on tap tonight."

"Thanks, sexy," I replied and winked.

Lynette let out a bark of laughter then walked over to help someone else. I turned to look out over the room. Two pretty blondes with matching black halter tops and red leather miniskirts were sending me flirty little smiles. They weren't twins but they were trying real hard to be. The matching outfits were a nice touch. Not to mention they had some killer legs. They weren't in Harlow's league, though . . .

*No! Fuck no!* I interrupted my own thoughts. I wasn't going to compare girls to Harlow. Those two were hot. They had nice plump tits about to fall out of their barely there tops. And the spiked heels were doing it for me. I shoved off from the bar.

"Figured those two would get your attention," I heard Lynette say in an amused tone.

I glanced back at her. "You know me well."

She just shook her head and fixed another drink.

Both girls tried to strike sexy poses as I approached them. They wanted it. This would be too damn easy. I needed easy tonight.

"You two here all alone? Looking like that?" I asked then took a sip of my drink. I wasn't going to give them any dumbass lines.

They giggled and glanced at each other. "Yes," they both replied.

So they were doing the answer at the same time thing. They had this twins bit perfected. I was impressed.

The band began to pump out a deep, heavy, sexy sound and I set my beer down. "Dance with me," I said and walked past them onto the floor. I didn't have to look back to know they were following me.

I wanted to see how good these two really were. They were promising a lot with those bodies and the way they were dressed, but their dance moves would tell me if they were worth my night. Besides, I wasn't drunk yet. I needed more alcohol for this.

"I'm Carly," the one with dark brown eyes said as she moved her body close enough that it pressed her tits out over her top even more.

"I'm Casey," the other one said as her body pressed against my back.

They had even chosen names that matched. Cute.

"Show me what you got, girls," I said as I slid one hand on the hip of the girl in front and took the girl's hand from behind me and wrapped it around my waist.

This was what I was telling myself I wanted. So I needed to fucking learn how to enjoy it again. Casey moved her hand down to rest over my dick and rub it as she moved her body against my back. I slipped my hand down over Carly's ass and let two fingers tuck underneath the hemline and tease the bare skin just under there. She had nice skin. Her breasts were pressed just under my mouth and with each move of our bodies I let myself focus on how good it would be to suck on those nipples. My cock started stiffening under my jeans as Casey kept rubbing.

I moved my legs farther apart and let her slip her hand down and grab my balls through my jeans. These two could give me some relief tonight.

"Feel good?" Casey asked in my ear.

"When your mouth's on it it'll feel better," I replied.

"I like it on my knees," Carly replied, licking her lips.

Yeah, these two would do.

# Harlow

Adam had been polite and attentive during dinner. He hadn't mentioned my dad or Mase once, which was a relief. It helped wash that worry away. Old habits die hard, and I was good at putting up walls when I was suspicious of guys using me to get to my dad.

We had watched an action movie because we both liked them. It was nice not to be "on" and worried about conversation for two hours. Then he had taken me home. Nan's car was gone and so was Mase's truck. I could invite him in, I guessed. Was that what I was supposed to do?

"I had a good time tonight," I told him as we walked toward the door.

"Me, too. I'm hoping we can do it again," he said with sincerity in his voice.

"I'd like that," I answered honestly. Because it was true. I had been nervous but the date had been easy. It had also given me something to do tonight.

I reached into my purse and pulled out the keys. "Would you like to come in for a drink? I have coffee," I suggested, not sure if I should be offering something stronger.

Adam grinned. "Yeah, I would. I wasn't really ready to say good-bye just yet."

I sighed with relief. I had done the right thing.

I opened the door and held it for him as he walked inside. "Come on in," I said.

He let out a low whistle. I glanced around. The place was kind of impressive for a house on a beach. "Nan has expensive taste," I explained and set my purse down on the table by the entrance. "Kitchen is this way," I said before walking toward it.

"You adjusting to living with someone you don't get along with?" he asked.

"Yes and no. It is what it is. We're working through it but ignoring each other," I replied. We entered the kitchen. "You want coffee or something else? Nan has a full bar."

"I need to drive home so coffee is good," he said.

I kept myself busy making the coffee and let Adam look around the place as he waited. "Is your brother staying here, too?" His question immediately made me tense. I had to remind myself that he was just trying to make small talk. Talking about Mase did not mean he was interested in my dad.

"He's staying here while he's visiting."

"A family gathering," he said with a smile.

I wouldn't think about that. I would not. I had to learn to trust people. Just because he was mentioning my family did not mean he was a fan of my father's. I had to overcome that insecurity.

"Not exactly," I replied, and pulled two cups down from the cabinet.

I heard the beep that sounded when an entry door or window opened and I froze. If it was Nan this could be bad. Then

I heard her voice laughing and a deeper voice. I felt sick to my stomach. *Please, God, don't let that be Grant. Not right now. I can't deal with that.* I wasn't ready just yet.

Her heels clacked against the marble as she walked down the hallway. They were headed this way.

"Nan," I explained to him as I poured a cup of coffee.

"Ah," he said simply.

"Cream and sugar?" I asked.

"Black is good," he replied.

I handed him the cup as Nan came staggering into the kitchen on the arm of a tall blond guy with a dark tan. He was dressed in a pale pink polo and a pair of plaid shorts. If he weren't so attractive the outfit would have looked ridiculous on him.

"Well, hello," he said, smiling at me in a way that made me uncomfortable. Then his gaze moved to Adam and his eyes widened a bit. "Adam, hey," he said as Nan looked sourly at both of us.

"What are you doing here?" she snapped.

"I live here, and he's my company," I replied, stirring the sugar into my coffee and praying she would just go away.

"Pull in the claws, kitty. It's your sister and Adam. Be nice."

"She's not my sister," Nan said angrily.

I wasn't in the mood for her stupid temper tantrums. I was getting sick of it.

"Then you probably should move out of the house my daddy paid for," I said, and took a sip of my coffee.

The hate sparking off her eyes told me I'd pushed the right buttons. Good. She needed to grow up.

"How dare you!"

"How dare I what, Nan? Remind you that we share a father who owns this house? It's as much mine as it is yours. If you want to argue, then please call him. I'm sure he'll clarify that for you."

The smart mouth was coming from somewhere. I wasn't sure where; it was as if I'd been possessed and had no control over my words.

The tall blond guy laughed, then patted Nan's arms as if to soothe her. "She's your sister, all right. That mouth says it all. Calm your sexy ass and leave her and Adam alone. We aren't here to drink coffee," he said, then winked at me as if I wanted to know about his and Nan's plans. "I'm August, by the way," he said.

He was the golf pro I had heard about. I was just glad he wasn't Grant. More glad than I wanted to admit. "Harlow. Nice to meet you," I replied.

"Don't talk to her," Nan spat.

"You get mean when you drink tequila. I told you I was going to stop letting you drink so much," August said.

"No, she's mean all the time. Tequila has nothing to do with it," I assured him.

Adam laughed this time, and I saw August hold back a smile. "I think I'll stop things before we have a fight on our hands. Come on, Nan, let's go upstairs."

The beep sounded again and we all turned to see who was here.

The heavy sound of boots told me it was Mase before he walked into the kitchen.

"Shit, now *he's* here," Nan complained, which only made me smile.

Mase stepped into the kitchen and around Nan and August with a glance at them before he looked at me and Adam. "What's up? Am I missing a family fight? I hate to miss those."

"I'm taking this one upstairs to keep any swings from breaking out," August told him.

Mase leaned against the counter in front of me before crossing his arms in front of his chest. "She can take swings if she wants, but she won't touch Harlow. Not if she wants to keep her bones in working order," he drawled as if he were bored.

August's eyebrows shot up. "Dude, Harlow isn't innocent here. She was mouthing off pretty good, too."

Mase glanced back at me over his shoulder. "Did you talk back to her?" he asked.

I nodded. No use in lying. A grin broke out on his face. "Well, I'll be damned. That's my girl." he turned back to August. "You can go on and take up with that one all you want. But when she's stomped you under her spiky heels and crushed you, then you'll see what a stupid idea this was."

"Ugh, I hate both of you. Come on, August. Let's go," Nan grabbed his arm and they left the kitchen. We could hear Nan's heels as she stormed up the stairs like a preschooler.

"That was . . . uh . . . interesting," Adam said, then took a drink of his coffee.

"Ain't it though. This place is a damn zoo," Mase replied, and looked back at me. "Got any coffee left?"

I nodded and fixed him a cup then walked around the bar. It was awkward now. I wasn't sure what to do with Adam after all that.

"I'm Harlow's brother, Mase."

He was introducing himself to Adam. I was a horrible hostess.

"Adam. Nice to meet you," he replied.

"You two have a good night?" Mase asked.

"Yes," we both said and I blushed.

Mase chuckled. "Well, I'll head on up to bed. See you in the morning. Nice meeting you, Adam," he said, kissing the top of my head, then heading for the stairs.

Once his heavy footsteps hit the stairs I looked over at Adam. "I'm sorry about all that. Maybe asking you in was a bad idea."

"No. I, uh, get it now. Why you don't like staying here. She's mean as a damn snake. I am trying to figure out why August is messing around with her. I wonder if she even knows he has a little girl. Surely he isn't letting her near his kid when he gets her on his weekends."

Whoa . . . Nan was dating a man with a kid? I couldn't imagine that.

"I hope he doesn't. I'm afraid Nan would see a kid as competition for his attention. She's that immature."

Adam nodded and frowned. "I was thinking that, too."

I drank some more of my coffee and considered inviting him into the living room or just saying good night. I was tired and after all that I wasn't sure I wanted to make this last any longer. Especially if Nan started getting loud.

"I'm getting tired and my head is a little scattered."

Adam nodded and gave me an understanding smile, then stood up.

"I get that. I would be, too."

I set my cup down and led him back to the door.

"Thanks again for tonight, and I'm really sorry about all this."

Adam didn't respond right away. Instead, he stared down

at me a moment as if he were deciding something important. Then he bent down slowly and in that brief moment I knew what was about to happen. It would be my first kiss since Grant. I had kissed Grant a lot during those two weeks. I didn't want to compare him to Grant, but I was afraid I wouldn't be able to stop myself.

When his lips touched mine they weren't as soft but they were warm. He moved over my mouth gently and it was pleasant. He didn't try for anything more. When he pulled back and smiled at me I knew that nothing would ever be as good as Grant's kisses but that I could live with this.

"They are as soft and plump as they look," he said, then shook his head with a grin on his face. "Good night, Harlow." He opened the door before I could say more and stepped outside, closing it behind him.

He wasn't Grant but he was nice. He wanted me. And the smile on his face made me feel special. As if I had been something special for him. Grant Carter was made for women's fantasies. Adam was more real. He wasn't the kind I would need to worry about getting in too deep with. He was just someone to spend time with.

# Grant

"You have got to be fucking kidding me," Rush's voice broke into my dreams and I slowly peeled open my eyes to see tits in my face. Confused, I looked down and saw two long pairs of legs draped over me.

Carly and Casey. I had forgotten. Damn, they were still here. I'd passed out. Shit. I would've preferred to send them home. Then I remembered Rush's voice and jerked around to look at the door. Rush was glaring at me with disgust. He wasn't looking at the two naked women in my bed. Kudos to him, because they had nice asses. I knew that firsthand.

"Get rid of them and meet me on the balcony," Rush said and walked off.

Why was he so pissed off? This is what I did.

I disentangled myself and stared down at the two girls I'd spent my night with. Several condom wrappers littered the room and bed. They'd been full of energy. "Time to get up, girls. It's going-home time," I said, jerking the covers back and slapping both their asses. They grumbled and I couldn't remember who was who anymore. I was pretty sure at one time last night I was just calling them both Harlow. It was a low moment.

"I got company. Get dressed. I'll have a cab waiting on you in five minutes outside. It was fun," I told them and flipped the lights on to help.

"Ouch," one said, covering her eyes.

I waited until both of them were up and looking for clothing before I left them to finish. I headed outside to see why Rush was here.

Opening the door, I stepped out into the sunshine.

Rush glanced back at me. "Two of them? Really? That's fucked up."

I cocked an eyebrow. "Don't preach at me about two at a time. You did it all the damn time back in the day."

Rush shook his head. "I was stupid. You're stupid."

"Watch it. I happen to think it was pretty damn smart. They were nice and jiggly and helped me release some tension."

Rush turned his head to look at me. "I thought you had a thing for Harlow," he said.

I did . . . but I couldn't. I had explained this to him.

"Wanting Harlow is one thing. Sure, I want her. Who the hell wouldn't? But the thing is, I care enough about her not to mess with her. I'm not going to get serious. I can't have what you have with Blaire. It isn't me."

"Bullshit," Rush said, turning to look directly at me. "I had a drunk-off-his-ass idiot rambling on about how special she was and how he just wanted to talk to her and how much he missed her smile. That shit don't go away."

I hadn't realized I'd said I missed her. I did. Even with her here, I missed her. She made me laugh and her smile always made everything else seem unimportant. "She went out with Adam last night."

"The tennis pro?"

"Yeah," I replied, feeling sick at my stomach. What if Adam kissed her? What if he touched her?

"So, you fucked two strangers in your own damn bed."

"Because she went out with Adam," I replied. That was the truth. I wouldn't have gone looking for distractions had she not been on a fucking date with fucking Adam.

Rush let out a sigh. "Harlow is the most sheltered person I know. She has been protected and guarded her entire life. She's the only child of Kiro's to make it into the news. So he hid her in North Carolina with her grandmother. He hated the way the news wanted to know everything about her. He used his money to keep the world out of her life. Once her grandmother died she was thrust into his world and did the only thing she knew to do. She hid away in her room. Now she's here and she needs friends. She can't stay home and hide. She has Nan there. So, sure. Someone asked her out. She went. Why the hell not? You haven't asked her out. You haven't done shit."

"I'm scared of her." There. I said it.

Rush frowned. "You're scared of her? Harlow? Or are we talking about Nan?"

"I'm scared of Harlow. Of what I could feel for her."

"You're afraid you'll fall in love with her," he said, finally understanding.

I just nodded.

"Why? What's so wrong with that? It's a hell of a lot better than what I walked in on this morning."

I gripped the railing in front of me. I hated that I was about to admit this. It made me sound so weak. "What if I lost her? Like Jace."

"You could lose anyone. You could lose me, but you don't keep me out."

It was different. I looked at him. "What if you lost Blaire?" I asked. Surely he feared that.

Rush frowned. "It would be the hardest thing I'd ever have to face. Losing her would take my soul. But I can't not love her for fear of losing her. What kind of life is that? I wouldn't know how amazing it feels to wake up with her in my arms. I wouldn't get to enjoy watching her laugh and play with Nate. It's worth it. Letting something like that stop you is letting fear control you. Don't do that to yourself. Every moment I get with Blaire and Nate makes a life without them seem shallow and lonely."

I could see it on his face. He didn't fear losing her. It didn't haunt him. He loved his life now. Focusing on what could happen wasn't holding him back. Was that what life was about? Taking chances?

"If you think she could be the one then it's time you take a chance. If I lost all that I have tomorrow, I wouldn't regret one single minute. Ever. They're what makes my life worth it."

"My dad thought he was in love twice. Both times he was burned, and I paid the price. And I look at his life and where he is now, and it's sad. I don't want that."

Rush shook his head at me as if he didn't understand me at all. "The two women your dad loved were nothing like Harlow. Your dad didn't choose well. Harlow is a good choice. The man who owns her heart will be lucky. She is honest and kind. I've never seen her be anything but both of those things. So, if she's the one you allow yourself to fall in love with then I'd be more than happy for you."

He was right.

A heavy weight that had been sitting on my chest slowly lifted. What he was saying made sense. And I didn't have to hurt myself to protect myself.

"I may have pushed her too far away," I said, letting reality sink in.

Rush shrugged. "Maybe. Maybe not. Maybe you never stood a chance to begin with. But is she worth trying?"

I nodded. "Yeah, she's worth begging," I replied.

Rush sat down and propped his feet up on the railing. "Then I guess you need to stop having threesomes in your bed with strangers and work on getting Harlow to give you another chance."

That sounded easier said than done. I had told her I didn't want to have anything more than a friendship with her. She'd agreed and left it at that. Now what? I should just tell her I changed my mind?

"I don't think she's going to let me in that easy. And then there's that brother of hers who doesn't approve of me."

Rush chuckled. "Mase? Yeah, he'll be hard to win over. Good thing is you won't have to kiss him and beg for forgiveness. Just focus on Harlow."

For the first time in months I had hope. The idea of being near Harlow again and spending time with her was more exciting than anything else I could think of . . . except getting her naked.

# Harlow

A far-off ringing interrupted my dreams. Forcing my eyes open, I realized the sound was my phone. I rolled over and saw Dean Finlay's number on my screen. This could only be about my dad. Rush's father only called when something was up with Kiro. I sat up and quickly answered.

"Hey. What's wrong?" I asked, then glanced at the time. It was a little after three in the morning.

"He's missing again," Dean replied.

This was not the first time my father had gone missing. Unfortunately, Daddy would get so high he would do stupid things like go off with women he didn't know and sober up in their bed, oftentimes cities away from where he was supposed to be.

I stood up and went to my closet for some clothes. "How long?" I asked.

"After the concert last night he was partying with some groupies. I left him to go to the limo and rest. That was the last time I saw him. Trac was still in there with him and so was Wayne. Wayne was too trashed to remember anything. Trac said he left with two women. One had red hair, the other had long, curly brown hair. He didn't think anything of it."

Trac Trace was the bass guitar player and Wayne Rolls was the lead guitarist. I shoved my legs into a pair of jeans. "Where was Hail?" I asked. Hail Holloway played the keyboard. He was also the most responsible.

"Hail had already left for the night. He knows nothing."

"I'm getting dressed. Where are y'all right now?" I knew Dean had called because getting me there was the only way to find Daddy. He went off the deep end sometimes and I seemed to be the only one who could bring him back. Dean said once it was because I looked just like my momma.

"I hate for you to come out here all alone. Isn't safe," he said with a worried tone. "I'd send for Rush but he ain't gonna wanna leave Nate and Blaire."

"Mase is here visiting. He'll probably come with me. Where are y'all?" I asked, then buttoned up my shirt.

"Vegas," he said with a sigh.

"I'm on my way. Not sure when I can get a flight out but I'll be there. Keep me posted."

"I've already sent the jet. It'll be at the private strip in Destin waiting on you in about thirty minutes. Your daddy wouldn't want you in a commercial airplane."

"Thanks, I'll try calling him. If he's gonna answer anyone's phone call it'll be mine," I said.

"Yeah. Keep trying him. I'll see you soon, kid."

"Bye," I replied, then hung up and grabbed a suitcase. I had clothes to pack. I didn't know how long this would take. I also needed to wake up Mase.

Opening my door quietly, I walked down to Mase's room and knocked several times before I heard him grunt. Good, he was in there.

"What?" he grumbled.

I opened the door slowly and peeked inside. "Dad's missing. I gotta go to Vegas and help find him."

Mase sat up and rubbed his face hard with both hands in an attempt to wake up. "You have got to be shitting me. How old is he, eighteen? Fuck. How does he just up and go missing? He's Kiro Manning, for fuck's sake."

Mase had no idea how common this was. "It's something that happens with him on tour. I'll find him or he'll eventually answer my calls. I just have to go. The jet is picking me up about twenty minutes from here."

I watched as Mase battled with himself on what to do. He didn't like being around the band. He rarely came around anymore. Looking for Dad also wasn't something he wanted to do.

"I'm going, too. You can't go alone to Vegas. Let me get dressed and grab some shit."

I didn't tell him he didn't have to; I just nodded and closed the door behind me. I still needed to pack and brush my teeth and hair. I dialed Dad's number on my way back to my room and it rang three times then went to voicemail.

⊞

Once I had my overnight bag packed I headed down the hall and for the stairs. I needed some coffee and I knew Mase would, too. Waking Nan up to tell her was pointless. She would be mad that I'd disturbed her. Might as well not even tell her we were leaving. She probably wouldn't notice.

Just as I put the coffee into the filter there was a light knock on the front door. What the heck? I glanced at the time and it was only three-forty-five. Who would be here this early?

I closed the lid to the coffeepot and pressed brew before going to the front door. It was too dark to see outside. I turned on the outdoor lights and saw Grant standing outside with a thermos in one hand, looking wide awake.

Opening the door, I stared at him, completely confused, but I couldn't just leave him out there.

Grant grinned at me. "You ready?"

What? Was I dreaming? Was Daddy really not missing? Had this been some elaborate dream where I ended up in bed with Grant again? I had those often enough.

"Dean called Rush who called me. Can I come in?" he said, stepping by me and into the house.

"What?" I finally managed to ask.

Grant held up his thermos of coffee. "I'm ready to go find Kiro. I'll even drive us to the airport."

Mase's heavy footsteps broke into my thoughts and I turned to see him walking toward us. "Is this a damn search party?" Mase grumbled, dropping his bag at his feet and looking from me to Grant.

"Looks that way," Grant said.

"I, uh . . ." was all I could think of to say. I still hadn't figured this out.

"Go get you some of that coffee I smell, Sis; you need it to make coherent sentences. I'll deal with this," Mase said.

I didn't want to leave Grant alone with him but, honestly, I didn't know what else to do.

So I went to get the coffee.

# Grant

"Explain this," Mase said, standing with his feet apart and his arms crossed over his chest. He was Harlow's older brother and possibly the only person who had ever stepped into the father figure role in her life. I respected that.

"I want to go with her. I have a lot of shit to make up for. I'm starting now."

Mase frowned and continued to stare at me. "What the hell does that mean? Last I heard you were fucking Nan. What do you have to do with Harlow?"

She hadn't told him anything. I wondered if she had done that to protect me. "I was scared of having feelings for someone. Harlow stirred things in me I wasn't familiar with and it made me run. I've decided I don't want to run."

Mase took a step toward me. "You need to be real damn sure of that. 'Cause she likes you more than she wants to and I don't trust you. Not at all. If you want to go help find our sorry-ass father then fine, but I'm going, too."

I preferred to have her alone but this was okay. At least I was near her. I was tired of not being near her and watching her from afar.

"Understood," I replied.

Harlow walked back into the foyer carrying two mugs of coffee. "Here," she said, handing one to Mase.

"Thanks. He's going with us. He likes looking at you or some sappy shit like that."

Harlow's eyes went wide and I bit back a smile. That wasn't exactly what I'd said but the look on Harlow's face was perfect.

"Oh" was all she said.

Mase picked up his bag and then looked at Harlow. "Where's your bag?"

"I left it in the kitchen. Let me get it."

"I'll get it," I said, heading to the kitchen before she could finish her sentence. If I wanted to gain her trust back and even slightly crack that wall she had up around herself I had to do anything I could to let her know I was serious.

"I'm confused," I heard Harlow whisper as I left the room. I just smiled. Good. Confused was a good thing.

A Louis Vuitton duffel bag was sitting on the floor of the kitchen. I went and picked it up. The bag was worn out. I had no doubt this had been a gift from Kiro and she'd carried it for years. This wasn't something that Harlow would buy for herself.

I brought it back to the door and then opened the door. "Time to go," I said to both of them, still holding her bag. She glanced down at it and then back at me.

Mase made an amused sound in his throat and rolled his eyes at me as he walked out the door. Harlow followed him but stopped as she got close to me.

"Thank you," she said simply, then went outside.

This was going to be good for us.

⌗

Mase climbed into the front seat and I doubted it hadn't been on purpose. He didn't want me close to Harlow. He was going to make this hard on me. Fine. I could handle it.

"You good back there?" I asked Harlow, looking back to make sure she had enough leg room.

"Yes, thank you," she replied as a blush touched her cheeks. Damn, she was beautiful.

I turned back around and cranked the truck. "Rush said this was normal for Kiro. Is there a process on how to find him?" I asked, trying to make conversation.

"Yeah. Harlow calls him. He finally answers and she goes to get him. She's the only one he listens to," Mase replied.

I didn't like the idea of this all falling on Harlow's shoulders. The man had three grown kids. Why did everything have to be Harlow's responsibility?

"You can't call him and get him?" I asked, unable to keep the annoyance out of my voice.

"Dear ol' Dad has a favorite. He only listens to her."

"That's not true. You have your mother and you don't really need him. You have a good life. Then there's Nan, and she doesn't make it easy on him. I'm just . . . I'm just the one that . . ."

"You're just the special one. He loved your mother. She was his world and when she died you became his world. That's just the way it is, and I'm damn happy he gives a shit when it comes to you," Mase told her.

Harlow didn't say anything. She stayed quiet. I wanted to ask her more. I wanted to know how she was feeling and if she was worried. But Mase was sitting beside me, and now wasn't a good time.

"I need food. That jet better be stocked," Mase grumbled.

"It always is," Harlow replied.

This wasn't the first time I had been on Slacker Demon's jet but it was strange getting on it with Kiro's kids. It had always been with Rush. These two had a dynamic that I'd never witnessed before. Until Mase showed up in Rosemary I wasn't even aware they were close. I thought Kiro's elusive son stayed away from that whole world.

"Have you two always been close?" I asked.

"Yes," they both said.

"Grandmama always took me to stay at the ranch with Mase and his parents when I was a kid."

"Parents?" I asked, because that didn't make sense since his father was Kiro.

"My stepdad and my mom. He's more like my father than my own father," Mase said with his head resting on the seat and his eyes closed.

I hadn't realized that. Interesting.

"Harlow's visits were always something I looked forward to. I thought having a sibling was so cool. Especially one as proper and sweet as Harlow. Getting her all muddy and talking her into riding a horse or feeding the cows was always entertaining."

Harlow let out a small laugh from the backseat.

Maybe having Mase around wasn't so bad. At least I'd get a chance to know her better.

# Harlow

As soon as we got on the jet, Mase ate a bowl of oatmeal and went to bed. He was not a morning person. I sat down on the leather sofa beside the window so I could look out while I thought about where Dad could have gone instead of the fact that Grant was here. With me.

I didn't turn to see what he was doing or where he was going to sit down. I wasn't sure what to say to him now that we were alone. I also hated that my heart sped up when he smiled at me.

His warm body sank down beside me close enough that his arm was brushing against mine. "Hey," he said simply.

Ignoring him was impossible and it was rude. I wasn't rude. "Hey," I replied, glancing over at him then back out the window.

"You worried about your dad?" he asked.

Not really. This was common. "No. Just frustrated that he never seems to grow up."

"You not gonna look at me?"

I didn't want to. He made me forget that he was dangerous. "Probably not," I replied honestly.

Grant chuckled. "That's a shame. I like looking into those eyes of yours."

I closed my eyes and swore silently. *Why, Grant? Why are you doing this to me? It isn't fair.*

"Are you going to hate me forever?" he asked.

I didn't hate him. That wasn't what this was about. Did he not get that? He had laid the terms down. I was just protecting myself from him.

"I don't hate you. I just know where I stand with you and I'm being careful not to think too much about it, or you, for that matter."

He didn't say anything. Good. I'd shut him up. Maybe he would move and I wouldn't have to keep smelling him. All warm and delicious. I knew how that skin felt against mine and I did not need reminders.

"I made a mistake, Harlow. I was scared and I fucked up."

I finally turned to look at him. We'd already had this discussion. I didn't want to have it again. "I know. You told me already. I get it." I started to turn away again but Grant grabbed my chin and gently turned my face back to his.

"No. We haven't talked about this. I told you bullshit that isn't true. I told you I wasn't ready for a relationship. That was a lie. I was fucking terrified of loving someone so much and then losing her. But I'm not anymore. I can't keep doing this to myself."

I didn't reply because I had no idea what he was talking about.

"I want you. I've wanted you since the moment I laid eyes on you. When I was buried inside of you I knew then I was sunk. Those pretty hazel eyes and angelic smile had started digging inside me and making themselves at home in my heart. But that night . . . you claimed me, and I can't shake it. I can't forget it."

Oh. I stared up at him as his words sank in. Did this mean

he wanted this with me? Or was he just saying this because he wanted to have sex again?

He lowered his head until his lips were barely brushing my ear. "You're all I want. Forgive me for running? Please."

I moved away from him, putting some space there between us. "Don't. I'm not ready to just forget that you slept with Nan or that you didn't call me for two months."

Grant frowned and ran his hand through his long hair, making it even more tousled looking. "I did call. Ask Dean. He'll tell you. I don't know why you didn't get calls to your phone but I was calling the hell out of it. I thought you had found out about my drunk screw-up with Nan and were done with me. Your dad threatened to call the cops if I showed up at your house. I started drinking a lot to forget you, and yeah, Nan happened to be there."

Had he really tried to call me? Why would Dad keep me from him? Unless he knew about Nan and Grant. That would be a reason for Dad to threaten Grant. Was he telling the truth?

"I want to be near you. When I am, everything else fades away and I can't concentrate on anything but you. That's what scared me, but I've decided I was stupid to be scared of that. It's special. You're special."

My grandmama would tell me to ignore the sweet talk and walk away. But then my grandmama had never laid eyes on Grant Carter. He was too appealing for words. I missed him. This. Being with him. I missed it. He had shown me how to enjoy life, if only for two weeks. I had felt like I was finally living when I was with him.

"I don't think I can trust my good sense with you," I told him honestly.

"You'll find out you can trust me. I'm not a bad guy. Deep down you know that. I just made a very bad decision."

Taking chances had never been my thing. I wasn't a risk taker. I was careful. I didn't get hurt. I protected myself. I had walls. Grant had made it past my walls once. Letting him in again was asking a lot.

He moved over to me and put his head on my shoulder. "I'm not above begging," he said.

I shivered from the tingle of his breath against my skin. This was a bad idea. Grant was good at sweet-talking. With his looks and his mouth he could talk a girl into anything. If I let myself care about him any more it would only end in heartache.

"Don't beg. Just give me some space. I need to think," I replied, pressing myself further away from him. The fact that I wanted to crawl into his lap and wrap myself around him was not good. I used to be stronger than this. He talked about me making him weak; if he only knew how weak he made me.

Grant gave me this sad look that only made his face more appealing. I closed my eyes and took a deep breath. "Don't. You've been sleeping with Nan. I heard you. Do you have any idea what that feels like? To know that the loud screams that kept you up at night were actually images of someone——" I stopped myself. I was going to say too much.

"It keeps me awake at night. I hate knowing you heard that. I don't even remember much about that night. But knowing you heard us . . . it kills me."

I looked out the window so I could open my eyes. I didn't trust myself with those eyes of his locked on me. "Put yourself in my shoes. What if you had heard me having sex with another man . . . one you hated. How would it make you feel?"

Grant didn't reply. I thought maybe I had shut him up and he was going to leave me alone. I was relieved and disappointed at the same time.

Grant moved closer to me again and his hand reached up and brushed the hair on my neck away. "The idea of some other man touching you makes me so fucking insane, I want to destroy shit. I can't imagine it, and just thinking about it makes me shake with fury."

I could feel the stiffness to his body as it brushed against my side.

"Your date with Adam haunts me. I can't stand the idea of him touching you," Grant's finger trailed down my bare arm. "I don't do possessive and crazy. Never have. But you . . . I want to wrap you up and run off with you so no one can touch you again. Just me. Always me."

Grant's head dipped down and the tip of his nose grazed the skin on my neck. "You smell like heaven and hell all wrapped up into one," he whispered.

My heart slammed against my chest and my legs felt weak. Did he mean all that? I turned my head to look into his eyes, and the determination and desperation told me that he meant every word. Grant Carter wanted me that much. As hard as it was to believe, he had called me and I hadn't known it. I couldn't convince myself he was lying. He was so determined for me to believe him. I wanted to believe him.

The memory of how good Grant could make my body feel was replaying vividly in my head. I didn't want to remember, but he was making it very hard.

"If you don't trust me, I understand. Just let me near you," he said as his hand slipped under my shirt and rested on my stomach. "I'll prove it to you. Just let me. Give me a chance to prove it to you."

His hand played with the skin on my stomach and I forgot to breathe.

"I don't want to be another Nan to you," I told him honestly. I had witnessed firsthand how easily he had slept with Nan then ignored her and her feelings the very next moment.

"You're nothing like Nan. What she and I had was shallow and based on her selfishness and neediness. She has no feelings for me and she made sure to kill all feelings I had for her."

I let his hand to continue to touch my skin and send tingles through my body. This might come back to haunt me, but I was good at reading people—and I believed Grant Carter.

"So fucking soft," he murmured in my ear, and I let my head fall back to give him more access to my neck because I was incredibly weak when it came to wanting what this man could give me. This wasn't smart. I was making a huge mistake but I couldn't seem to stop myself. I loved how he made me feel. My body wanted more. Even if my head was screaming at me to stop this.

He let out a pleased growl and his lips found my arched neck and took small nips as he made his way down to the top of my shirt. His hand was there, unbuttoning it, and I didn't care. I wanted his mouth on my breasts. Grant had given me orgasms I hadn't known existed, and I wanted that. He made my body do things I didn't know it could do, and I wanted that.

"So beautiful," he said in a reverent tone as he pulled my bra down and his hands covered my breasts. I moaned in relief. The ache that had settled in them was somewhat eased by his touch. I wanted more, though.

Grant grabbed my waist and hauled me into his lap until I was straddling him and my bared breasts were in his face. "Fuck, yes," he said before his mouth was on my nipple, sucking. His other hand was pinching and twisting my other nipple. The sensation was causing the wetness between my legs to grow as I squirmed. A new ache was taking over. I sank down onto his lap and the hard erection in his jeans pressed against me, causing me to cry out in pleasure.

Grant stopped sucking, and his eyes were fiery blue pools as he gazed up at me hungrily. "You need me to touch your sweet little pussy?" he asked as his hands began unzipping my jeans. I only managed to whimper. I shouldn't be doing this but I couldn't stop.

The simple truth was I was horny. I hadn't understood that term until Grant Carter entered my life. But this man made me lose it. All that control I possessed he made me forget in seconds.

"Put your hands behind me and lift up," he ordered. I didn't argue. I wanted his hands on me. The excitement made my heart race and my body tremble.

His hand slipped into the front of my jeans and two fingers slid into my panties until they rubbed right against my clit. I bucked and moaned.

"Fuck," he growled, and jerked his hand out. I started to beg him and he stood up, holding on to me. I wrapped my legs around his waist as he stalked to the back of the plane. Then he stopped and looked at the closed door to Dad's room. Mase was in there sleeping. I had forgotten about Mase, and I was pretty sure Grant had, too.

He looked at the room beside it and I knew even if we were quiet Mase would hear us. Grant turned and went the other way to the private bathroom and opened the door and slammed it closed behind him.

"Get them off," he said in a heated voice as he jerked his shirt over his head.

I glanced down at my jeans and started to fumble with them. Before I could get very far he had stripped and taken over, pulling my jeans and shirt off. Once we were both naked his mouth crashed down on mine and his tongue invaded me. Hot, minty, and hungry. I clung to his shoulders and kissed him back just as fiercely. I had missed this. The heat, the passion, the need all wrapped up into this one act. Grant's hands cupped my bottom as he pulled me closer and continued to take nips and licks at the corners of my mouth while destroying me with a kiss I knew no one could ever live up to.

When he pulled back he looked into my eyes then pressed one more small kiss to my lips before picking me up and sitting me on the counter. "I want inside you again, but I want to taste you. I've missed how sweet you taste. But you have to be quiet." He gave me a wicked smile. "Can you be quiet while I kiss this sweet pussy?" he asked, slipping a finger into me and causing me to cry out.

"I don't think you can. My sweet girl likes to be loud. I can't kiss it if you're gonna scream," he said as he kissed my neck and continued to run the tip of his finger between the slick folds.

I wanted his mouth on me. I wanted it more than I wanted to breathe. "I'll be quiet," I promised.

He grinned but didn't look as if he believed me. I held my breath as he kissed his way down my body and pressed one simple kiss to my bare mound.

Then his tongue stuck out and he slipped it right over my clit. I slapped my hand over my mouth and threw my head back as the pleasure grew.

He stopped and I reached for his head to hold him there.

"If you scream I stop," he said, looking up at me with a sexy smile that made me want to do anything he asked.

I nodded and held my hand over my mouth.

# Grant

This was not what I had intended to do. I wanted to talk to her and ease her into talking to me. Get Harlow to smile at me and trust me as she had before I screwed it all up by being a coward. But then she'd made me think about someone else touching her. Someone else knowing how incredible it felt to be inside her and knowing he was the one making her cry out. Fuck no. I couldn't allow myself to think about that. If she had thought about sleeping with someone else, I needed to make sure she remembered just how it was between us. I wasn't losing her. Not again.

The taste and smell of her made me forget everything around me. I'd almost forgotten her brother was in the damn bedroom. Small noises escaped from behind the hand she held so tightly across her mouth. I couldn't help but grin. She was so damn adorable.

Bringing her to an orgasm like this would make her drop her hand and grab my hair and cry out. I knew that. So as much as I wanted to, that wasn't happening. I needed to have my mouth close enough to smother her cries when she got off.

With one small kiss to her sensitive skin, I leaned back, causing her to reach for me and pull me back. I loved seeing proper, sweet Harlow get sexually demanding. It was hot as hell.

"Shhh . . . I'm gonna make it feel good, sweet girl. Just wait," I promised her, reaching over her head into the cabinet, knowing there would be condoms somewhere close by. This was Slacker Demon's plane, after all. The second door revealed an open box, and I grabbed one. Harlow watched me as I slipped it on, then I grabbed her hips, sliding her closer to the edge of the counter.

Her eyes went wide and locked with mine as I eased inside her. It was so incredibly tight I wanted to make a noise. I bit my bottom lip as I sank all the way in. She was like a hot, slick glove that squeezed me just right.

"If you move I'm gonna get loud," she said, breathlessly.

I bent down and covered her mouth with mine before sliding back out and letting the exquisite feel of her send tingles up my spine. Harlow moaned into my mouth as I began pumping my tongue into her mouth with the same rhythm as our bodies.

Harlow clawed at my back and I relished it. She'd leave marks that I would feel later. I wanted that. I grabbed handfuls of her hair and let out a groan into her mouth as her hips began meeting each thrust. Her knees lifted even higher until they were covering my ribs. That was my undoing. I was too close and she felt too damn good.

"Let go," I muttered against her mouth before covering it again to muffle her sounds.

At my words, her tight warmth clenched me so tightly I lost it. Harlow's cry as I reached my release made me come even harder. Feeling her body jerk and tremble under me made want to shout. This was mine. How had I thought I could let this go?

I broke the kiss and buried my head in her neck as I gasped for air. Her nails gently raked down my back one more time, then she let out a long, shaky breath. Her legs fell from my sides and I stayed there inside her, reluctant to leave her warmth.

"I can't believe I just did that," she said quietly.

Me either, but I wasn't going to say so. I didn't want her regretting this.

"You're amazing," I replied, lifting my head so I could see her face. The flush on her cheeks and chest only highlighted the sated look in her eyes.

"I'm not like this. I don't just do this," she said.

Here came her self-doubt. I stood up and pulled her up with me. "You do this with me. That's all that matters. We're attracted to each other. We have feelings for each other. This is okay. It's not like I'm a one-night stand."

Harlow ran her hand through her messed-up hair and gazed up at me. "Are you sure this doesn't make me a slut?" The true concern in her eyes was the only thing keeping me from laughing out loud.

"Baby, it's only been me. You've only been with me. Twice. That does not make you a slut. Never. Don't consider it."

Harlow chewed on her bottom lip as she thought about my words. Finally, she sighed. "Okay. I guess you're right. But . . . it's not like we're in a relationship, and I just . . ." She paused and looked down at us. I was still inside her and I could see that realization in her face as her pink cheeks turned even redder.

I eased out and groaned from the release of her warmth. Harlow watched me in fascination. If she didn't stop, I was going to be ready to go again in less than five minutes. I reached over and grabbed some toilet paper and eased off the condom before looking back at her.

She jerked her attention off my cock and then smiled at me shyly. "I forgot what I was saying."

A loud knock on the door made her jump and I swore.

"Get your damn clothes on and get the fuck out of there," Mase demanded loudly from the other side of the door.

Shit. Not what I wanted to deal with right now.

"Let me talk to him first," she said, jumping down off the counter and reaching for her panties. Her angry brother might be outside, but I wasn't letting him ruin this for me.

I took her panties from her hands and bent down to put them on her. Once I had them pulled up and in place I did the same with her jeans. She cooperated silently. When I fastened her bra I finally allowed myself to look at her. She had on enough clothes now that I could focus.

There was a softness there I hadn't seen before. I wanted to keep her right here, locked away from everyone else in this moment. She slipped her arms into her shirt and I buttoned it up before pressing a kiss to her cheek.

Then I quickly grabbed my jeans and jerked them on and pulled my shirt on over my head. We both slipped on our shoes. I ran my hands through her tangled hair until I had it looking as if she hadn't just been completely fucked in the bathroom.

"Let's go," I told her and opened the door so she could step out.

"Maybe you should stay in here," she said quietly.

I shook my head. I wasn't scared of the cowboy. "Hell, no."

Harlow let out a sigh and we walked into main cabin of the

plane. Mase was drinking coffee and sitting by the window, but he was facing us.

"Not sure why this surprises me. I saw it coming a mile away," Mase said as he glared at me.

"You don't understand. It wasn't just . . . it was . . . we were . . . ," Harlow stuttered.

"I screwed some shit up. Harlow and I are working through it. I'm winning her trust back."

Mase snarled. "No, you're fucking her in the damn bathroom on a plane."

I took a step toward him and Harlow reached out and grabbed my arm. "You don't understand, Mase."

He raised his eyebrows, then took another sip of his coffee. "You're a grown woman. If you want to make a mistake, I can't stop you."

The fact he was calling me a mistake pissed me the hell off, but I held my tongue.

"Don't say things like that. You don't understand. But you're right. I'm a grown woman, and as much as I love you this isn't your business."

Mase smirked. "Bet our father will disagree with that."

Harlow moved this time. "You will not tell Dad any of this. We aren't kids."

Mase took another long drink of his coffee. "Easy, tiger. I'm just teasing. Besides, he'll figure it out himself. First, we just have to find his sorry ass."

# Harlow

Grant had taken a seat on the couch and pulled me down beside him with his arm wrapped firmly around my shoulders while he talked to Mase as if my brother hadn't just caught us in the bathroom.

Men.

The rest of the flight went quickly, but then Grant had kept me very distracted for the first long portion of the trip. When we arrived in Vegas, Grant took my bag and we headed to the limo that Dean had sent to pick us up. I didn't have to ask to know they were at the Hard Rock. It was their favorite place to stay in Vegas. I preferred the Venetian.

Grant slid in behind me and sat close enough that our bodies touched from shoulder to ankle, even though Mase sat across from us and there was plenty of room for him to scoot over. I liked it, though. He was determined to stay close to me.

"You called him since we landed?" Mase asked as he leaned back and stretched his legs in front of him.

I quickly pulled out my phone and turned it on to call Daddy. It rang three times and went to voice mail again. "Still not answering," I said.

"He's an ass. I can't believe we came out here to look for our forty-five-year-old father. This is ridiculous," Mase grumbled.

I knew Mase didn't respect Dad. He held him to the level of his stepfather and that was unfair. Dad was a rock star. He was a legend. His world was different. You had to take into account that if he wanted something, people fell all over themselves trying to give it to him.

"He's still our father," I said, trying not to get defensive. Grant reached over and squeezed my hand. It felt as if I had an ally. Someone who understood. No one really understood my life and choices, not even Mase. Just knowing that someone might felt . . . well, it felt freeing. As if I wasn't alone.

"Yeah, he is. Lucky us," Mase replied, staring out the window.

Grant's hand tightened on me and he pulled me closer to him. I didn't want to like this or need it. But right now I was giving in to it.

My phone rang, startling all of us, and I fumbled with it to see it was only Dean.

"Hello," I said, hoping he was about to tell me Dad was back at the hotel.

"Have you landed?"

"Yes, we're on our way to the hotel," I replied.

"Has he answered any of your calls?"

There was something off in Dean's voice. Did he know something?

"No . . . has he called you?" I asked.

Dean didn't reply right away. I started to get worried.

"No, he hasn't. But when you get here we need to talk about something before you go looking for him."

That sounded as if he knew something. I didn't like him being so secretive. It was only making me nervous. "Okay. I should be there in just a few minutes," I replied, when I wanted to demand he tell me now what it was he knew.

"See you in a few, kid," he said before he hung up.

I held the phone in my hand and stared at it a moment.

"You forgot to tell Dean you brought his other son with you," Mase drawled.

I glared at him and Grant just chuckled. I was glad Mase wasn't getting to Grant. That wasn't something I wanted to think about right now. I was afraid I had a much bigger problem. The foreboding sound in Dean's voice was all I could focus on at the moment. Something was wrong. He would tell me if something had happened to my daddy . . . wouldn't he? I dropped the phone to my lap and placed a hand over my stomach. He had to be okay. He had to.

⌘

When we arrived at the Hard Rock, we were sent right up to the penthouse that Dean and Kiro always used. The rest of the band stayed in another one. Dean opened the door, a frown creasing his forehead. I studied him closely. He didn't look like someone who was about to tell me my dad was dead. He just looked concerned.

"We need to talk," he told me. I nodded, because I already knew this. I hadn't said anything to Mase and Grant in the car because I wasn't sure I could without choking up. I was scared. I hated to admit it but I was scared of losing Kiro.

Grant's hand was suddenly in mine and Mase was at my other side, his hand holding my arm as if I needed support to stand.

"Is he alive?" Mase asked, and I realized he knew nothing but was reading the tension in the room, just like I was. Whatever it was, Dean needed to tell me, even if he didn't want to.

Dean's eyebrows shot up and then he realized how his words had sounded and an apologetic look crossed his face. "Hell, yes, he's alive. I'm sorry, Harlow, I didn't mean to scare you, sweetheart. Normally, when he does this and I know where he is, I don't call you. I just deal with it. But when he ran this time I decided it was time you knew. You're not a child anymore. Kiro still treats you like one but he needs you more than he realizes." Dean paused and started pacing back and forth in front of us. He fisted and unfisted his hands at his side and stared at the floor.

Although I knew Dad was alive, I was now dealing with the fear of this big secret. Could he be sick? Was he hiding something like that from me?

"I don't want to be the one to tell you—hell, he should have told you years ago. This isn't right. But you need to know. I need you to know. I can't deal with him anymore. I need help. You're the only one that can help him, I'm afraid. It's getting harder and harder to make him leave once he's there." Dean's ramblings made no sense. He continued to pace the floor as if he could walk a hole through it to sink into. Whatever this secret was, it was bad. My knees started to feel weak.

Dean motioned to the sofa and waved his hand at it before running a hand through his hair. "You need to sit down," he said.

Different scenarios began running through my head. My dad was in rehab, or he had a secret family I didn't know about, or he was terminally ill. I let go of Grant's hand and walked over to the sofa and sat down, never taking my eyes off Dean. Grant was right beside me. I wasn't sure if I wanted anyone near me now. I started to feel smothered. Or my nerves were just making it hard for me to breathe.

"Didn't expect to see you, Grant," Dean said, acknowledging Grant.

I could see the look in Dean's eyes, and I realized he knew exactly what had happened with those phone calls I never received. He didn't approve of me and Grant, and that surprised me.

"Tell her whatever it is, Dean. She needs to hear it," Grant replied.

Dean started to sit down then stood back up and ran his hands through his hair. "Damn, this ain't gonna be easy," he muttered and looked over at Mase.

"Get to it, Dean," Mase demanded, taking a seat across from me. I was thankful he hadn't sat down on the other side of me. I was having a hard time getting air.

Dean nodded, then looked at me. "You know the story of how your mother was in a car accident when you were a baby?"

I nodded. It was how she died. She had left me with Dad and gone to the store. A truck had run a red light and hit her. She died instantly. My grandmama had told me the story one day when I was old enough to ask. She never wanted to talk about it, though. She wouldn't even look at me when she told me. I knew it was because losing her daughter had to hurt her. So I never asked her again. The fact that he was asking about my mother only made my anxiety worse. I gripped the edge of the sofa and tried to calm myself.

"She didn't die in that car accident, honey. She was in a

coma. For five years. Your dad refused to take her off life support, and one day she woke up. Except she didn't remember anything. Not you, Kiro, or even her own name. She also couldn't eat or drink or speak. And . . . she was paralyzed. The doctors soon realized she hadn't just suffered memory loss; her brain was traumatized. She was no longer mentally complete. She would never be able to relearn simple things again. She would be stuck in this state for the rest of her life. She got very agitated when your dad tried to bring her home, and the doctors warned him that if he did take her the trauma could send her back into a coma, and she might never wake up. So he had to leave her there."

I shot up off the sofa and walked away from everyone to the other side of the room. I couldn't breathe. This wasn't true. This was not true. It couldn't be true. My grandmama would never lie to me. She wouldn't do that. My mother was dead.

Grant was immediately beside me, his arm around my waist.

"I don't believe you," I said angrily, glaring at Dean. He was a liar. Why was he trying to hurt me like this?

"Holy shit," Mase said, standing up and swinging his gaze from Dean to me. I could see it in his eyes. He believed Dean. Didn't he know this was a lie?

"It's time you saw her. I think you're going to have to be the one to get him. He hates going on tour because he can't see her when he wants to. She's in the finest facility available in L.A. When we come to Vegas, he's close enough to run back and check on her. We have to leave the States from here and hit the U.K. He doesn't want to leave her. He's gonna need you to get him. We can't go without him, and seeing her only upsets him more."

I jerked away from Grant's arm. I didn't want anyone to

touch me. I needed space to breathe. Once I managed to force oxygen into my lungs, I put both of my hands on the wall and closed my eyes. Could this be true? Mase thought it was. He didn't have to say anything—it was all over his face. And Grant wasn't calling Dean a liar. He had been there to comfort me.

How could that be hidden from me all my life? Wouldn't my grandmama want to visit her daughter? There was no way. This made no sense. I didn't look at Dean. I didn't look at anyone. I stared at the wall in front of me and took a deep breath. "This isn't possible. I would have figured it out. My grandmama would have wanted to visit her only child." I wanted to yell at him and throw things, but I balled my hands into fists and focused on calming down. Let him explain that. Let him tell me my grandmama had gone the rest of her life without visiting her only daughter.

"Texas, Harlow. Your grandmother took you to Texas to stay with Mase," Dean said quietly. His words were gentle, yet it felt like he had slammed his fist into my gut.

She . . . she was going to see my mother. Oh my god. I doubled over from the pain. She had never stayed in Texas with me. How could she lie to me? Why? Why? Didn't they want me to see her, too? She was my mother.

I heard Mase and Grant both say my name but I shook my head. I didn't want them to try and soothe me. There was no way to ease this pain. I turned to see them both moving toward me, and a scream bubbling to the surface broke free. "NO!" I didn't want them near me. I held out both hands to keep them back. They both froze. I didn't focus on the pain in Grant's eyes and the sadness in Mase's. This wasn't about them. This was mine to deal with. Alone.

"Where is she?" I asked Dean, looking back at him. The fury and betrayal building inside me were solely focused on that man at the moment. He was the only one around that I could lash out at. He had known, yet he had let them lie to me.

"The limo will take you to her. Your father took it to L.A. The driver knows where to go," Dean said, dropping his head and letting out a sigh. He hadn't wanted to tell me. I should be thankful he had. But right now I had no room for thankfulness in my heart.

Grant started to walk toward me and so did Mase. "Stop. Both of you. Don't come near me. I need to be alone. I want to go alone. Just stay," I demanded. I didn't wait for their response. I turned and headed for the door.

I had to get to that limo. If this was true, then it changed everything. My father had lied to me my entire life, and my grandmama. How could I trust anyone?

How could they keep my mother from me?

# Grant

I had never felt this helpless. The door slammed behind Harlow as she fled the suite. She didn't want me with her. She didn't want Mase. She was just going alone. How the fuck was she supposed to deal with this alone?

I glared back at Dean. "I can't believe this shit!" I roared, wanting to throw something. "You just blurted out that her mother was alive and in a special home with no preparation? What the fuck were you thinking?"

"What he said," Mase said in an angry growl.

Dean sank down onto the chair behind him. "What was I supposed to do? Kiro won't leave. When it finally dawned on me where he might be, I called the place and sure enough he was there. He said he wasn't going on tour. He wasn't leaving her that long. She gets anxious and difficult if too many days go by and he doesn't come to see her. The doctors say she expects it. If she doesn't see him then she gets upset."

Fuck me.

I walked over to the windows overlooking Vegas. How did he survive this? Seeing the woman he obviously still loved, knowing she would never talk to him again? It seemed almost worse than death.

"Someone should have told her before now. She's twenty years old! She's been robbed of knowing her mother her entire life!" Mase sounded as if he was ready to put his fist through a wall.

"Kiro was afraid seeing her like that would upset Harlow, and Harlow would, in return, upset her mother. He does everything he can to protect Emily. The media have never gotten ahold of this story. No one knows about her but us. To everyone else, she's simply dead. Kiro loves Harlow, but when it comes to protecting her mother he will do anything and everything. No matter the cost. Even denying Harlow the opportunity to see her. But you're right. It's past time someone told her. Kiro should have told her."

I couldn't just stand here and wait on her. I couldn't be left to wonder if she was okay after meeting her mother for the first time. I looked back at both men. "I'm going."

"What? You're just leaving? What happens when she comes back? You not ready to face that?" Mase asked, glaring at me.

"I'm going *to* her. I'm not leaving her. Someone needs to be there when she meets her mother."

Mase's angry expression changed to one of respect. He nodded. "Good."

I didn't ask if he wanted to come. I didn't want him to. Three was a fucking crowd.

# Harlow

When I walked into the large white home, which could only be described as a mansion, I was met at the door by a lady in a nurse's uniform. "Can I help you, Miss?" she asked, not allowing me to enter the building.

Apparently The Manor in the Hills was harder to get into than a military base. I had shown the man at the gate my ID and Social Security card. It had taken him ten minutes to make a phone call and discuss my information before opening the tall iron gates that surrounded the place.

"I'm Harlow Manning. My father is here . . . and . . . my mother," I replied. Saying that my mother was here felt strange. I'd had plenty of time during the ride to process all of this. Part of me understood why Dad and Grandmama had done this, but the other part of me hated them for it. It was like being robbed of something you could never get back.

The lady used the mini iPad in her hand to type in something. I assumed it was my name. "I will need to see your ID, please."

Again? Really? I pulled my wallet out of my purse and handed her my driver's license. She looked from me to the picture several times then typed in the info from my card and waited. After what seemed like forever she finally stepped back.

"Regina," she called for one of the ladies behind the desk. "Please take her to Mrs. Manning's room. Mr. Manning is in there and he's expecting her arrival."

So my dad knew I was here. Good.

I followed Regina through an area that looked like the lobby of a five-star hotel. We stopped at the elevator and she pressed in a code. The doors opened and we stepped inside.

Regina then put in another code before locking her gaze on me. "Whatever you do, do not upset Mrs. Manning. Mr. Manning's presence keeps her calm, but if at any time she feels threatened, she gets very agitated and we have to sedate her. Mr. Manning hates that."

My heart was beating rapidly in my chest. I was nervous. I hadn't been nervous until now. Knowing I was about to see my mother and that she would be this . . . person . . . not like the smiling woman in the pictures . . . unresponsive . . . Was I ready for this?

And my dad. The way everyone described him with her didn't sound like him at all. Kiro Manning did not get emotional. He screwed girls my age and he drank too much. He didn't sit by a woman's bedside and take care of her. It was as if I had walked into another life.

The doors opened and I followed Regina into the hallway. There was only one door on this floor. I wasn't surprised. Dad didn't do normal. Regina walked up to the door and knocked twice, then waited.

When the door opened I saw my father standing there. His hair hadn't been brushed in what looked like days, and he also hadn't shaved. He was wearing one of his tight T-shirts and a pair of jeans that were too tight for the average forty-five-year-old man. But he was Kiro. It was expected of him.

"Thank you, Regina. You may leave us," he said in a defeated tone.

I just stood there and stared at him. I didn't know this man. He looked like my dad but he also looked broken. I had never seen him look broken.

"I told her you were coming. I tell her about you every time I visit, so she knows about you. I think she's excited to see you but I need you to be calm. Do not show emotion; it will upset her. Do not discuss this shit in front of her; she will get upset and I don't want her fucking upset. I hate it when I can't calm her. I hate those motherfuckers and their damn needles getting near her. So you stay calm. You keep your questions to yourself and we will talk where she can't hear us. I know you're angry; I can see it in your eyes. But understand me: no one upsets Emmy. No one. Not even you. I won't allow it."

The fierce, protective look in his eyes was something I had never seen. The emotion in my chest wasn't something I wanted to examine right now. This was a side of my father I had never known.

"Okay," I said simply.

He nodded and stepped back. I walked into the room and it was as elaborate as the rest of the place. A chandelier hung in the entrance. Tall windows straight ahead were framed with elaborate crown molding.

"This way," he said as we walked past a tall, marble fireplace and white leather-tufted sofas that set off a seating area. We entered another room, and this time my attention wasn't on the décor; my eyes fell on a sheet of long, dark hair, which looked as if it had just been brushed. It draped over the back of what I assumed was a wheelchair, though it was unlike any I'd ever seen; it was made of soft, tufted leather, though the wheels were unmistakable. It faced tall picture windows, which looked out over rolling hills and a stream that ran nearby.

My father walked over to her and picked up a brush that was sitting on a chair beside her. Had he been brushing her hair before I arrived?

"Emmy, sweetheart, remember I told you that Harlow was coming to visit? She's a big girl now. She's very excited to see you. I've brushed your hair and you look beautiful."

Was that my father talking? Never in my life had I ever heard him speak in that tone. All I could do was stare at him. This wasn't Kiro. This wasn't my dad. My dad didn't talk that way. He didn't brush women's hair. He had never even brushed my hair as a child.

He looked up at me, then slowly turned my mother's chair around to face me. My heart slammed hard against my chest. Breathing became difficult again, and I feared I was about to have a panic attack. This was too much. I was expected to remain calm, but how could I? This was my mother.

My eyes locked with hers. I held my breath as I slowly took in the woman in front of me. I had seen her pictures, and I could still see that same young woman in the one in front of me. She was cared for well. There was a vacancy in her eyes that couldn't be ignored, but what looked like a smile touched her lips.

"Hello," I said. I couldn't say "mother." I didn't know her. The woman I had always thought of as my mother was an image of a young woman with laughing hazel eyes and a big smile. One that was full of life. That was my mother. This woman . . . she wasn't someone I knew.

"Harlow, this is your mother, Emily. Emmy, this is Harlow. Remember that sweet baby girl you held? We look at her pictures and talk about the things we did and places we went? She was too small when she was born, and we were so scared we would lose her. But we didn't. You loved her too much to let her die. You did a good job, honey. She's all grown up now."

Emily Manning continued to stare at me. I wanted to accept that she was the woman in the photos I'd spent my childhood staring at and daydreaming about. But then that broke my heart even more. The happy, vibrant woman was gone. This was what was left.

"She's old enough to come see you now. Would you like that? If I brought her here with me sometimes?" Dad asked as he pulled the chair up beside her and held her hand in his. "I think it would make you smile more. You know I love to see you smile."

This wasn't happening. I was asleep. Nothing seemed real.

"Come over here so she can see you better, Harlow. She doesn't do well with far distances," my dad said without taking his eyes off Emily's face.

I was afraid to argue with him. It was obvious he would move heaven and earth to make sure she was happy. I sure didn't want to be the one to upset her.

I walked over to her, and she followed my every move with her eyes. Her eyelashes batted quickly and she made a grunting noise.

"That's close enough," Dad said. "Don't make her nervous."

I stopped.

"She looks like you. Can you see that? She has your beautiful mouth and hands. And her hair—that's all you. God knows mine is shit," he told her affectionately.

Her body leaned over toward Dad. I wasn't sure if she just slipped or if she was trying to get closer to him. "It's okay. See, I have you right here with me. I wouldn't let anyone in here hurt you, would I? You know I take care of my favorite girl," he said, pressing a kiss to her head.

The emotion in my chest exploded and I understood it now. This wasn't about me. This wasn't about what I had been denied. The bitterness of betrayal faded to sorrow in that moment. Not for me—not because I hadn't been given a chance to know my mom—but for my dad. Tears pricked my eyes and I knew I was going to cry. He was killing me. His devotion and obvious love for her was breaking me in two.

"I need to go into the other room a moment," I told him as my eyes filled with tears.

"Go on," he said as he turned Emily back around to face him.

"We're going to let her get a drink and rest. She's traveled a long way to see you today," I heard him explaining to her. Did she even understand him? Was he just talking to her to make himself feel better because he missed her so much?

By the time I walked into the sitting room area, tears were streaming down my face. I covered my mouth to hold in the sound of my sobbing. My strong, hard, powerful father, who loved to tell the world "fuck you" and live like he had no worries, was sitting in there holding my mother's hand and treating her like a queen. As if she were the most precious thing in this world. I had always known he loved her. He made sure everyone knew that the day he lost her marked him for life. But the scene I'd just witnessed? Oh, God, my heart hurt so much.

People saw him as a legend. He had it all. They worshipped him. Yet none of them knew. I hadn't known. I had always seen him as strong and impossible to hurt. I knew that wasn't true anymore. That illusion was gone. My father hurt. He hurt more than I could have ever imagined.

I sank down onto the sofa and buried my face in my hands and cried. I cried for the woman in there whose life was cut too short. I cried for the little girl who never got to know her. But mostly I cried for the man who would always love her, even if she would never again be the one he fell in love with.

# Grant

The moment I got into the rental car my phone rang. I reached for it and saw Nan's name on the screen. I started to ignore it but decided it was time to deal with her. I wasn't going to hide the fact I was seeing Harlow. Besides, she was with August.

"Yeah," I said. She must've had some reason for calling, so I'd let her get that out.

"Where are you?" she demanded.

"Why?"

"Because Harlow's gone, you're gone, and Mase is gone. Where the fuck are you?"

"You need to keep up with your roomies better," I drawled, bored already by this conversation.

I needed a cigarette whenever I talked to her. I was doing good. I hadn't had a smoke in two months. I wasn't about to let Nan send me backpedaling.

"I don't give a shit where those two are but I want to know if you're with them. I won't let that happen. Do you understand me?"

I understood that she was delusional, as always.

"Nannette, if I start sleeping in Harlow's bed, there ain't a damn thing you can do about it. So back the fuck off. It's over. I'm tired of being your backup."

The boiling rage implicit in her silence made me smile. I liked pissing her off.

For so long I had just wanted to make her smile. I had wanted to save her from herself. But she'd made sure to destroy all those feelings in me. Sleeping with one man after another and rubbing it in my face, then calling me the moment she needed someone. I had let her use me, and slowly it had eaten away at me. Being needed was something I thought I wanted. I thought it would make me feel like I had a purpose. What I hadn't realized was I had become Nan's bitch. That was a sour pill to swallow. Backing out of her life hadn't been easy, but once I had managed to kill my feelings for her and accept that she was bitter and angry, and that I could never change that, I had been a happier person. Sleeping with her when I was drunk was just easy. I knew what to expect in the morning. I knew I was no longer in danger of falling in love with her.

"Is this because I'm screwing around with August? You're being childish. I told you I just wanted to do the friends with benefits thing for a while. I don't like serious, and you wanted serious."

I'd been fucking insane. She'd saved us both from hell—I should thank her for that.

"I'm bored, Nannette. The benefits thing is over. We're in the past. I don't want it from you anymore. You can fuck whomever the hell you want to, and I'm okay with that. Hell, if he needs a condom I'll tell him where I left my stash."

Nan squeaked in disbelief. "You think she's sweet and pretty, but that'll get old, too. She's uptight and boring. When you're done trying to fuck Harlow, don't come running back to me when you realize it wasn't worth the effort."

I didn't take the bait. She was fishing. I wasn't stupid and I wasn't about to give her anything to throw in Harlow's face later. Nan played games. Mean, brutal games.

"Who I decide to spend time with is my business. I'm not yours, Nan. Never was. Now, if you're done I have important things to get to."

"Where are you?!" she screamed into the phone.

"Not in Rosemary," I replied, then hung up the phone and dropped it. Nan had been a hard lesson to learn. She was the kind of girl her father had warned me about. Loving Nan would only lead to disaster. Good thing I never really fell in love with her . . .

My phone rang again before I could think too much about Nan.

This time it was Rush.

"Hey," I said, thankful for someone I could actually talk to.

"Just talked to Dad," was his only reply.

"Yeah. It's fucked up. I'm headed there now. She wanted to go alone but I want to be there when she leaves."

"You and her talk things out before all this shit happened?"

We talked it out, all right. We talked it out in ways I hadn't expected.

"Yeah, we did. We weren't done but then Dean dropped this on her and she was gone."

"I'm having a hard time believing this, and it ain't even my momma. I can't imagine Harlow is handling this well. She seems so breakable."

I pushed back the possessiveness that rose up in me. Thinking about Harlow being breakable upset me. I didn't want to think about that. Not when I wasn't there to catch her.

"Not gonna lie. I'm pissed at your dad. He just blurted it out—no preparation or anything. That kind of shit needs to be eased into. He didn't ease into it."

Rush sighed. "Yeah, well, he's not exactly good with words. He just says what he's thinking."

That excuse wasn't enough for me. Dean was on my shit list.

"Nan is looking for you," Rush said.

"She called me," I replied. This was not something I wanted to talk about with him. Nan wasn't one of my favorite people but she was still his family.

"She'll eat Harlow alive. Be careful."

Not what I expected him to say but I agreed.

"I know. I won't let Harlow get hurt."

"If you do then Kiro will never accept Nan. She needs him to accept her. She might not deserve it, but she needs it."

I should have known his concern was more for Nan than Harlow.

"I won't let her near Harlow," was my only response.

"It would be nice if you wanted into the panties of someone who isn't Kiro's offspring. Less complicated."

I just laughed. Yeah, it would be, but Harlow . . . well, she was Harlow.

# Harlow

"You can't go in there looking like that," Dad said as he entered the room. "You'll scare her."

I lifted my tear-streaked face to see my father. I would never see him the same way again. No matter how many girls he screwed around with and how many crude things he did or said. All I would be able to see was the man in there holding my mother's hand.

"I came here angry. At you. At Grandmama. But now, I'm just . . ." I shrugged. I couldn't say heartbroken. I didn't want him to know his pain had shattered my heart.

"I was protecting her. You were a kid. You wouldn't have been able to understand, and you would have upset her. I couldn't let that happen, Harlow. I love you, kid. I've always loved you. You are the only piece I have of the woman I met and fell completely in love with. But she's still here, even if that spirit is gone. And I'll protect her with my life. She'll always come first. Even before you."

I just nodded, because I got it. Before I arrived, I'd thought there was nothing he could say that would prevent me from hating him. What I hadn't expected was that all it would take was to see him with her. He hadn't needed to say a word to me.

"How often do you come see her?" I asked.

Dad walked over to the fireplace and leaned against the stone. "Three, four times a week."

"And that's why you left Vegas? Because you're about to leave the States on tour?"

He frowned. "She doesn't do well when I'm on tour. The doctors have to sedate her some days because she gets so agitated. She needs me. She may not be the woman, mentally, that I fell in love with but her heart knows who I am. She wants me close. I can't do that again. Seeing her smile when I walk into her room makes everything else less important."

I would not cry again. He didn't want my tears. I was sure he had cried enough for both of us over the years.

"The band needs you. Maybe you can just fly back a few times and visit so it makes it easier on her."

He nodded. "I've been thinking about that. I just don't know if it'll be enough."

I couldn't stand here and tell him to sing for millions of strangers when his heart was in that room with my mother. It wasn't my place. I didn't understand his torment. I never would. I hadn't lived it.

"I know I can't let the guys down. They need me. But this is my last tour. I've decided I can't keep doing this. I want to be home. I want to be close to her."

"I'm sorry, Daddy," I choked out because I didn't know what else to say.

His eyes lifted from where he had fixed them on the floor and he looked at me.

"For what?"

I bit my lip and sucked in a sob and prayed no tears would fall. "For losing her."

A sad smile touched his lips.

"I used to be sorry. Hell, I used to hate the world. I hated life. But then I'd see you and I knew I had to live. You shouldn't have lived, but you did. She would want me to live, for you. For the baby girl her love had saved. I also knew she wouldn't want you in my life if I was going to continue being Kiro. She would want you to grow up in the house she grew up in with the mother she adored. So I did what I knew she would want. And you grew up to be her spitting image, inside and out. I get accused of loving you more than my other kids, and I do. I fucking do. You're mine and Emmy's. I didn't love Georgianna—she was a groupie. I didn't love Maryann—she was just a fling. So no, I don't love their kids the way I should. I only have one heart, and your mother takes up most of it. I don't have a lot of room left for anyone else. You're the only one I would even consider making room for."

I knew he loved Mase. The jury was still out on Nan. But I also knew he was trying to tell me that my mother was and would always be his heart.

I stood up and walked over to him. I wrapped my arms around his waist and laid my head on his chest. I didn't say anything. I had no words.

His arms slowly came around me. "I never meant to hurt you by keeping her from you. But it's what I had to do. I know you're all grown up now, but when I look at you I still see my little girl in pigtails. Every time I tried to tell you, I got high instead. I wasn't brave enough to hurt you. I hope you can forgive me and your grandmama. She agreed with me that you didn't need to know about your mother until you were grown. You were sick, baby, and I knew I couldn't lose you, too. That would have destroyed me."

I tightened my hold on him and buried my face in his chest and sobbed quietly. I couldn't hate him for this. It wasn't fair, but I understood. "I love you," I told him.

"I love you, too. And that woman in there adored you. She never left your side when you were in the hospital. She believed you were our special gift. I remember the look on her face when you took your first step. You were her angel from heaven, and when I lost her I knew I had to protect you."

I closed my eyes tightly and fought off the tears. I wanted to get control of myself so I could go back in there and see her again. When my sobs finally eased and my tears dried up, I gazed up at my dad. "Can I go back in there?"

He reached up and wiped my face then nodded. "Of course."

# Grant

A phone call from Dean had gotten me past the large iron gates of Manor in the Hills. I didn't intend to go inside. I just wanted to park and wait on Harlow to come outside. She'd been here at least two hours by now. I closed the car door and stepped around the front of the car so I could see the front doors. When she came out, I would be here.

If she didn't want to see me, fine. I'd just follow the limo back to Vegas. But if she needed me, I was available. I was stupid enough to think that because I had gotten her to fuck me in a bathroom, all was forgiven. I still had a lot to prove to her. And if she would give me a chance I'd always be there when she needed it.

I hadn't been waiting but ten minutes when the door to the Manor opened and Harlow walked out. From here, I could see she'd been crying. I made my way toward her. She didn't notice me at first. She was wiping her eyes and walking down the steps when I made it to the bottom. Her eyes lifted and widened when she saw me standing there. This was it. She was going to yell at me to leave or she was going to—

Harlow ran down the stairs and threw herself into my arms and began sobbing. I held her against my chest tightly and closed my eyes. I was immediately thankful I'd come. I'd been right. She needed me.

I didn't ask. I just let her cry and held her. Both her hands grabbed fistfuls of my T-shirt as her body shook. My chest ached with each pitiful noise that came from her. I wanted to fix this. I wanted to go inside and fix anything that upset her, but how the hell did I fix this? I couldn't.

"He . . . he brushes her hair," she said as a sob racked her body again.

He brushes her hair. What? Was she talking about her dad? I didn't ask. I just let her talk.

"She smiles at him," she choked out.

Yes, she was talking about her dad. I tried to imagine Kiro brushing a woman's hair, one who couldn't speak or move. It didn't seem like those two things went together. I couldn't see Kiro brushing anyone's hair but his own, and that was rare.

"Oh, God, Grant, my heart hurts so bad. He's so sweet with her. It's like there's this man I never knew existed. She can't do anything. Nothing. I don't even know if she even understands what he's saying, but he talks to her like she understands everything. He still loves her. Completely. And he gets nothing in return."

I glanced up at the mansion in front of me and tried to imagine what she was telling me, but I couldn't. I'd seen Kiro fuck a woman on his pool table who I was pretty sure was barely nineteen. He was drinking vodka straight out of the bottle and smoking a joint at the same time as he did this. It was forever burned in my thirteen-year-old brain.

I held Harlow and ran my hand down over her hair, trying to soothe her even if it was impossible. She didn't say anything else. Finally her sobbing eased off and she let go of my shirt and smoothed it out where she had wrinkled it. Not that I gave a shit. She could have the shirt if she wanted it.

"You're here," she finally said, looking up at me with a wet face that was still breathtakingly beautiful. How did she do that? Always so damn perfect. She made it hard on a man.

"I thought you might need someone."

She gave me a shaky smile. "You were right."

I reached up and wiped away the tears still clinging to her cheeks with my thumbs. "If you ever need me, I'm here," I told her.

She sighed and closed her eyes briefly. "That doesn't help," she said.

"Why?" I thought having me at her beck and call would be pretty damn helpful.

"I'm trying to keep you at arm's length. Being sweet makes it hard."

So that's what this was about. Well, she hadn't seen anything yet. I was gonna make it even harder before it was over.

"I thought we had gotten rid of that arm's-length thing in the bathroom on the plane," I replied, trying to get a real smile out of her.

She cocked her eyebrow. "No. That was because you're ridiculously sexy and you give me really amazing orgasms."

I could work with that.

"Anytime you want one of those all you have to do is crook that pretty little finger," I replied, and this time she did smile. A real smile. One that lit up all the darkness in her eyes.

I reached down and laced my fingers through hers and she let me. "I drove a rental car. You want to ride with me?"

She glanced over at the limo. "Yeah. I do. Dad wants to stay until tonight and I need to leave him the limo."

Good. I wanted her beside me.

"You ready now?" I asked.

She glanced back at the house. "Yeah, I am. I can't take any more today. And he needs his alone time with her. I think she needs him, too."

I wasn't sure what all went on in that room today, but I knew it had changed things for Harlow. Her life was forever different. The crying wasn't over, either. I had a feeling more mourning would come. And I intended to be there. She wasn't going to deal with this alone.

⊞

We were headed back to the desert and I had let Harlow pick the music. I also left her to her thoughts. She needed to think and process all she had seen today, and I understood that. I glanced over at her every once in a while to make sure she wasn't crying.

"I'm not going to break down again," she finally said.

"Do you want to talk about it?" I asked. Harlow wasn't a big talker when it came to her feelings, but after today I felt like she really needed to talk. Keeping that bottled up wasn't good for her.

"I was so angry at him. At everyone who had lied to me. But then . . . I saw him with her. No one could have prepared me for that." She shook her head and looked down at her clasped hands. "It definitely changed a lot between us today. I've always known that Dad loved me more. I hated to say that out loud, but I knew it and I felt guilty about it. Now, I get it. I don't think it's *me* he loves more. I'm just the kid that she gave him. I'm his connection to her."

I thought about Mase and how distant he seemed when he talked about Kiro. As if Kiro wasn't his father at all. And then there was Nan. I knew Kiro wasn't a fan of hers. Harlow, however, needed Kiro and she loved him. I didn't argue with her, but it was more than just her mother that made Harlow the favorite child.

"This is his last tour. He hates leaving her. I couldn't even argue with him. The world may want Kiro, but Kiro wants to be with her. Even like she is . . . he wants to be near her." Harlow let out a soft laugh. "And to think I thought my dad's heart had been buried with my mom."

I glanced over at her. "Do you plan on going back to see her?" I asked.

Harlow nodded. "Yes. She can't talk to me and I don't even know if she realizes who I am, but I know about her now and that's enough. I want to . . . I want to be the one to tell her about my life. And maybe she is truly smiling when people talk to her. If I spend more time with her, then maybe I will find a way to have some relationship with her."

I could hear the hope in her voice. She wanted to know her mother. It made sense. I just wasn't sure I could personally handle it if she left there broken every time. I reached over and tugged her hands free from each other and laced my fingers through hers. "I'm always here to go with you. Don't think you have to go alone. I will gladly wait in the car until you're ready to leave."

A soft smile touched her lips, and she laid her head back on the seat and turned to look at me. "Thank you," she said simply.

"Anything you ask, Harlow. Anything you ask," I told her.

She squeezed my hand. "I can't get the image of Dad talking to her out of my head. He was so gentle and sweet. Kiro is never sweet. Thinking about it just makes my heart hurt all over again."

"Tell me what I can do to distract you and I will. I can sing pretty damn good, but I suck at telling jokes so that's all I have to work with at the moment."

Harlow smiled but she didn't say anything. She just kept staring at me, making it hard on me to keep my eyes on the road.

When I pulled onto a long stretch of road, I was relieved that I would be able to look at her more often. It was too damn tempting not to. Before I could glance her way, Harlow leaned over and slid her hands between my legs. My entire body went still and my focus was shot to hell. I gripped the steering wheel with both hands and took a steady breath. Her mouth was at my ear before I could form words and her hand was rubbing my instantly hard dick through my jeans.

"Pull over," she said before pressing a kiss to my neck, then taking a lick. *Holy motherfucking shit*. What was she doing?

"Harlow, baby, what are you doing?" I asked. I knew she was trying to find something to take her mind off today's traumatic events, but I wasn't sure this was the right thing to do. Even though my dick disagreed with me.

"I need you to make me forget today," she said in a husky whisper.

Oh hell. This was a bad idea, but her hand felt so fucking good. I decided pulling off the road may not be a bad idea. At least then I could focus on controlling myself and talking to her. I pulled the car off the road.

Harlow leaned over in her seat. I thought she had changed her mind until I saw her unbuttoning her jeans and pulling them down her legs, along with the panties I'd already seen once today.

I was frozen in shock until she crawled over the seat and straddled me and lifted her shirt to pull out her breasts from their confinement. "Are you going to make me beg?" she asked as she sat there, looking at me.

Beg? What had I been going to say to her? I couldn't remember. "Harlow, I don't think this is what you really want," I managed to get out.

"Please. Don't tell me what I want or need. I am tired of people deciding what I need. I'm a grown woman and right now I need you to help me forget. Give me something else to think about."

I gazed up into her eyes, and the pain there was my undoing. How was I supposed to tell her no? She needed me. Wasn't that why I came? To be there for her however she needed me? Even if my brain was screaming that this was a terrible idea, I reached up and cupped her face, brushing my thumbs across her still tear-stained face. She was special. "I'll do whatever you need me to," I told her before pressing my mouth to hers.

I tasted her sweetness and wished I could take away all her sadness. Pressing a kiss to each corner of her mouth, I trailed my tongue along her bottom lip and shivered as she sighed. Her tongue found its way into my mouth and she got her own taste.

I could do this for hours. Once, this was all we had done and I had loved every minute of it. Holding her close and being this connected was more powerful than anything I had experienced. Until I'd been inside her.

She rocked her hips in my lap and I moved my hand down

to slip it between her legs. The wetness that met my touch surprised me. I had worried she was forcing this as a way to forget the pain. But she was ready, and the pleased hum that vibrated against my mouth told me she wanted more.

"Yes, that's good. I need more," she said as she started riding my hand. Holy fuck, where had this come from? I was gonna come in my damn jeans at this rate.

I slipped my hand out of her and she groaned in protest until she saw me quickly unbuttoning my jeans and jerking them down until I was free.

"Oh," she said in excitement and grabbed on to me with both hands, then brushed the tip of my swollen head with her thumb. I reached down and stilled her hands.

"Baby, you're naked and begging for me to touch you. I'm about to explode. You can't touch me. As good as that feels, I'm too damn close."

Her small frown turned into understanding as she took in my words, and her eyes got big in surprise. "You mean you're about to come?"

Fuck. Did she have to say that word? Her mouth saying words like that was gonna kill me. "Yeah. Real close."

"I wanna see it," she replied.

"Harlow, sweet girl, that's messy and we're in a car. I swear to you, I'll let you see it up close and personal if that's what you want, but not in the car where I can't clean up."

She glanced over at her purse. "I have tissues in my purse."

Was she serious? Or had I just died and gone to heaven where sweet, dirty-talking angels asked to see your come?

"Please, Grant. Let me play with it until it comes. I'll clean it all up," she said.

I gritted my teeth as my cock jumped in her hands. He liked that idea a lot. Too much. She wasn't gonna have to play long.

"But I thought you wanted me to fuck you," I managed to say.

"I do. We can after I see it. We can get it hard again, can't we?"

I glanced down at her bare pussy and decided, yeah, we could get it hard again real easy. "Yeah, I'm sure you can. I'm fucking positive you can."

She beamed at me and reached for her purse, leaving her round, bare ass stuck up in my face. I reached over and squeezed it and she squealed before sitting back up with an entire pack of tissues in her hand. "See," she said, smiling. Then she dropped them in the cup holder and reached for my erection again. I laid my head back and closed my eyes. If I watched her do this I was going to embarrass myself and shoot off too damn quick. And my girl wanted to play.

"It's so soft. I thought it would feel rough or something, but the skin on it is soft, even though it's hard and looks swollen. Does it hurt?"

She was not asking me this. Motherfucker. "It hurts a little but it's a good hurt, and you're making it feel real damn good. So fucking good."

"Really?" she asked innocently, and I opened my eyes to look at her.

She was staring down at my dick and gently toying with it. I would lose my mind like this. I reached down and took her hand and wrapped it around me. "Squeeze it," I instructed her.

She did, but not hard enough.

"Harder, baby," I told her.

She did. Yeah, that was it. "Okay, now move it up and down like this." I held her hand and kept it squeezing me tightly and moving up and down. "You do that and you'll see some come real damn fast."

Harlow bit her bottom lip and focused on doing exactly what I told her. I couldn't stop looking at her. She was so sexy. I reached over and touched the wetness between her legs, causing her to stop a moment and moan in pleasure.

"If you get to play, so do I," I told her.

"Okay," she said, breathing out and pulling harder on me as I ran my finger around her clit, feeling it swell under my touch.

"Oh, that's . . . it's so good," she moaned, tugging on me harder.

I needed a taste. I brought my fingers to my mouth and sucked her moisture off them as she watched me. Her tongue came out and licked her lips. My balls drew up and I knew I was there. I started to cover myself to keep from getting any on her, but she wanted to see this, so I laid my head back and cried out her name as I came undone in her hands.

She made a surprised sound but kept holding on to me while I shot all over her hands and arms. My hips bucked, relishing the feel of coming so she could see it. When her hand touched the tip of my head to touch the come, still slowly leaking out, I grabbed her wrist and cursed. "Fuck, baby, don't. Too sensitive."

Her breathing was fast and hard like mine. This had turned her on. I looked down at her hands and saw myself all over her. She wasn't wiping it off, she was studying it, too. Her breasts were bouncing with each hard breath she took. Fuck. I was already getting hard again.

I grabbed the tissues and started cleaning her off.

"Can I do that again sometime? I liked it. I liked the face you made when you did it," she said. Her blunt admission made my already stirring cock begin to rise.

Only Harlow.

"Baby, anytime you want to touch my cock it's yours. You can make it do whatever the hell you want it to."

She smiled and lifted the hand I hadn't cleaned to her mouth and licked my come off her finger. I stopped moving. I stopped breathing.

"I like the way it tastes," she said before licking another spot clean off her hand.

I was dead. That was the only explanation for this. I had made it to a place where little, sexy, dirty angels made men's fantasies come to life.

"Next time, will you do it in my mouth?" she asked, holding out her hand for me to finish cleaning it.

"You wanted me hard again. Well, you fucking well achieved it," I told her, wiping the come off, then grabbing a condom from my wallet and jamming it on. "I can't take you talking like that. Now I need you," I told her as I lifted her hips and slammed her down on me, causing her to scream out.

"You want to play with my cock, baby, then you can fucking play with my cock," I told her as I lifted her hips and slammed her back down.

"Yes!" She threw her head back and shoved her tits in my face. Both large, pink nipples right there for me to latch on to. I began to suck one and she grabbed my head and held it there. "Harder. Suck me harder," she said, and I bit down on the hard bud, unable to control myself.

"Oh, God, Grant! That's so good. More," she begged as I

switched breasts. She started to take over, lifting her hips and slamming back down on me.

"Is this what you wanted?" I asked her as she rode me harder.

"Yes!" she screamed.

"Say it. Tell me what you want." I needed to hear that sweet mouth talk dirty.

She opened her eyes and looked right at me, then licked her lips. "I want you to fuck me hard," she said slowly, and I let out a growl I didn't recognize and began pumping into her as hard as I could. Her breasts bounced in front of me, making the scene even more erotic.

I had never imagined Harlow like this. But damned if I didn't like it. She'd just taken amazing sex and made it mind-blowing.

"I'm gonna come," she said, grabbing my hair and burying my face in her chest. I liked it there just fine. I took a bite of her swollen breasts and she cried out my name and began trembling over me. She clawed at my back again and said my name over and over.

I grabbed both her tits and squeezed as my release hit me and I pumped into her, wishing there was no barrier. I wanted to mark her as mine. I wasn't sharing this. Ever.

# Harlow

I was a slut. Or trauma made me a slut. I wasn't sure. I hadn't been able to look at Grant since I'd basically raped him, then moved over to my seat and pulled my pants back on. He had kept his hand on my leg or his fingers laced in mine, but he didn't force me to talk.

I figured either he didn't realize I was a slut or he was feeling sorry for me today. My face heated at the memory of him coming on my hands and me tasting it. I knew about blow-jobs. I knew women must like it to do it. So I was curious. But now that I had made him come in my hands and tasted him, I was embarrassed. I didn't do things like that. It wasn't me. I had just needed to be reminded I was alive. Grant made me feel alive and as if nothing could touch me.

I had today, though, and it had been good. He'd made me feel good. My left breast still stung from the bite he took out of me. I tried not to smile thinking about his mouth leaving a mark on my boob. I liked that too much.

Maybe I liked being a slut. I was embarrassed, sure, but I felt really good. My body was still humming from the orgasm he'd given me.

"You going to sit over there, silent, and smile like that the rest of the way home? 'Cause if you are I'm gonna have to pull over again."

I laughed and turned to look at him. His sexy grin was on his face as he watched me.

"I wasn't smiling," I told him.

He glanced back at the road. "Yes, sweet girl, you were smiling like a very happy girl."

He was right. I was happy. How was I happy after everything I'd learned today? I never thought I'd be happy again when I walked out of that place, but then Grant had been there and he'd let me cry all over him. He'd made me happy.

"Thank you," I finally said.

Grant glanced back at me and frowned. "Please tell me that you didn't just thank me for sex."

I shook my head. "No. I mean, it was incredible, but no. I was thanking you for coming to get me. For being there."

His hand slid up my thigh and took my hand again. "You're welcome."

I couldn't figure Grant Carter out. Two weeks ago I thought he was a guy who wanted nothing but sex from me, and once he'd got it he'd left. Then I thought he was hung up on Nan. But now . . . now I wasn't sure what he was doing. He had come with me in the middle of the night to Vegas to find my dad. Then he had come after me so I wouldn't be alone when no one else had thought to do that. Then we'd had the most amazing sex in the world. I didn't have anything to compare it to but I was pretty positive that it didn't get better than Grant.

"Why are you here?" I asked. I needed to know. If this was all about the sex I couldn't say that I wasn't going to still have sex with him, because I liked it. No. I loved it. He was addictive. But I needed to prepare my heart and emotions.

"Because you are," he replied.

That didn't make sense.

"I don't understand that," I told him.

Grant squeezed my hand. "I screwed up with you. I got scared and I screwed up. So I ran because I'm good at running. I always fucking run from things. But when I saw you standing in that kitchen at Nan's I realized this time I didn't want to run. I wanted to stay. I just needed the guts to do it. You're worth fighting demons for."

I sat there, unable to think of a response to that. Grant Carter was known for his looks, his sexy body, tattoos, and smooth talking. That was no secret. I'd heard the rumors and experienced the smooth talking more than once.

As much as I wanted to believe what he was saying, I was a smart girl. I had been burned already. Grandmama always used to say, *Fool me once shame on you. Fool me twice shame on me.* I tried to live by that motto. But Grant made it hard.

"I don't trust you. I may never be able to trust you again. But I do like you. You make me smile when I need it. I don't want to keep you at arm's length, because I want more of . . . well, you know. I just can't promise you that I'll ever get over the past."

Grant didn't reply right away, and I wondered if he was going to tell me to take a hike, that I wasn't worth this. I wouldn't blame him if he did. I was more high-maintenance than he first assumed.

"You'll trust me again" was all he said. His hand never left mine and I didn't argue with him. There was no point.

⌗

Mase called me when we were right outside Vegas. His mom had called and his stepfather had broken his leg falling off the tractor. He had just left Texas on a commercial plane back to Rosemary to get his truck and go home. He had wanted to wait for me, but he said his mother sounded tired and worried. He needed to get her some help, then he'd be back for me. He sounded upset and questioned me about how I was after seeing Emily. I assured him that I was okay and Grant was with me. That hadn't eased his mind. "You need to be careful with that one. Let me bring you to Texas with me. I can help Mom and take care of you."

He had meant well, but I wasn't moving to Texas. Not now. I was ready to see where this thing with Grant was going first. I explained that I wanted to stay in Rosemary and if I needed him I would call. But I wanted him to stay with his mom and stepfather for right now. He seemed mollified by that and said he'd be back to Rosemary as soon as he could to check on me.

Grant had seemed silently pleased with Mase's departure. I didn't comment on that, though. Dean had apologized to me for telling me everything the way he had. I had hugged him and assured him it was okay. I needed to know, and I was glad I had witnessed Dad with Mom. I would never have believed it if I hadn't. However, Grant didn't speak to Dean, and I found that odd.

Once we were on the jet headed back to Rosemary, it dawned on me that I hadn't slept in more than twenty hours. Grant seemed to read my mind. He took my arm and led me back to the bedroom and began taking off my shoes.

"Lie down," he said in a husky whisper, and I did. I wasn't about to argue.

He slipped off his boots and crawled up behind me and pulled me against his chest. We didn't talk, but we didn't need to. This just felt right. My eyes closed and I let the exhaustion of the day take over.

# Grant

We slept the entire flight home. On the drive back to Nan's house, I stopped and got us coffee and sausage biscuits at an all-night drive-through. Harlow looked adorable and rumpled, and I was having a hard time looking at the road and not her.

Pulling into the driveway, I was instantly annoyed to see Nan's car. Sure, it was the middle of the night and this was her house, but I'd been hoping she wasn't there so I could crawl into Harlow's bed with her and go back to sleep without its being an issue.

I parked the truck and turned it off then looked over at Harlow.

"I'm gonna shoot it to you straight. I want to go inside and get back in bed with you and finish sleeping. I don't give a fuck that Nan lives here."

Harlow glanced at the house then down at her hands and sighed. "I don't know if that's such a good idea. She won't handle it well if she sees you're here with me."

I reached over and grabbed her chin so she would have to look me in the eyes. "I don't care what she does or says. I won't let her hurt you. And I'm not going to let her control this."

"But you were just in her bed a week ago," she said. The pain in her eyes as she reminded not only me but herself made me hate myself.

"I was drunk and stupid. It didn't mean anything. With you, it always means something."

Harlow gave me a small smile and opened the door to my truck. "I guess this is going to get back to her eventually. We might as well not hide anything," she said and stepped down.

I didn't wait for her to change her mind. I grabbed my bag and hers and got out of the truck.

She glanced back at me as she climbed the steps and I enjoyed the view of her ass in those tight jeans.

"Are you gonna sleep in your boxers?" she asked.

I hadn't thought of that. I shrugged. "Yeah, probably."

She smiled. "Good. I like the way you look in boxers," she said, then finished walking up the stairs.

Yeah, I was smiling, but I was also thinking about what she was going to sleep in. Suddenly, sleep was the last thing on my mind.

Harlow opened the door and we walked inside. I could tell she was trying to be quiet, but honestly, I didn't give a shit. Unless Nan came out screaming and ruined my chance to see Harlow in those cute little pajamas I'd seen her in the first day.

When we got to Harlow's room she closed and locked the door, then glanced over at me. "I need to take a shower and get the travel off. I feel yucky."

"I need one, too," I replied, and opened the door leading into the bathroom for her. She paused and looked at the door, then me.

"Are we . . . are you going to . . ." she stopped and I fought to keep from laughing.

"Sweet girl, if your sexy ass is getting in a shower in the very next room, I'm getting in it, too. That's a sight I don't intend to miss."

Harlow looked unsure, and I wondered what was wrong now.

"I . . . that seems so revealing and personal. I don't know if I can do it."

Would she always make me want to laugh? God, I hoped so. Even if she wasn't so perfectly packaged, her being so damn adorable would be enough. "Baby, I've had you naked and spread out open for me on a bathroom counter with my head between your legs. It doesn't get any more personal than that."

She ducked her head and I heard a soft laugh. "Yeah, I guess you have a point."

"Hell yeah, I have a point. Now get in there and get naked so I can help wash you," I told her.

She stepped into the bathroom and I followed her. I didn't even try to hide the fact I was watching her take off every damn stitch of her clothes. It was something that would never get old.

"Are you going to wash my back for me?" she asked with a teasing tone in her voice as she stepped out of her jeans.

I grinned and pulled my shirt off. "Sure, I'll wash your back. But I'm also washing those nice big tits and that pussy I'm such a fan of."

She closed her eyes tightly. "I hate it when you call it that."

Laughing, I let my jeans drop and went to turn the shower on. The prim and proper thing was part of her sexiness. Knowing I could get Miss Prim and Proper to do things like lick my come off her fingers was hot.

I turned back around to see her standing behind me, looking at my bare ass. She had her arms wrapped around her chest—as if that covered anything.

"It's warm, come on." I held out my hand and she stepped forward and slipped hers in mine, letting her breasts free. They bounced and my cock was at full attention.

"Harlow," I said.

"Yes?"

"I'm gonna fuck you in this shower. If I don't, we won't get any sleep in that bed."

Her breathing picked up and that was all I needed. "I don't know how to do that."

"Oh, trust me, baby. I know exactly how to do it."

She tensed and turned toward the water so her back was toward me. What the hell had I done now?

I placed my hands on her arms to keep from putting them in other places. "What is it?"

She shrugged and stepped farther into the water and tilted her head up to let the warm stream pour over her face and hair. I forgot what I was doing for a moment. I just watched in fascination. I was pretty damn sure I could spend the rest of my life standing right here and watching this.

When she stepped back and ran her hands down her hair, I grabbed her and pulled her back against me. "I don't speak silent, Harlow. I need you to tell me what's wrong. Your back is rigid and your body is telling me something's wrong."

I was expecting more silent Harlow.

"Maybe I don't like to be reminded about the fact you've had sex with a lot of other girls before you had sex with me."

Well, hell.

I'd never thought of that.

No girl had ever cared before.

I was an ass.

I turned her around to face me. Her wet eyelashes stuck together and water dripped from her smooth skin. I'd made her insecure. I never wanted to do that. "I'm sorry. I shouldn't have said that. I didn't think anything of it, but I understand why you're upset. I can't change my past," I told her, reaching up to touch her face because I couldn't stop myself any longer. "But you're different. This thing we're doing is different."

She pressed her lips together and tilted her head into my hand like a kitten. "I just hate not knowing what to do. Being with you is amazing but you're all I know. I have no experience so I have no idea how to do things to make you feel good. I can't compete with your past."

She really had no clue. I pulled her against me. "God, Harlow. You're going to kill me," I said, holding her while I tried to get my emotions together. "Sex is a way to get pleasure. It never meant anything more to me. Just a way to feel good. I didn't put anything else into it. I just gave and took what I needed. And maybe when I first saw you that's all I wanted. At that engagement party I got a look at those legs of yours and I wanted you naked and under me. I won't lie. But then I got to know you. I saw something precious that I wanted to taste. I wanted to hold it and I wanted to touch the special that I saw there." I pulled back and looked down at her. "When I was inside you for the first time I realized I had found something I'd never felt, and it was terrifying. The pleasure wasn't shallow and I wasn't untouched. Something inside me turned over and I became addicted. To you. I don't have any other explanation for you right now. But never compare yourself to anyone else I've ever been with because you're all I want and all I see."

Harlow didn't respond. Instead, she pressed a kiss to my chest and continued to press kisses until she was on her knees in front of me. She looked up at me through wet lashes. "I don't know how, but this is all I've been able to think about since that car ride."

I was pretty damn sure I had forgotten how to inhale. Her hands held me and she squeezed just the way I'd taught her to. "Anything you do will be fucking perfect," I rasped out.

My plan had been to wash her body and send her into a crazed frenzy with my hands before I pressed her against the wall and slid back inside her. But she wanted to suck my dick. How did I get this? Her? What did I ever do right to get this kind of reward? Harlow wasn't meant for guys like me.

All thought left the moment her lips pulled me in and she began to suck as if she knew exactly what she was doing. There was no pattern or rhythm to it. She just took me in her mouth like I was a treat and she was enjoying herself. I didn't instruct her. Hell, I was afraid to. I wanted inside her, and if she got any better that wasn't happening in the shower.

She licked the head and looked up at me, smiling. "Is this okay?" she asked.

I realized I was holding my breath and sucked in some air. "No fantasy I've ever had can compare to how this feels."

She opened her mouth and started to pull it back into her mouth. But I couldn't let her do that right now. I wanted inside. I'd be more than willing to let her have at it another time for as long as she wanted, or until I blew.

"Up," I told her, reaching down. She let it pop out of her

mouth and I groaned. She stood up, frowning at me as if she wasn't sure what was going on. I grabbed her face and covered her mouth with mine. The musky taste on her lips made my pulse beat faster. That was me. She tasted like me.

I grabbed her hips and pressed her against the wall and spread her legs before sinking into her tight warmth.

"Oh, God!" she cried out, grabbing my arms.

I picked her up and began to pump in and out of her while she moaned and begged for more. The little uptight Harlow was gone when she was like this. She was my wild, sweet girl. When she raised her knee and wrapped a leg around my waist and clawed at my back, I knew she was close.

I wasn't wearing a fucking condom. Shit!

Harlow screamed my name and grabbed on as she found her release. I let her ride it out while grinding my teeth and holding back. When she started squeezing my dick with her tight little hole, I pulled out and covered her thighs with my release.

She was still holding on to me but she went still as the warmth of my come ran down her legs. Her eyes lifted to mine and went wide. She was just now realizing we had done this without protection. But I'd pulled out in time and I knew I was clean.

"I'm clean. I swear. I get checked regularly and I always wear a condom."

"You're sure?" she asked, still standing very still.

"Very sure."

"I didn't realize, but it felt different. Better."

God, yes, it had felt like fucking nirvana. I had never had sex without a condom. I had no idea this was what all the fuss was about. Holy hell, I wanted that again.

"Let me wash you," I told her, stepping back.

She immediately looked down at her legs and then back up at me. A small smile touched her lips. "I feel kind of marked."

I stopped reaching for the soap and stared at her. Had she really just said that? "If you like being marked then I'll mark you any damn time you want me to," I told her before taking the soap. "Turn around. I'll start with your back," I instructed.

# Harlow

When I opened my eyes Grant's arm was wrapped around me and I was nice and warm, tucked against his chest. I glanced at my closed door. The clock beside the bed said it was after eleven in the morning. Nan would be awake by now. Was I ready to face this?

"Stop thinking so hard," Grant mumbled sleepily.

He wasn't at all worried about Nan. I didn't understand their relationship at all. If I was smart I wouldn't be snuggled up in bed with someone who had any kind of relationship with Nan. But having the willpower to ignore Grant's sexy smile and smooth-talking ways was almost impossible.

"I won't let her do anything to hurt you," Grant said into my hair.

That wasn't what I was worried about. I could take on Nan if I had to. I was more concerned with making a choice that would eventually break my heart. Could I love Grant? Was I falling in love with him? Was it fair for me to love him?

Yes. I was positive I could love him. But I wasn't in love with him right now. This was simply attraction, and possibly a crush. He flashed his smile and I did dumb things. That would be considered a crush, right? And if he wasn't in love with me then would it hurt for me to love him? Even if he didn't know my secret yet?

"Turn around and look at me," Grant said, letting his tight hold on me go so I could actually move.

"Why?" I asked.

"Because I don't like where your head is. I need to fix it," he replied.

He had no idea where my head was. And he really needed to get over wanting to fix everything for me.

"I'm not worried about Nan," I told him. Okay, maybe I was a little. I didn't like confrontations, and the one I had waiting on me when we left this room was going to be dramatic.

"Then why are you so quiet?"

"I'm trying to figure out what we're doing. If I'm headed for possible heartache in the future," I replied honestly. There was no reason to lie to him. I wasn't one for pretenses.

"Turn around," Grant growled, pulling my arms around him this time.

This was a bad idea. His face looked even better all sleepy. His eyes weren't fully awake, which only made his long lashes more obvious. And his hair was all messy. Made a girl want to run her hands through it.

"I don't do relationships. Closest I got was with Nan, and that was because she was so damn needy. I liked being needed. No one ever needed me. She did. But then she was also crazy as fuck and heartless, and that ended things for me. So what you and I are doing right here is a first for me. I've never wanted to wake up and cuddle with a female in my life. I've never missed her when she wasn't around. You're all I can think about, Harlow. Where I'm headed is new to me, but I damn well want to go there as long as that's where you'll be. You're worried about getting hurt, but I don't think you understand yet that you're holding all the damn cards, sweet girl. All the damn cards."

I stared up at him and let his words sink in. Why me? What was it about me that made this man want to do something he had never done before? Was I needy? Did he think I needed him? Because I was pretty damn self-sufficient.

"I'm not needy," I told him.

He grinned. "I already figured that out. But I am—at least where you're concerned."

And there went my resolve to strengthen one of the walls I had built around myself. Instead, it crumbled a little. This man knew exactly how to make me weak.

I started to say more when a loud banging noise sounded at the door, followed by "Grant Carter, get your fucking worthless ass out here NOW!"

And there was Nan.

I jumped out of bed, thankful to be wearing my pajamas and not naked, like Grant had wanted. "She figured it out," I whispered.

Grant sighed and lay on his back as if he didn't care. "Go away," he called back.

She started banging on the door again. "I will not go away, you motherfucker! Get out of there now! I won't let her do this. She has it all, why the hell does she have to take you, too? Stupid slut!"

My eyes went wide. I'd never been called that, and I wasn't sure how I felt about it.

Grant sprang out of bed and stalked to the door. The murderous look on his face had me backing up against the wall.

Maybe I wasn't as brave as I thought I was. Grant was an even-tempered guy, so I'd never seen him look so . . . *pissed*.

He jerked the door open. Then he reached for her. I watched as he grabbed her shirt and pulled her close to his face. "Don't ever call her that again. Do you fucking understand me? Ever." He let her go and she stumbled backward, and then he slammed the door in her face. The sound of the lock turning echoed in the silence around us. I think he had shocked her into silence, too.

His shoulders were rising and falling hard as he laid one hand on the door and stared down at the floor.

I didn't move and I didn't speak.

Finally, he turned to me, and the anger I had seen earlier was gone. He looked like Grant again. Fun-loving, easygoing Grant. "I'm sorry," he said simply.

I didn't know what to say to that. "Okay" didn't seem like the right word to use here. I just nodded.

"She just wants to hurt you. I've tried to talk to her and help her see that nothing is your fault, but she won't listen. If I could muzzle her I would."

A mental picture of Nan muzzled made me smile. Grant smiled back at me in return and then walked over to me. "She should've never called you that. You're so far from that, and she knows it."

He was talking about the slut comment. Was that what set him off?

"I think you scared her. She's not saying anything." I wasn't even sure she was still there.

A frustrated frown touched his forehead. "She isn't done. She's just too mad to react right now. I've never been that tough on her. I typically just walk away and let her talk. But that," he shook his head, "that shit was going to be dealt with."

"Are you trying to fix things again?" I asked, wondering why he thought he had to fix all my problems.

He grinned and bent down to press a kiss to the corner of my mouth. "No, sweet girl, I'm just correcting a wrong. No one can fix Nan."

I was afraid he was right.

# Grant

All I wanted to do was get Harlow naked and back in that bed. But I was behind on work and we both needed to leave the room and get this Nan shit over with.

I let Harlow get dressed while I cleaned up in the bathroom. I couldn't watch her dress because we'd end up back in bed. Screw work. Once we were both dressed, I opened her bedroom door slowly, just in case Nan was standing out there, waiting to pounce.

Harlow waited behind me and I was pretty sure I heard a sigh of relief when we saw the hallway was empty. I reached back and took her hand as we walked out of the room and to the stairs. I didn't think Nan was going to jump out of a damn corner and attack, but I still felt safer with Harlow as close to me as possible.

I wasn't going to let Harlow stay here alone until I was sure Nan was over this. I didn't know what she'd say to Harlow, and I wasn't going to let her lash out at her without me there to protect her and shut that shit down.

"Hungry?" I asked her as we reached the bottom step with no Nan sightings.

Harlow jumped when something made a loud noise in the

kitchen. Guess we wouldn't be eating here. "I, uh . . . probably not a good idea," she said, staring at the kitchen.

"Want to just leave?" I asked.

Harlow shook her head. "No. I live here, too. I want coffee before I leave. I won't hide; this is my home, too."

The way her shoulders straightened reminded me that behind the sweet face was a spine of steel. She'd been through a lot. I just nodded and let her lead the way.

If she was getting coffee then so was I.

Nan was standing in front of the microwave and turned to glare at us when we entered the kitchen. Her eyes dropped to our joined hands, and her glare turned to pure hatred.

"You have got to be fucking kidding me. Really, Grant? Holding hands? My God, you have lost your mind." She snarled and jerked the microwave open and pulled out a small bowl.

Harlow let go of my hand and walked over to the coffeepot. I had to make myself stand still and not run after her to guard her. She wanted to do this and I was going to let her.

"He gets bored easy with your type. I don't know what he's telling you but he likes excitement, which you could never give him. Don't let that little heart of yours get involved, because you're not Grant Carter's type," Nan said in a haughty tone as Harlow went about making coffee and avoiding her. When she set her mug down, she turned and gave Nan her full attention.

"He may get bored with me, but that isn't your business. It's mine," Harlow replied.

I had already realized I would never get bored with her. She was so damn fascinating, no one could get bored with her.

"Grant likes to fuck. He isn't into hand-holding and talking about your feelings. He likes it rough. Right here across this counter, he's thrown me down and ripped my panties off and fucked me. He loves it, and he'll be back for more."

Yeah. That was enough. I started walking toward Harlow to get her the hell out of there before Nan gave her any more details I didn't want her to hear. She didn't do well being reminded of my past sex life.

"Then I guess that makes you the slut, Nan. Not me. Because I'd never give you details. That's just trashy." Harlow picked up her mug, then turned to me. "Ready?" she asked, as if Nan hadn't just given her a play-by-play of something I didn't want her to know.

"Uh, yeah," I replied, and glanced back at Nan, who was seething. That only made me smile. Damn, my sweet girl could cut deep with no drama. She just did it with ease.

I slipped my hand around her waist and led her to the door, where she grabbed her purse and keys. When we stepped outside, she moved away from my touch and looked back at me.

"That's done now. I told you I could handle her. I missed tennis so I need to talk to Adam and apologize. Thanks for going with me yesterday. It meant a lot," she said, then pressed a kiss to my cheek and started to walk toward her car.

What. The. Fuck?

I went after her and grabbed her arm to stop her. "Hey, wait. What was that?" Because it sure as hell felt like a brush-off. And that wasn't fucking happening.

She smiled at me sadly and shrugged. "My way of putting distance between us. I need it."

Distance? "What the hell? I thought after yesterday that we had moved past distance."

She tucked a strand of hair behind her ear. "I don't do this. I've never done this. That's probably why I'll have the image of you jerking Nan's panties off and screwing her on the counter forever etched in my brain. Before, it bothered me; now, I have visuals. So I need distance."

I wanted to hurt someone. Particularly a certain redhead in that damn house. "Harlow, don't do this to me. That was before. I didn't know. I was fucked up. It was after we found Jace's body, and I lost it there for a while."

"I'm sorry, Grant. But I can't. I've been protecting my heart for years. I can't stop now. You're dangerous. That sexy smile and those sweet words are hard to resist, but I can't let something that could possibly destroy me into my life."

No. Fuck no. She was not going to do this. "I'm not going to go away. I want you, Harlow. Just you."

She reached up and brushed her thumb over my bottom lip. "I believe you right now. What scares me is who you'll want in a couple of weeks."

Then she turned and opened her car door and got in. Had I not just told her this morning that I had never felt this way about anyone? Were Nan's fucking words that powerful? My chest ached and I put my fist on it to ease the pain. I wouldn't let Harlow do this. I just needed to find some way to prove to her that I was serious. Completely serious.

# Harlow

I watched Adam finish his session with a lady I didn't recognize. I tried to focus on apologizing to him and not on what had happened this morning. The fact that I had just reacted like a jealous girlfriend was eating me up. I wasn't that girl. I didn't let something like Grant's past sex life make me punish him. I could lie to myself and say I had meant what I said, but the truth was I did it to get back at him. For what? Screwing around with Nan? When had I gotten so shallow? Was I acting like Nan? Oh, God. I felt nauseated.

Adam glanced over at me and I smiled. I would think about Grant later. I would work this out in my head. He didn't deserve what I had done this morning. We were seeing where things could go with us. I knew about him and Nan. It wasn't a secret. I'd heard them my first night back here. I had just gotten all territorial and been a bitch about it.

I was horrified with myself.

Adam ended his session and he waited until the lady he was working with walked out of the gate before following her out. He came over to me.

"You're late," he said with a smile I didn't deserve.

"I slept in late. I'm sorry. Long day yesterday. I had to see my dad about family stuff."

"It's okay. Life happens. I hope everything is okay."

I nodded. It wasn't, but telling him the truth wasn't going to happen. "Everything is fine. I just wanted to make sure you knew why I wasn't here. I didn't want you to think I was just blowing this off and had no thought to your time."

He grinned. "How do you expect anyone to get frustrated with you? Has anyone ever? I'd find it hard to believe."

I thought of Nan. He had no idea.

"It happens," I assured him.

"Send them my way and I'll correct that."

Adam really was nice, and so less complicated than Grant. But the excitement and bone-melting passion weren't there.

"I was about to grab some lunch. Want to eat with me? Make it up to me that you stood me up?" he said.

I was hungry, and company during lunch sounded nice.

"Yes. I'd love to," I replied.

"Good. The restaurant here okay with you?"

I had never actually dined in the restaurant here. "Sure," I told him. I just needed food. I wasn't picky.

He held out his arm for me to take it. So nice. I slipped my hand over his arm and he led me up the stairs and toward the doors to the club.

The hostess obviously liked Adam. She couldn't keep from smiling at him. I was worried she was going to trip walking us to a table.

"Your server will be with you in a moment," she told Adam. As far as she was concerned, I didn't exist.

When she walked away, I picked up the menu and tried to hide my grin.

"You find that amusing, don't you?" Adam said, smiling over at me.

I pressed my lips together to keep from laughing and nodded.

"She's cute and we went out once, but she isn't really my type."

No wonder she'd ignored me. I just nodded again and went back to looking at my menu.

"The boss is on his throne," Adam whispered, and I glanced up. What was he talking about? He tilted his head slightly to the left. "You see the dark-headed guy up there in that round booth talking to Rush Finlay?"

I didn't want to look. Especially if Rush was up there. He would see me staring. I gave it a few moments, then quickly glanced over my shoulder. Rush wasn't paying attention to us. He was talking with the dark-headed man. I had seen him before. "Yes," I replied.

"That's the boss, Woods Kerrington. He owns the whole damn place. Nice guy if you don't piss him off."

He was young. I wanted to look back again just to make sure I had seen him correctly, but I didn't. "Is he young? He looks really young."

Adam took a drink of his water and nodded. "Yeah. Like twenty-five or something. His dad owned the place and died of a heart attack a while back. Now the place belongs to Woods. Finlay is a good friend of his and is on the board of directors. Rumor is so is Dean Finlay. When that got out it was really good for business. Everyone wants a glimpse of the famous drummer."

I didn't know all that. Interesting.

"Good afternoon. My name is Jimmy and I will be your server today. Can I get you mineral water or sparkling?"

I looked up at the tall, attractive blond who was smiling at me. "I would love mineral, please," I replied.

"I'm good with this," Adam replied. "What is the special today, Jimmy?"

"A cold crab bisque with raspberry salad and seaweed-wrapped grouper, fresh off the boat."

Adam frowned and I decided I was sticking with a sandwich.

"I'll let the two of you look over things and I'll be back with your mineral water," he said, then quietly walked away.

"You into seaweed?" he asked me with an amused smirk.

I laughed and shook my head. He must have been thinking the same thing. I had eaten some strange things while living in L.A., but seaweed was not one of them.

"I think I'm going with the chicken pecan salad on a croissant," I told him.

"I may have moved to pecan country but I still don't eat them," he replied.

I closed my menu and glanced up just as Grant walked into the dining room. His eyes were focused on someone else and it gave me a moment to prepare myself. Would he say anything to me? Or had I made him mad? Did he decide my drama wasn't worth it? I watched him as he walked over and sat down beside Rush at Woods Kerrington's booth. Woods said something to Grant and he forced a smile that didn't meet his eyes.

I had started to look away when his head turned and his eyes met mine. We both froze. I wasn't doing anything wrong, but why did it feel as if I was? His eyes flickered to Adam, then back to me, and a hard edge transformed his face. He wasn't happy. Well, crap.

I quickly looked back at my menu and counted to ten. My heart was beating fast, which was ridiculous. I shouldn't be nervous. We hadn't left things in a good place this morning, thanks to me. So me sitting here, having lunch with Adam, was no big deal. Right?

The chair beside me pulled out and I swung my gaze up to see Grant sitting down.

Okay . . . wrong. This was apparently a big deal.

He didn't look happy but the tight smile on his face was trying to say otherwise.

"Hello, Adam," Grant said before turning his intense blue gaze to me. "You could have asked me to lunch," he said simply.

Technically, I hadn't asked Adam. He'd asked me.

"You're here with friends," I told him, hating how my voice gave away how nervous I was.

Grant leaned closer to me. "I would drop anyone and anything the moment you called."

There were those words again. The ones that managed to slide through you and turn you into a bowl of jelly.

"I, uh, Adam asked me to lunch. I was hungry," I said, unable to look at Adam. I had no idea what he was thinking and I didn't want to know right now.

"Looks like we have three guests now," Jimmy said as he set the water in front of me.

"Mr. Carter, would you like me to get you something to drink?" Jimmy asked.

Grant didn't take his eyes off me. "A sweet tea, please, Jimmy," he replied.

"Yes, sir," Jimmy said, and left without taking our orders.

"I guess I need to make sure I ask before Adam next time," Grant said, then leaned back in his seat and put his arm around the back of mine in a possessive move. "So, Adam, how's tennis going? Like the new job?" he asked in a polite tone.

Adam looked nervous. He glanced back at Woods's table then back at Grant. I wondered if they were watching us. "Yes, sir. I'm enjoying it. The town is great."

Grant touched my bare shoulder and he began to trace circles around it in a gentle caress. Adam noticed. This was becoming more and more awkward.

# Grant

I could feel Woods and Rush staring at me. They had tried to stop me. Not that I listened. It wasn't like they wouldn't have done the same thing. Sitting here eating and letting Adam the tennis pro hit on my girl. Hell, no. That was not happening.

Harlow was stiff as a board. I hated that she was so uncomfortable, but she shouldn't have come to lunch with Adam, the fucking tennis dude. This morning had fucked up my day. If Harlow thought we were going to bed tonight with this shit unsettled, she was wrong.

I listened as Harlow ordered a sandwich and ignored Jimmy's amused grin. He knew what was going on. He probably talked to Rush and Woods about it when he was filling their drinks.

"I want to show you something when lunch is over. Do you already have plans?" I wanted to add that she needed to take a break, but I didn't want to sound like an ass.

Harlow glanced at me. "No, I don't have anything to do."

"Good," I said, leaning in to wrap one of her strands of hair around a finger so I could feel its silkiness. "I'm sorry." I said the words without thinking about them. But I was sorry. I was sorry about this morning. I was sorry about how uncomfortable she was right now. But I wasn't sorry that I was making sure Adam knew Harlow was not available.

"Adam," Woods's voice caught my attention and I looked up to see that he'd walked over to the table. "Nelton is double booked. It was an accident. He needs help with Mrs. Venice before she causes a scene. If you could please help, I will have your lunch brought to you. It's on the house today."

He'd just made that bullshit up. I had to cough to cover my laugh. Guess he did have my back after all.

"Yes, sir," Adam replied, standing up and looking over at Harlow. "I gotta go. Next time," he said, then turned to leave.

Woods didn't say anything else before he went back to his table. Rush was staring down at his drink, grinning. He was in on this, too. I coughed again to cover my laughter.

"That was a setup, wasn't it?" Harlow said, looking at me with her eyebrows drawn together.

"I assure you, when Adam gets out there he will have someone to teach," I told her. Woods would've made a phone call to be sure of it.

"But Woods made that happen," she said. Harlow wasn't stupid.

"Yeah, he did. I didn't ask him to, though. That was all him, and probably Rush, from the look on his face."

Harlow glanced over at them and they both quickly looked away from us.

"Guess it's nice to have friends in high places," she said, turning back to me.

I had been ready to thank Woods but if she was pissed, I wasn't gonna be thanking him. "I had nothing to do with that," I repeated.

She sighed and relaxed. "I think I believe you. And honestly, I don't know how Adam was going to eat with you rubbing on me and glaring at him anyway."

"I didn't glare," I replied with a relieved grin.

She rolled her eyes and picked up her glass. "Yes, Grant, you did."

Maybe I had, but I didn't like the guy. He wanted what I wanted. "I want to talk about this morning and I want to show you my place. You've never been there and I want you there."

She took a sip of her water, then set it back down before looking at me. "I acted like a jealous girlfriend and I hate that. I've never acted like that before. I'm sorry. We aren't exclusive. You have a past that isn't my business, and when Nan threw the bait out there I took it. I shouldn't have."

Not what I'd been expecting her to say. Again, Harlow wasn't like the other girls I knew. Also, we needed to discuss that "exclusive" comment. Because lunch with Adam was one thing, but I'd be damned if she intended to go out with that prick again. "What Nan said was mean and bitter. You didn't like it and that's normal. As for exclusive, I am very, very exclusive. Since yesterday on that plane, I knew I wasn't touching anybody else."

Harlow tilted her head to the side and studied me silently. Had she thought I was going to go screw other people now? Really? Was my reputation that bad?

"Okay" was all she said. If there one was thing about Harlow that drove me nuts, it was her one-word answers, like "okay," when I wanted a few lengthy sentences. Dammit. Girls liked to hear themselves talk. Why didn't she?

"Could you elaborate on that?" I asked, reaching over to

take her hand in her lap because I just needed to touch her.

The corner of her mouth turned up. "What else do you want me to say? You aren't going to sleep with anyone else while we're doing . . . this thing we're doing. And I won't have lunch with anyone else," she replied.

I needed more than that. "Lunch? That's it?"

She shrugged. "It isn't like you have to worry about me sleeping with anyone else. I don't do that."

No, she didn't. And damned if that didn't make me want to pull her into my lap and growl at anyone who looked her way like a damn dog with a bone. "Dates?" I asked. She'd been on a date with Adam.

She frowned. "I said no lunch. That meant dates, too."

"Just wanted to clarify," I told her, and leaned over to press a kiss to her lips. I had sat here and stared at them long enough. My eyes lifted and I saw Woods and Rush watching me. They were enjoying this a little too much.

# Harlow

Grant's apartment was just outside Rosemary. It was small and I was surprised by that, but then again I wasn't. His place looked like him. The furniture was worn and it was everything a bachelor pad should be, from the dartboard on the wall to the empty pizza boxes on the counter.

"I should've cleaned up before I brought you here," he said, walking up behind me. I stepped back until I was touching him.

"I like it just like this," I replied.

Grant's head dipped to my shoulder and he kissed my neck. "And why is that?" he asked.

"Because it's you. It's comfortable and real."

Grant's arms came around me and held me. "I don't know if I want you thinking of me as comfortable. That sounds real close to boring."

Grant was anything but boring. "Well, you're not that."

He moved a hand down to the bottom of my skirt and tugged it up. "I feel the need to prove just how exciting I can be," he whispered in my ear.

I didn't want what we were doing to be all about sex. I wanted something deeper than that. But then maybe that was what Grant wanted. I liked it . . . no, I loved it. He made me feel amazing, but was that all we would ever be? When this was over, would I have been just another girl he had sex with? Or would he remember me for other things?

"You tensed up. What's wrong?" he asked.

Nan's words replayed in my head. He would get bored with me. He would want something exciting. Was she the exciting one he wanted? Did I even want to be that? I wanted Grant. Who wouldn't want Grant? That was a given.

I had always been boring. I was sick of being boring. I was sick of being forgettable. No. I wouldn't bore Grant. When we ended it, it would be mutual, not because I'd been the boring prude that Nan accused me of being.

I reached for his hand and slipped it up higher as I spread my legs.

"Make me forget the image of you on that counter with Nan," I told him boldly.

Grant looked pained, and he moved his hand from between my legs and cupped my face instead. "I've already forgotten it. I'm sorry she said that to you."

He was taking care of me again. Treating me as if I would break. I shook my head. "No. I haven't forgotten. I can't get it out of my head. I don't like thinking about you and Nan together. I'm jealous that she had you first. I want to be more . . . I don't want to be forgettable."

Grant scowled. "You could never be forgettable. You've claimed me in ways Nan never did. Nothing about you, Harlow . . . nothing is forgettable. Don't ever think that."

His words were always so sweet. His way with words was his greatest talent. "Then do this for me. I want to see a kitchen counter and remember us on it. Not you and Nan. That hurts too bad."

A low growl came from Grant's chest and he grabbed my panties and pulled them down, "I can't stand the idea of you ever hurting because of me. I fucking hate that. I want to make you happy. I wish I'd never been with anyone before you." He stopped and took a deep breath. "I'll make you forget it but know that I forgot every other woman I've ever been with the moment I slid inside you the first time."

Before I could react, he ran a finger along the edge of my heat. "Do you know why she told you about the counter?" he asked in a husky voice that always made me shiver.

Yes. To hurt me. But I didn't say that. Instead, I shook my head.

"Because I had taken her and closed my eyes," he breathed against my neck. "And when I came it wasn't her name I yelled. It wasn't her I was fucking."

My breathing became heavy and I let my head fall back on his chest. His finger pushed up inside me. "It was your name I cried out. I was drunk, but even drunk it was you I was fantasizing about. Once I got a taste of you, nothing else worked for me. You were all I could think about."

That wasn't what I expected to hear, but it helped make that image in my head much more bearable. I let my panties shimmy down my legs and stepped out of them.

"I don't want you fantasizing about me with her or anyone," I said, turning to look at him as I pulled my shirt off.

Grant picked me up and sat me on the counter before he started unbuttoning his jeans. His eyes never left mine. I reached around and unsnapped my bra, then let it fall forward slowly. His eyes dropped to watch me and the heat in them made me smile. It eased the jealousy of him touching Nan.

He didn't even step out of his jeans. He pulled me to him and started to sink in before he stopped. "Motherfucker, I almost did it again," he swore.

He reached over to a drawer that was full of junk and pulled out a condom. I didn't want to know why the heck he had a condom jammed in there, but then again this was Grant we were talking about.

"I don't like condoms," I said.

Grant took a deep breath and closed his eyes. "I don't either, but I need to get checked again, then we need to get you on birth control before we go without one."

He was right and I was glad he was strong enough to think about it. Truthfully, I was so ready to feel him inside me I wouldn't have remembered.

This time when he grabbed my hips he sank inside me and bit down on my shoulder with a loud groan. That was exciting. Really exciting. He licked where he had bitten me then looked into my eyes. "I don't have to pretend. I'm right where I want to be," he said and slid his hands up my sides and covered my breasts. "Damn, these are nice."

I leaned back on my hands and lifted my knees up his sides. "Don't be gentle with me. You want to fulfill a fantasy, then use me to do it," I told him. I didn't want him using someone else to take my place. I was burning that out of his mind right now.

Grant swore and his hands clamped onto my hips and he began slamming into me over and over, his eyes never leaving mine. I slid a leg up and draped it over his shoulder.

"Holy fuck!" he yelled and grabbed my leg. He was losing his control, and the wild look in his eyes made me want to push him further.

I lay back until I was lying on the countertop and put my other leg over his shoulders. He turned his face and bit my leg while holding my gaze. I cried out. This was better than I imagined. Having sex in the kitchen was a major turn-on.

"Come here," Grant ordered, pulling my hips up so close that my legs were draped over his back completely now. "You drive me fucking insane. Your plump little lips and big, round nipples, and these long-as-hell legs. All I want to do is stay buried inside you. You got me, Harlow. You fucking got me, baby. I . . ." he paused and groaned as the tremors of my approaching orgasm squeezed him. "I can't fight this. I don't fucking want to," he finished, then both his hands landed on each side of my head. "Come with me," he whispered, and I broke apart into a million pieces. I screamed his name and bucked underneath him while he chanted things about how tight I was and how good I felt. Every word out of his mouth sent me crying out in pleasure again. He had magic words. That was the only way to explain it.

# Grant

I watched as Harlow stood outside on my balcony in nothing but one of my T-shirts. Her back was to me and the wind was making her hair dance around her shoulders. I had held her before I'd gone to clean up after our counter sex. Then I had to catch my breath.

I'd almost told her . . . I had almost fucking told her I loved her. Never. Had I ever. Almost. Told a girl. I loved her. Not even if the sex was hot. It had never even come to my mind, much less my mouth.

So now I had to figure something out.

Did I?

Was I in love with her?

She wrapped her arms around her front and leaned over to look down, causing the T-shirt to ride up and give me a glimpse of her ass. I was in love with that ass. I was in love with those legs of hers, too. But was I in love with *her*?

I watched her silently and felt the protective streak in me roar to life when I thought of someone looking up and seeing her in my T-shirt, looking like a sex goddess. I didn't want anyone looking at her. She was mine.

She was mine.

Holy fuck.

She was mine.

I wasn't ever letting her go, and I sure as hell didn't want anyone else touching her. I wanted to hold her and keep her safely with me. It was irrational. It was . . . it was . . . I was in love with her.

I took a deep breath, preparing for the moment of panic to come along with this realization. But it didn't come. I felt complete. The heavy weight I thought would come with this feeling wasn't there. Instead, I could breathe deeper.

I moved from around the counter and went straight for the door. When I opened it, Harlow turned to smile at me. It was that perfect smile that could fix the world's problems. I picked her up and carried her over to the lounger and sat down, cuddling her against my chest. I was feeling a little like a caveman at the moment, and I just hoped I didn't beat my damn chest.

Harlow didn't ask questions; she just tucked herself under my chin and wrapped her arms around me. Mine. All mine.

I was just going to have to convince her of this first, because although I had this figured out, I knew she didn't. She didn't trust me. Not with her heart. Even if she owned mine.

"Thank you," I said into her hair.

"For what? Hot counter sex?" she asked with a smile in her voice.

"For you," I replied.

She didn't say anything else. That was Harlow. She didn't ask a lot of questions. She didn't want to always talk about things. She just took it in and accepted it. I just hoped she accepted that she was mine. Or more accurately, I was hers.

We spent the rest of the afternoon sitting there, talking.

She told me about her grandmama. There was no wonder she was special. She'd been raised very differently from the other females in my life. She also did an adorable impersonation of her grandmother.

I told her about my dad and what it was I did exactly. Back when Dad married Georgianna, he had worked in construction. Now he owned his own construction company. His company was all over the Southeast. I helped him handle the Florida Panhandle. I managed things and checked on things when he needed me. I also dealt with phone calls he didn't have time for.

I left out the fact I had ignored two of my father's phone calls today. I wasn't in the mind-set to talk business, especially when I'd just figured out I was in love. I needed to adjust to that first.

⌗

"I'm hungry," Harlow said as she sat with her legs in my lap on the sofa.

I knew I didn't have anything here to feed her. "Me, too. Want to get some Chinese?" I asked while playing with her little silver toe ring.

"Can we get takeout?" she asked.

I was all about keeping her to myself. "Sure. I can call and order it and they'll deliver."

She didn't respond right away. She fiddled with her fingernails as if they had her answers. "Are you going to take me home tonight?" she asked, then glanced up at me.

"I was waiting until I fed you and buttered you up with a fortune cookie before I brought this up, but I want you to stay here tonight. I don't want to take you back to Nan's."

She let out a breath and smiled. "Good. I don't think I'm ready to walk back into that just yet. I'll deal with it tomorrow."

I took her ankle and pulled her closer to me, making her squeal in surprise. "I'm all about keeping you here all the time. But tomorrow morning I have to do some work before I get fired. You don't have to leave. You can stay right here. I just need to catch up on some things. Then I have a board meeting at the club at four."

She scrunched her nose. "I didn't think about how I was keeping you from work. I'll leave in the morning. I have tennis anyway."

Tennis.

I hated fucking tennis.

"I can be more fun than tennis," I told her, crawling on top of her.

"Is this about Adam?" she asked, grinning up at me.

"Hell yeah, it is."

Harlow laughed and shoved at my chest. "I don't want Adam. I think I made that clear today. And yesterday, a few times."

She had a point. But I wanted Adam to know it. "Okay, fine. Go to tennis, but if I come to watch while I work, don't get pissed."

Her eyes went wide. "You wouldn't do that."

I bent down to kiss the corner of her mouth. "Yes, sweet girl, I would."

# Harlow

It was three days later before I went back to Nan's. Grant convinced me to come back to his place every evening. When he wasn't working, he was with me, and sometimes when he was working he was with me. Like during tennis every day. Grant sat on the porch that wrapped around the main clubhouse. He drank coffee and worked on his laptop.

Adam got the hint. He would've been an idiot not to. Grant made it very clear, going so far as walking me to the gate and kissing me until I lost my breath before sending me to each session.

Today, however, I had to go back to Nan's. I couldn't move in with Grant. We had to get over this hurdle with Nan. This was my house, too. I also wanted to talk to Mase without Grant around so I had privacy if Mase wanted to ask me about Grant.

When Grant got a call to drive two hours south to check out a site for his dad, he wanted me to go with him. But I needed some space to think. I felt like we'd gone from taking things fast to super overdrive. My heart was having a hard time keeping up.

I knew the moment I'd given myself to Grant that I had deep feelings for him. Then he'd destroyed them. I had thought it would take a long time for those feelings to come back, or even resurface. But I was finding out how wrong I was. They were coming back hard.

✥

While watching Grant brush his teeth this morning as I shaved my legs, I realized that this felt right. It was easy. And it scared me. He was making me picture a future for us. But what kind of future could I give him? Not the one I'm sure he always wanted. He wasn't in love with me. Falling into the daily everyday details of life with him was dangerous. Before, I was worried about getting hurt. Now, I knew I was going to get hurt. It had gone too far.

And I didn't know what to do about it.

I was hoping Mase had some wisdom to share.

Nan's car was gone when I pulled up to the house, and I breathed a sigh of relief. This was good. Maybe she was gone on one of her trips. I headed inside and stopped by the kitchen to get myself a bottle of water before going up to my room.

My room was just like I left it. Nan must have told the house cleaner not to go into my room. Not that I cared. I didn't have a messy room, just an unmade bed. I set my water down on the table and sat down.

Mase answered his phone on the second ring.

"About damn time I got a call from you," he grumbled into the phone.

"Sorry. I've been busy," I replied.

"Don't need to know. I already got an idea of the busy you've been."

My cheeks turned red. I hated thinking about what he'd heard on the plane.

"How are things?" I asked him.

"Working my ass off. With Jim down, I'm having to take up all his work. The man works hard. I wake up early and fall into bed late."

"How much longer will he be in a cast?"

"Six weeks. I can handle it. Hard work never hurt me."

The idea of Kiro's only son working hard on a ranch in Texas wasn't what the world would imagine.

"What about you? Nan eat you up yet?" he asked.

"No. I'm too tough for her. You know that."

"Bullshit. She sees you with Grant and she's going apeshit on your ass. He better be ready to make sure you come out without a scratch."

"She knows, and he handled her. I haven't seen her in a few days."

"Good. Maybe she'll stay gone."

I hadn't called him to talk about Nan. I needed guy advice. "Do you think it would be stupid for me to have feelings for Grant?"

He didn't reply right away. I was worried he was about to say what I already feared. "I was under the impression that, for you to do what I heard on that plane, you'd already have feelings for him."

"Well, yeah, I already had feelings for him, but I mean . . . you know, *feelings* feelings."

Mase chuckled. "Are you trying to ask me if it's smart for you to fall in love with Grant Carter?"

Well, yeah. "I guess," I replied.

"No. It's probably the dumbest thing you could do. But it's done. You were in love with him when you decided to sleep with him. That's who you are, Harlow. So you've done it. You need to be worrying about what you're gonna do when this ends. How will you handle it?"

I sat there staring at the mirror in front of me. He was right. I had been in love with Grant for months. I didn't want to admit it because it was pathetic. You didn't fall in love in two weeks. But I had done just that. Then he'd left.

"I don't know," I said.

Mase grunted, and I could tell he was moving something heavy. "You pack your shit and come to Texas. I'll handle the rest. That's what we'll do."

I realized talking to Mase about this was pointless. I wasn't moving to Texas and I wasn't letting him seek revenge. "Never mind. I'll figure this out. Thanks for listening."

"I'm here, Sis. Anytime. Just call me."

"I know. Love you."

"You, too," he replied.

I hung up and dropped the phone beside me. Where did I go from here?

I was in love with Grant. Full-fledged in love with him. I wanted him forever. I wanted to see his smile every morning. I wanted to know what it was like to be in his arms every day. What had I done?

# Grant

It was after nine when I rolled back into Rosemary. I had tried calling Harlow twice and she hadn't answered. If Rush hadn't told me that Nan was in New York with Georgianna, I would be panicking. But I knew Harlow was home alone. I kept telling myself she was asleep or left her phone upstairs.

By the time I pulled into Nan's driveway I was jumping out of the truck and running to the door. She was gonna have to start answering her phone when I was gone from now on. We'd talk about that. First, I just needed to see her face and know she was okay.

The door was locked. Good girl. I rang the bell and waited. I was about to ring it again when the door opened and a sleepy-looking Harlow answered. A smile touched her lips and she ran her hand through her hair. "Hey," she said sweetly.

I walked inside and closed the door behind me, then covered her mouth with mine. It was so soft and plump, free of lip gloss, and I wanted a taste. It was all I'd thought about on my drive home.

She slipped her hands up my arms and held on. The little blue polka-dotted boxers and matching tank top she was wearing shouldn't have been so damn sexy. But on her, they were that and more.

When I pulled back to look at her I smiled. "Hey."

She giggled and laid her head on my chest. "Sorry, I fell asleep on the couch watching season one of *How I Met Your Mother* on Netflix."

I wasn't sure what the hell that was but I nodded anyway. "Where's your phone?"

She frowned. "I think upstairs."

I pulled her closer. "Next time I'm gone, keep it with you. I broke every damn speed limit out there trying to get back because you wouldn't answer."

She leaned into me. "I'm sorry. I didn't think about it. People don't normally call me."

That, in itself, boggled my mind. Why didn't people call her? Didn't they want to hear her voice? Be near her? The world was full of idiots.

"I call you. I need to hear your voice when I'm gone," I told her.

The grin that lit up her face made my heart swell. "Okay."

I was going to have to tell her soon. I needed her to know how I felt. She wasn't going anywhere. I was keeping her. I wasn't letting her go. I'd chase her all over the damn world if I had to.

"It's been a long day, and right now I want to crawl into bed with you," I told her instead.

"Mmm, okay," she said before slipping her hand in mine and turning to walk toward the stairs.

At this moment, life was good. I had my girl and I was about to hold her all night. Before Harlow, I didn't get it. Why Rush and Woods would let one woman control their emotions, lives, actions.

But I got it now.

It made complete sense.

This little woman had me wrapped around her little finger, and she didn't have a clue.

I was going to have to tell her. I just didn't want to scare her off. I needed to let her fall in love with me, too. When I knew she was mine and my feelings wouldn't send her packing, I would tell her.

"I don't think Nan is in town," she said, glancing back at me.

"She's not. I talked to Rush."

Harlow didn't reply but I could see her body tense. What the hell was that about?

When we got to the top of the stairs I tugged her back to me. "What? Say what you're thinking."

"I'm not thinking anything," she replied, but the look on her face mimicked her body language.

"Yes, you are. Tell me or we'll stand right here all night."

She let out a sigh and looked away from me. "You talked to Rush about Nan," she mumbled.

"Of course I did. I had left you with your crazy-ass half sister to drive two hours away and I wanted to make sure you were okay. I called Rush to send Blaire over here to stay with you, and he told me there were no worries. Nan had gone to New York."

Her shoulders relaxed and then drooped. "I guess I'm not dealing well with this thing yet."

She was jealous, and that made me want to shout. I cupped her face in my hands. "My past with Nan bothers you. I know that and I'm going to do whatever the hell I have to in order to ease your mind."

She nodded, then let out a soft laugh.

"Why are you laughing?"

"Because I can't believe I'm acting like this."

Me neither, but I wasn't about to complain. I was thrilled.

"Would it make it better if I admit that I like it?"

She cocked one eyebrow. "You like me to act like a possessive, crazed girlfriend?"

"Hell yeah, I do. And nothing about you is crazed. But, baby, anytime you want to get possessive over me, then do it. Turns me the fuck on."

She laughed and slapped my chest, then turned around and started strutting to the bedroom.

"You left me," I called after her.

"Come and get me," she replied, and glanced back and winked at me.

Harlow just fucking winked at me.

"Get your ass naked and on that bed now before I rip that cute little outfit off your body," I ordered before going after her.

# Harlow

I didn't do well in crowds. I preferred to stay away from crowds. But I also couldn't tell Grant that I didn't want to go with him to a charity event at the club. He was on the board of directors and it was an annual ball held to benefit sea life along the gulf coast.

Kerrington Club had hosted this event for more than twenty years. Grant had told me he didn't really want to go either, but Woods wanted him there. So we were going. Tonight was held in memory of Jace. His parents would be there, and Woods had warned Grant they would play a video that wouldn't be easy to get through. Jace's death was still too fresh for all of them.

I spent extra time putting on makeup, mostly because I didn't do it often and I wanted to get it right. Choosing a dress hadn't been easy, either. I had several formal ones that Dad had insisted I buy to bring here. He had said there would be events I would need them for. When I didn't buy any, he'd had the personal shopper he hired for me bring several to me. I'd pointed at the few I liked and was done with it. I never expected to actually be wearing one. Now I was thankful Dad had made sure I had them.

I finally settled on the pale blue satin that hit right above my knees in the front and went longer in the back. I slipped on a pair of Daniele Michetti heels that consisted of barely there straps and tiny silver spikes. They were an impulse buy. I never bought things like this, but I'd seen them one day and couldn't resist. I hadn't even tried them on. I always got nervous in shoe stores.

I had only worn them around my bedroom. Tonight, I was being brave and wearing them in public. The dress called for it. I hoped if I dressed boldly then I would feel bold. By the time I finished curling, piling, and pinning the curls I'd spent over an hour working on, it was time for Grant to arrive. Nan was in her room, also getting dressed. We hadn't spoken earlier when she came in. She just walked past me as if I hadn't been there.

Grant had warned me she would be coming tonight. I had assured him I could get ready without him being my bodyguard. The doorbell rang right on time, and I stepped out of my room, grabbing the black and silver clutch that matched the best with my shoes.

Nan's door didn't open. I was relieved. Taking the stairs slowly, I headed to the door and then took a deep breath. Grant had never seen me like this. I wanted him to like it. No, I wanted his tongue to hang out. I was being vain. I had never gone to prom. This was that moment all little girls imagine.

Slowly, I opened the door. Instead of Grant, August stood there in a black tux, his hair styled perfectly. He blatantly checked me out, starting at my feet and going all the way up.

"Nan isn't ready yet, but you can come in and wait," I told him, stepping back and hoping to get his eyes off my body.

"I hope she looks half as good as you do," he said with a

wink as he walked into the foyer, his tall body making it seem smaller. Where was Nan?

"Um, can I get you a drink?" I asked, hoping to find a reason to get away from him.

"I'd love one. I'm sure she plans to keep me waiting another half hour. Glad I got good company," he replied.

I didn't like him. I turned and headed to the kitchen and felt like cursing when I heard his steps fall in behind mine. I had been planning on him going to the living room and waiting.

"I can get you a drink and bring it to the living room if you want to have a seat," I told him.

"You don't even know what I want." He was amused; I could hear it in his voice.

"Oh, sorry. What would you like?"

He didn't reply. When I stepped into the kitchen I battled my impulse to run back upstairs with the excuse that I'd forgotten something, leaving him to fix his own drink.

"Hard to believe you and Nan are related. She's not at all this polite and sweet," he said, pulling out a bar stool and sitting down.

I needed to get out of here. I would hurry and make his drink, then run. I turned and reached for a glass. "What would you like?" I asked.

He leaned forward and began checking my legs out again. "A lot of things," he replied.

I set the glass down. I was leaving him to help himself.

"Who's the lucky guy taking you to the ball tonight?" he asked.

"I am." Grant's voice startled me, and I spun around to see him scowling at August. I hadn't heard him come in, but then I had been focused on getting away from August.

"Don't blame you. She's the nicer sister," August said, dropping his gaze to my legs again.

Grant rounded the bar and was pulling me to his side before I could blink. "You ready?" he asked me.

I nodded. "Yeah." This was not the moment I had been daydreaming about. Grant looked like he was barely controlling his anger, not interested in how I looked.

"Hello, Grant," Nan drawled as she walked into the kitchen.

I turned to look at her in the short, tight red dress that hugged her every curve. She shouldn't look stunning in red but she did. Nan was what every little girl wanted to look like when she grew up. Her long red hair hung in soft curls and rested on her cleavage, which was right out there for the world to see and, no doubt, drool over.

"Damn, baby," August said, standing up with his mouth slightly open.

I glanced at Grant, who was also looking at Nan. The way I had wanted him to look at me. I closed my eyes briefly and took a deep breath. I didn't want to see that.

"You always did look good in a tux," Nan said, ignoring August and keeping her eyes on Grant.

This wasn't a game I knew how to play. My instinct told me to take off running to my room and lock myself up and let Grant have what he wanted while I got the heartbreak I knew was coming for me. But my pride wouldn't let me move. So I stood there, hoping he remembered me and had enough compassion to not totally humiliate me in front of Nan.

Nan's smile curled up evilly on her lips as she sauntered toward Grant, not taking her eyes off him and knowing she had his complete attention.

I was about to give in and flee. I could go to Texas. It wasn't so bad.

Grant slipped his hand into mine and started walking for the exit. I didn't glance back at Nan, although I heard her laugh an amused, knowing laugh, which shot a pain through my chest. Because she knew, just like I did, that she'd gotten to Grant.

Grant was silent until we got outside and down the steps to his truck. Once we reached it, he let go of my hand, but instead of opening the door he turned me around to face him.

"You look so damn beautiful, I'm not sure how you expect me to focus tonight," he said as his eyes finally focused on me.

This was what I wanted. The silly female in me wanted to see his appreciation, but now . . . it fell flat. I had seen the way he looked at Nan, transfixed. He hadn't reacted that way to me. But then I didn't look like Nan. Could I blame him? He was a guy, and Nan was breathtaking. I was just me.

"I wish we didn't have to go to this ball. I want to take you out and keep you all to myself."

I liked that idea. Facing a room full of people was not on my priority list. But I wasn't sure I wanted to be alone with him tonight. There was a wound I needed to lick now, and hiding out in my room with my books was more appealing.

"We will stay long enough to make Woods happy. Then I promise I'll make this night better," he whispered before pressing a kiss to my mouth and making a low growl. He jerked away and opened the truck door. "Get in before I change my mind and piss Woods off."

When he was ready to leave, I would make an excuse to come home and go to bed. Alone.

"How long was that douche there before I got there?" Grant asked as he pulled out of the driveway and onto the road.

"Maybe ten minutes. Not long," I replied.

Grant's nod was tight. He didn't like August, and I wanted to believe it had nothing to do with his dating Nan. But it was hard. He'd explained his relationship with Nan to me, but I wasn't sure I completely believed him. Especially now.

# Grant

Harlow was silent the entire way to the club, but I needed that time to calm myself down. Walking in and seeing that piece of scum looking at her chest had just about sent me over the damn edge. I should have been there earlier. I didn't like thinking about Harlow being at that house and August being able to show up at any time. What if he got Harlow alone? My hands clenched the steering wheel tighter.

That wasn't fucking happening. Nan's looks weren't enough, and I had no doubt August was figuring that out. Tonight she'd played it up big. Sure, she was gorgeous. Nan had always been gorgeous, but it was only her appearance. The moment she opened her spiteful mouth her outward appearance dimmed. It wasn't enough.

I knew she had misinterpreted the way I looked at her tonight. She was just glad to have my attention. She didn't understand what I was looking at. She thought she'd stunned me with her looks. I was past that. Nan was a part of my past. She always would be. We had bonded over our absent parents. Nan and I had grown up with absent parents, but I didn't let that define me. Nan did. She let it poison her. Tonight, I had seen only the bitterness and hate in her when she'd walked into the room. It was all there on her face, and I wondered how I had ever missed that. Was I that blind before . . . before . . .

Harlow?

Damn, I'd been a shallow fuck.

Glancing over at Harlow, I saw her hands clasped tightly in her lap. She was nervous. Her bottom lip was tucked between her teeth and she was staring straight ahead. Well, shit. I'd ignored her this entire ride and she had been sitting over there, nervous.

I was fucking this night up completely.

I reached over and pulled one of her hands free and slipped my fingers through hers. "Hey," I said, breaking into her thoughts.

She turned her head to look at me and a forced smile touched her lips. That wasn't going to work. If she really didn't want to go to this damn ball then Woods could get over it. I wasn't making her do this. I thought the fact she had dressed to make every man she passed drool meant she was ready for this. Maybe not.

"You okay?" I asked, squeezing her hand.

She nodded and didn't say anything.

"If you don't want to do this we'll go somewhere else," I told her, and waited to see what her reaction was. She stiffened. What the hell?

"Talk to me, Harlow," I said.

Her shoulders slumped and she dropped her head to stare down at her hands, still balled up in her lap. "I think maybe I should just go home. I don't want to be in the way."

What?

"Whose way are you worried about being in? Has someone said something to you that I need to fucking handle?"

She didn't look up at me. She kept staring at her lap. "No. I meant your way. I don't want you to feel obligated to take me. I don't mind going home. I'm good with that. Truly, I am."

She wasn't making any sense. Had Nan said something to her? I wanted her out of that bitch's house. We were talking about that later tonight. But right now I had to figure out what was wrong.

"I want you with me. If Nan said something to you . . ."

"Nan didn't have to say anything. You said it all with your eyes."

Wait . . . what?

I studied her, trying to figure out what that meant.

Harlow took a deep breath and then finally looked up at me. Her big eyes were so sad and broken, my chest felt like it was going to explode. I had to fix this shit. I didn't want my girl hurting. I jerked the truck over to the side of the road and threw it into park before reaching over to Harlow and pulling her close to me.

"You need to explain that because I'm not following you, sweetheart," I demanded.

Harlow kept her eyes fixed on my shoulder. "I saw the way you looked at her. I'm not blind. I know how beautiful she is. I know you were struck speechless. And it was obvious she would have dumped August for you. Who wouldn't?"

Well, fuck. I hadn't thought about Harlow thinking anything about me looking at Nan. I hadn't been impressed; I'd been disgusted with myself.

I slipped my hand under Harlow's chin and tilted her face up to look at me. She always looked down, and I wanted to see her eyes. I wanted to fix that sadness in them. I didn't ever want to make her sad.

"What you saw was me looking at Nan and seeing nothing but bitterness and cruelty in her eyes. I wondered how I had missed that for so long. I wasn't impressed with the way she looked. I had you standing there beside me, looking like an angel. No one can compare to you. You're not just beautiful outside, you're also beautiful inside. I see that and I cherish it. I just don't know why I screwed around with Nan. I guess you saved me."

Harlow continued to frown at me. "She's every man's fantasy."

I rubbed my thumb over her bottom lip and tried not to think about how sweet that mouth tasted. "She's every man's nightmare, sweet girl. Unfortunately, they don't realize it right away."

"I can't compete with her. I don't want to."

"There's no competition. She pales in comparison. I wish I knew what I could do to convince you that you're it for me. I don't see anything but a girl I once knew when I look at Nan."

Harlow dropped her gaze to study my shirt before finally lifting her eyes and giving me her first real smile. "I think I believe you."

She had serious trust issues, and I needed to remember that and act accordingly. Where Nan never needed reassurance that I wanted her, Harlow needed reassurance that she owned me. She was too innocent to see just how I really felt about her. Even if it was obvious to the rest of the world.

"I'll make sure you never doubt me again. Just know I can't see anyone but you. When you walk into a room, you light it up."

She leaned up and pressed a kiss to my cheek. "Thank you," she said, simply.

It was things like that that set her apart. She was like no one else I knew, and I was the luckiest son of a bitch in the world.

# Harlow

Blaire spotted me the moment we stepped into the ball-room, and she made her way toward us. I was relieved. Seeing a friendly face helped ease me into this. The black dress she wore danced around her legs as she walked. It also made her blond hair stand out even more. I glanced behind her to see Rush's eyes on his wife, watching her every move. The love and posses-siveness that was there on his face for everyone to see made my heart beat faster. That had to be an amazing feeling.

"I'm so glad you're here," Blaire said as she hugged me.

"I'm still trying to decide if I am," I replied.

Blaire laughed and glanced around. "They're not all bad." She turned to Grant and grinned. "You look happy."

"I am," he replied, and slid his hand around my waist.

"It's about time," she said.

"Yeah, it is," he agreed.

I felt like there was a private conversation going on here that I was being left out of.

"You thirsty?" Grant asked me, leaning down so that his warm breath tickled my ear.

"Yes," I replied. A drink in my hands would give me some-thing to do.

"Be right back," he replied, and stepped back to leave me with Blaire.

"So?" she asked, lifting her eyebrows.

I knew she wanted to know about Grant. From what I could tell she was close to Grant because of Rush. "I think he likes me," I replied, because I really didn't know what else to say.

Blaire's grin only got bigger. "I believe that's obvious, Harlow. If you aren't positive about it, though, I think you could just ask him and he would clarify that."

I turned to look back at the bar and saw a girl with dark brown curls and a low-cut white dress pressing very close to him as she talked to him.

"Ignore her. I assure you, he is. That's Katrina, and she's not one to worry about. It's just what she does."

I turned back around. "I can't figure out why he chose me. He gets attention from everyone. He's perfect. He can have anyone."

Blaire put a hand on her hip and stared at me in disbelief. "You're serious, aren't you?"

I just nodded. Why would I be kidding?

"Do you know what I thought the first time I saw you?"

"No," I replied, not sure if I wanted to hear this answer.

"I wanted to know who this beautiful woman walking into my fiancé's room was. I was instantly stunned by you. Then you opened your mouth and this sweet, kind personality of yours shone through. I wanted to get to know you. There's this draw to you that brings people in. So that's why Grant can't keep his eyes off you," Blaire said, glancing over my shoulder and grinning.

I turned around to see the girl still talking to him, but he was looking at me. I smiled and he winked. I had to learn to trust him. He deserved it.

"How did you learn to trust Rush?" I asked, looking back at Blaire.

She let out a sigh. "That was hard. Once I trusted him he blew it all to pieces. It was a long road after that, but I had to trust him. My heart wanted him, and in order for me to give in to that I had to trust him and believe he would take care of me."

"You're saying it's a decision you made," I asked.

She nodded. "Yeah, it is."

I could do that.

Blaire let out a sad sigh and I followed her gaze. Bethy stood in the corner in a server's uniform, talking to some lady who looked as if she was in charge of things. "I'm worried about her," Blaire said.

"I saw her last week at a bar. She was really down," I told her. I wouldn't have told just anyone, but I knew Blaire was her best friend.

"Losing Jace has completely changed her. I can't seem to reach her," she said. "She rarely takes my calls anymore."

"I can't imagine what she's going through," I said, remembering her words that night at the bar.

"Me neither," Blaire replied.

"Your sparkling water," Grant said, handing me the wine glass in his hand.

"I need to get back to Rush. You two have fun," Blaire said, then looked directly at me and smiled before going back to Rush, who was still watching her.

"There's Tripp. I didn't know he was in town," Grant said, staring at a tall guy with short hair and a tattoo visible above his collar. He didn't look as if he was happy to be here. And he also seemed to be worried about Bethy. He was completely focused on her.

"Let's talk to Woods and Della, then I can get away with talking to just a few other people before we escape this place and I get you alone," Grant said, pressing his hand to the small of my back and leading me toward the tall, tanned man who commanded the room with authority. I already knew who Woods was, but even if I hadn't, I would know he owned the place.

I noticed the woman on his arm. Her blue eyes stood out from a headful of long, dark curls. A soft smile touched her face as she stared up at Woods as if he had all the answers in the world.

Woods's gaze found Grant and he glanced at me then back to Grant. An amused smile touched his face, and I realized Woods knew something. "Grant, looks like your choice in dates has improved," Woods said.

"Yeah. It takes some of us longer than others," Grant replied as his thumb made small circles on my back where his hand rested.

The dark-haired woman let go of Woods and stepped forward to hold out her hand. "Hello, I'm Della. I've heard so much about you from Blaire. It's nice to meet you."

She was sincere, and I instantly liked her. "It's nice to meet you, too," I replied.

"I'm happy to see Grant is making wiser choices," Della said, grinning.

Apparently Nan was disliked by everyone.

Grant chuckled at her comment and I relaxed. I was worried he was going to take offense at everyone's bringing it up. "How long do I need to stay at this thing?" Grant asked.

The professional all-business demeanor in Woods's expression faltered a moment as he let his gaze travel over the room. "Give it at least thirty minutes—maybe an hour. Be sure to watch the video. I think it'll be the hardest part of the night. It'll mean a lot to Jace's parents for you to be here for that. People also need to see your face, since you're a board member. Then take off. Wish I could," he said in a low voice.

In that moment he reminded me of Grant and Rush. He didn't seem so powerful and serious. Della smiled at me. "I wish we could get out of here early, too."

"If you want to leave early, I'll find a way," Woods replied.

Della stared up at him and smiled brightly. "No. We stay. You can't leave early."

Woods leaned down to her ear. "I do what you want to do."

Della pressed a kiss to his cheek. "I want to stay."

"Liar."

Della just laughed and looked back at me. "I have to keep him in line."

"Glad someone does," Grant replied.

Woods's easy smile turned into a frown as he focused on something behind us. Grant and I turned at the same time. Rush was walking toward us with a look on his face I didn't understand.

Grant's hand dropped from my back, and he walked toward Rush before he could get to us. I wasn't sure if I should follow him or wait here.

"Something's wrong," Woods said before stepping by me and walking toward them.

I glanced back at Della, who was watching them, concerned. She wasn't following Woods so I stayed with her.

Rush shook his head and looked over at me, then nodded
his head for me to join them. Confused, I walked over. Rush
reached out and grabbed my arm.

"I need you to stay with Blaire and Nate. Grant needs to
come with me. Can you do that?"

I tried to nod but I just stood there, confused even more.

"It's Nan. But I need him for this. And you have to trust
him," Rush said.

Nan? We just saw Nan. She was coming here. "Okay" was
all I could say. They didn't look as if they wanted to answer any
questions. Grant looked angry and Rush was tense.

"I can't leave with you guys, but if it's what she says, then let
me know. I'll handle it," Woods said, then turned and headed
back to Della.

Rush motioned for Blaire and pulled her into his arms,
talking to her in hushed whispers. She nodded and glanced
over at me with a worried frown. "If you think that's necessary"
was her only response.

"I can't ignore it. I have to check," Rush told Blaire, who
didn't seem too sure that she agreed with him.

She kept her back stiff and nodded. Rush looked torn.
What in the world was going on?

"If you want to come, then come with me. Don't do this to
me," Rush said, closing in on Blaire and pulling her close.

She finally seemed to surrender and nodded. "Okay," she
said. Rush pressed a hard kiss to her mouth that had her melt-
ing further into him.

Everyone seemed to know what was going on but me.

Woods's head was lowered as he talked to Della. He was telling her. Rush was telling Blaire, but then there was me. No one was telling me. Grant wasn't even looking at me. His body seemed coiled tight, and I realized I had trusted in him a little too soon.

# Grant

I was doing this for him. He was my brother. At the top of all things that mattered was the fact that Rush was my brother. But, motherfucker, the look on Harlow's face when she heard Nan's name was going to screw shit up. I could see it, and I had to choose. I'd chosen Rush. He was family.

I was trusting Harlow to believe in me. To know why I was doing this. Who I was doing it for. I needed her to understand, because losing her wasn't an option.

"She'll understand. Harlow will listen when you explain, and she'll be okay with it. Blaire is probably explaining it to her now," Rush said as he sped toward Nan's house.

If this shit was real and August had just beat the hell out of Nan, then I was all for hunting him down and letting Rush get his vengeance. Nan was a lot of things, but first and foremost she was Rush's little sister. Rush didn't allow Nan to come between him and Blaire, and he protected Blaire from her. But if Nan was in trouble and needed Rush, he came. He was all she had. No one else gave a shit. I had once, but she'd made sure I didn't for long.

"If she's lying, it might be me beating the shit out of her," I warned him.

He let out a heavy sigh. "I know."

Rush wasn't blind to Nan's nastiness. He also knew that saving Nan and leaving Harlow wasn't easy for me. I wasn't married to Harlow. I hadn't made her promises with a diamond ring. Blaire had all that, and seeing Rush run off to save Nan made more sense to her. Nan was also Rush's sister.

I couldn't claim any of that.

Fuck, she better be telling the truth.

Rush pulled into Nan's driveway, and the fear that Harlow might not get over this hit me again as my gaze found her little black car. Fuck, I shouldn't have left her. But Rush had needed me. When he needed backup, I was it. That was what brothers were for. We had each other's back.

We both climbed out of the truck and headed for the stairs at the same time. Rush didn't knock; he slid his key into the door and opened it. I was surprised he had a key. That must be Kiro's doing.

"Nannette," Rush called out when he swung the door open.

I followed him inside.

"In here," Nan called from the living room. Rush stalked toward the sound of her voice.

He paused when he walked into the room, and I stopped behind him and looked over his shoulder.

She hadn't been lying.

Nan's lip was busted and a black eye was already appearing on her pale skin. Her bare arms each had handprints on them that would be bruises soon enough. Nan sat there with her knees pulled up against her chest tightly. Black streaks of mascara ran down her face. She'd been crying.

This wasn't the Nan I knew. It was the one I had known.

She reminded me of the little girl I had once felt sorry for. The one whose problem I had wanted to fix just as much as Rush did. The bitter, angry bitch wasn't in her eyes as she looked at us. Instead, she was scared.

"What the fuck," Rush growled and took two big strides until he was in front of her and sitting down on the sofa beside her. "August did this?" Rush asked. His fury was barely contained, and as I stood there and looked at her, my anger began to boil, too.

I didn't care what she had done. No woman deserved this. August was a dead man walking. If Rush didn't kill him, I would.

"Yes. He got mad because"—she glanced over at me and then back at Rush—"I was upset about Grant and Harlow. I didn't want to go, then he wanted to have sex and I didn't want to. He tried to force me, but I fought back. Then he just snapped, and when I woke up on the floor he was gone."

Rush's body went taut. "He knocked you out?" Rush asked.

She nodded, and her gaze shifted to me again.

"He's gotten angry before, but never like that. I didn't know he was like that. I knew his wife left him and it took him two years before he got to see his daughter again. I believed him when he said he never hurt her. That she was a liar," she said in a shaky voice.

"You need to see a doctor. If you were unconscious, you could have a concussion. Grant, take her to the hospital and have them check her out."

Me? "What? Why can't you?" I asked. I didn't need to be taking her anywhere. I was gonna beat the shit out of August, but that didn't mean I wanted to haul Nan around.

"I'm going to find August. I need you to take her to get checked out. Please," Rush said, standing up. "I'll call Blaire and explain."

Which meant he would make sure Harlow knew what was going on and why. I just hoped she understood. Rush believed Harlow was strong enough for this emotionally, but I wasn't sure I agreed. He didn't know how insecure she really was.

"Can't I find him?" I asked.

Rush shook his head. "No. I have Dean to make sure I don't serve time. You don't."

He had a point.

"He doesn't have to take me. I'm fine to stay here," Nan said.

Rush looked at me, silently pleading. Shit.

"Okay, I'll do it." I looked at Nan. "Can you walk?" I asked.

She nodded and stood up. "Just a little dizzy."

Rush put his arm around her and I let him help her to the truck. I wasn't touching her. I would help, but I wasn't touching her.

I followed them to his Range Rover. He put Nan in, then turned to me.

"I'll take Nan's car. Get her completely checked out."

"Call Blaire and check on Harlow for me," I replied.

He nodded. "Doing that now."

I didn't say thanks. He owed me that much. I walked around the Rover and opened the door. I climbed in and slammed the door to get out some frustration. It didn't help.

"You didn't have to take me," she said.

"Yeah, I did," I replied.

"Because you still care," she said with a hopeful tone in her voice.

"No, because of Rush," I replied, and turned to head for the hospital, which was a good thirty minutes away.

"Do you really mean that?" she asked.

"Yes, I really do."

"But you said once that you loved me," she said, sounding hurt.

I had been drinking. The sex had been great. "I was in lust. What we had was good at first. I'd enjoyed it. Then I realized you weren't the one. You were nasty and mean and shallow. And so was our sex."

She made a small gasp. I didn't care if my words wounded her. I knew she was hurt, and I hated that she'd messed around with someone who would hit a woman. That was it. Nothing more.

"Is sex with her better? She's too unpracticed to be any good."

That was what Nan would never understand. Sex would never be more than sex for her because she didn't have the heart to look deeper. To actually feel something for another person.

"Nothing can compare to Harlow. Nothing comes close to touching it" was all I said.

My private life with Harlow was just that: private. I wasn't sharing it with Nan.

# Harlow

I heard Blaire talking on the phone in the kitchen as I stood just outside on the balcony. She had explained on the ride over that Nan had been badly beaten up by August. Or that was what Nan had said when she called Rush.

I could see in Blaire's eyes that she wasn't sure she believed that story. But she had understood Rush's need to go. I also understood that he needed backup if it was true, and Grant was his brother—or the closest thing he had to one.

But the image of Grant holding Nan and comforting her was haunting me. I hated that I was being that selfish. I wasn't a selfish person. My feelings for Grant were making me different. I didn't exactly like some of the differences, either. If Nan had been beaten up by August, then she needed her brother and Grant. They were the only two men in her life she could trust.

"That was Rush," Blaire said from behind me.

"How is she?" I asked, unable to look back at Blaire. I was afraid she'd see what I was thinking in my eyes, and I was ashamed.

"She was telling the truth. Rush said he had beat her pretty bad, and she was knocked unconscious."

My chest hurt, but it wasn't in sympathy for Nan. It was for me. It was because I could see Grant slipping away from me. I hated myself for that. Was I truly that cruel?

"Rush is going to find August. He sent Grant with Nan to the hospital. He said he wanted her checked out."

So Grant was with her. Alone. This was it. He was a sucker when it came to Nan in need. I had seen how he had chased after her before when he felt she needed someone.

"Rush wanted you to know Grant didn't want to take her. He guilted him into it."

I could hold on to that for a little while. Maybe it would ease my fear. Or maybe preparing myself for the worst was the best way to protect my heart. Not that it would really make a difference. I was too far gone anyway.

"I used to hate her. I thought she was the bane of my existence. But over time, I've realized that Nan is just sad. She has pushed everyone away and made them hate her and her ugly heart. She does nothing to endear herself to anyone. She has to call Rush because he's her brother. He's the only one who'll come running. She didn't call Grant tonight because she knew he wouldn't answer, much less come to the rescue. But she knew Rush would, and she knew he would bring Grant. Even when she's at her lowest point, she manipulates people. Grant's smart enough to see that."

I hoped she was right.

"He saw something in her before," I said simply.

Blaire stood beside me. "He saw someone who was in need of fixing. Grant likes to fix things. When I first came here, Rush hated me. He wanted me gone. But Grant made sure that didn't happen. The next morning when I woke up, I was worried about how I was going to afford to get gas so I could find a job. When I got to my truck, there was a note on it from Grant. He'd filled my truck up with gas. It's just who he is. Nan is broken and she isn't fixable. Grant figured that out. He has you and he isn't going to mess that up."

I felt tears sting my eyes. I knew Blaire's history. She'd come here alone, lost but brave. The fact that Grant had made sure she'd had gas only made me love him more. I gripped the railing hard and closed my eyes. I would not cry.

"I'm in love with him," I admitted, in a whisper so low I wasn't sure she heard me. I hoped she hadn't as soon as I said it.

"I know. It's all over you when you're with him. But he's in love with you, too. I've never seen him look at anyone the way he looks at you."

I thought of Rush and the way he protected Blaire. The possessive gleam in his eyes, and the way he kept her so close to him. I didn't have that. She had something exceptional, and I had read too many romances. I wanted that, too. I hadn't realized it was real until I had seen Rush with Blaire.

That kind of love wasn't a fantasy. It was real.

"I want the fantasy. I want him to love me the way Rush loves you."

Blaire leaned into me and bumped my shoulder with hers. "He's headed that way if he isn't there already. You've gotten under his skin."

"He hasn't told me he loves me," I told her.

"He will," she replied. "When he's brave enough, he'll tell you."

I tried to believe that. I wanted to believe that.

"All my life I've seen my dad screw around with women and throw them aside as if they meant nothing. I worried that love wasn't real, or if it was that I didn't have the right genetic makeup to love like you love Rush. I had never been in love. I was so guarded. I worried that I wouldn't love because my father couldn't love. Then . . . then I saw him with . . ." I stopped. I didn't know if I wanted to share this with Blaire. I wasn't sure if I wanted to ever share what I had seen. "He loves my mom. Even though she can't speak or move, he wants to be near her. He brushes her hair." That fact still baffled me. I had never known he could be that way.

"My guess is that you're just like your mother. She inspired that kind of love and devotion from a rock star who could have anyone he wanted. It's a special gift, and you need to learn to trust that you're worthy of that love. Give Grant time. He's just now figuring things out, and I believe he's worth waiting for."

I nodded. She was right. He was worth it. I had to stop doubting him. Twice in one night. Another trait I had that I hated. I was insecure. Painfully so. It was time I overcame that. I didn't know if I had a long life with Grant or not. But I wanted him. I wanted this to be my life. When it was over, I wanted to know I had this.

It was time I told him my secret. He deserved to know.

✥

Three hours later, my phone rang as I sat curled up on the Finlays' sofa. Blaire had gone upstairs earlier when Nate had started crying. She said he was used to Rush rocking him to sleep, so she had to give him extra attention.

"Hello," I said, knowing it was Grant.

"Hey, you still at Rush's?" he asked.

"Yes," I replied.

"Good. I have to get Nan inside and make sure she gets into bed. Doctor says she needs to be woken up every hour. She's got a pretty bad concussion. I'll come get you as soon as she's in bed."

I wasn't going to dwell on the fact he was putting her to bed. I was stronger than that. "Okay," I replied.

"Harlow?" he said, the concern in his voice obvious.

"Yes."

"I'm sorry about all this. Please know it changes nothing. She's just Rush's little sister. Okay?"

"I know."

Grant let out a frustrated sigh. "I'll be there in a few minutes. I swear."

"I'm fine. Take your time," I assured him before hanging up.

The front door opened and Rush came walking in. He walked past the open doorway to the living room then stopped, backtracked, and looked at me. "Hey, you're still here," he said.

"Yeah. Grant just called."

"I needed his help tonight. That's the only reason he did this."

"I know," I said, even if I didn't completely get it.

"He wanted to come back to you," Rush told me.

"It's okay, Rush. I'm not upset," I assured him.

He looked relieved. "Nate asleep?" he asked.

"He was crying and Blaire went up to rock him."

"He wants me. It's our time. Tell Grant I said thanks," he told me.

"I will."

# Grant

Harlow came walking outside when I pulled into the driveway. She was still wearing that dress, but her heels were dangling from her fingers. I'd had plans for that dress, and especially those heels. Even if she hadn't meant to, Nan had ruined the evening.

I jumped out of the truck and walked around to open her door as she reached me.

She smiled up at me sweetly. The tired look in her eyes made me want to tuck her close to me and hold her.

"Hey," I said, taking both her hands and putting them around my neck.

"Hey," she replied, resting both her hands on my shoulders.

"I missed you," I told her, lowering my head until I could press my lips to hers. She opened easily for me, and I dove in, tasting her and reminding myself that she was mine. She trusted me.

"I missed you, too," she whispered against my lips.

"You're not mad at me?" I asked, needing reassurance.

"No," she said simply.

"It's time I get you tucked into bed, too. Except I want you naked and wrapped around me," I told her, and picked her up to set her in my truck. "And I want you to wear those heels for me."

She scrunched her nose. "To sleep in?"

"No, I want you in those heels while I bury myself inside you," I informed her.

Both her cheeks flamed red as she flushed and nodded.

That was my girl. She wasn't hurt or mad. I had never been so fucking relieved.

I patted the seat beside me in the truck and Harlow slid over. She leaned against me and let me hold her close. Having her here made everything easier. I pressed a kiss to her head. "Thank you," I said.

"For what?"

"For being so damn perfect for me."

Harlow turned her face to rest on my shoulder. Her breath was warm on my skin, and getting her to her bedroom was becoming a top priority.

"I'm not going to lie. I was upset. I didn't like that you went to Nan's rescue. It was selfish of me, and I hated that I had that ugliness inside. I won't ever react that way again. I don't want to be that way."

She was so damn honest. And she was also wrong. There wasn't an ounce of ugliness in her. I slid my hand over her bare thigh. "Harlow, I don't think you could be selfish and ugly, even if you tried. You reacted that way because you felt possessive of me, and that makes me the luckiest damn man in the world. You should have been upset. Hell, baby, I was upset. I was so damn torn. I didn't want to be there, but Rush needed me."

"And I resented that. So I was selfish."

Laughing, I slid my hand up her thigh. "I tell you what. You can be selfish anytime you want to with me. It turns me the fuck on."

Harlow eased her legs open. "Why?" she breathed as my hand brushed her already-wet panties.

"Because I want to belong to you. I want you to care when I leave. If you would've come after me I would have gladly let you go with me. I can't tell you no."

She moved against my hand and made a soft moaning sound in her throat. "Then fuck me in the truck before we go inside. I need you," she said, throwing her head back and crying out as I slipped a hand inside her panties.

"Looks like I'm gonna get to live out that fantasy with you in this dress after all," I told her and reached for her shoes. "I want these on you first," I told her.

She laughed and slipped them on before crawling into my lap.

✿

When the first alarm went off an hour after Harlow and I lay down to go to bed, I quickly turned it off and started to get out of bed to wake Nan. Harlow's hand reached out and grabbed me and pulled me back down.

"No. I'm doing this," she said and started to get up.

"Stay in bed. I don't want you dealing with this," I argued. Nan was not her problem.

Harlow pushed her long, thick hair out of her face and frowned at me. "You said that it was okay for me to be possessive. Well, I don't like the idea of you going into Nan's room with her in bed and waking her up. You stay here in my bed, and I'll go wake her up," she said.

Smiling, I lay back down. "Okay. Fine. You win," I replied.

She had a point. There was no way in hell I'd let her go in another man's room at night and wake him up to check on him.

She nodded and grabbed my discarded white tuxedo shirt and put it on without bothering to button it; she just held it closed and went out the door.

Little, sweet, sexy woman was going to make sure she checked on Nan while showing her just whose bed I was in. Made me grin. I liked knowing she had some fight in her. With a sister like Nan, she needed it. I hated to think of Nan hurting her in any way.

To think I almost lost this because I was worried about loving her and losing her. The fear of death had gotten its claws in thick. I had Rush and Blaire to thank for showing me that loving someone like this was worth it. I just had to find a way to tell Harlow exactly how I felt. I didn't want to scare her off. The way she was looking at me lately, I wanted to believe she felt the same way.

The bedroom door opened and Harlow rolled her eyes. "She's fine. Bitchy as ever. Said she wanted you to check on her next time," Harlow said before dropping my shirt and crawling back into bed to snuggle up against me.

"What did you tell her?" I asked.

"I told her to get over it. I was keeping your sexy ass safely tucked in my bed." Harlow replied as she threw one of her long legs over mine and burrowed into me.

I held her against me and went back to sleep with a smile on my face.

# Harlow

Rush found August. Even if Woods hadn't fired him, he wouldn't have been able to work. Rush managed to break the arm he hit Nan with and told him to leave town. Either Rush had an in with the police department or August had run scared. I'm not sure what exactly happened. I didn't like talking about Nan with Grant.

Nan left town again, which was a normal thing for her, from what everyone said. She would be back when she was over the thing with August. I was just glad to have Grant alone. He seemed more relieved than I was.

The only thing standing between me and Grant now was my secret. The one that I had kept to myself most of my life. The one that made people treat me differently. And the one that kept me from telling him I loved him.

He hadn't said he loved me. Was it fair to love him if I couldn't give him things he deserved? For so long, I had lived without thinking about it because my grandmama hadn't allowed me to use it as a crutch or an excuse. But now . . . I couldn't do this without being honest. Telling Grant the truth was going to be hard. He would either understand or see this as a deception.

If I just had some more time. I didn't want to ruin things. His heart was safe, even if mine wasn't. I glanced back at Grant, who was on the phone with a construction site that we were headed to three hours out of town. He had wanted me to come with him, and I didn't want to be away from him. We hadn't been talking much on the ride because he'd been driving and making notes and talking on the phone to different people. I had even heard him argue with his father. It was a nice look into a different side of his life. He wasn't like the other social-ites in Rosemary—he actually had a job. A regular job for a blue-collar company. I liked it.

He finally dropped the phone onto the notebook and looked at me. "I swear, if I'd known they were gonna keep me on the damn phone all day I wouldn't have dragged you out with me."

"I just like being with you," I told him.

His face transformed into a smile and he reached over and laced his fingers through mine. "I love having you with me. Makes everything better."

He loved having me with him. He didn't love *me*, but he loved having me around. That was new. I couldn't keep the silly grin off my face.

"I'm starving. You ready for some lunch?" he asked, pulling off at the next exit.

"Yes, I'm getting hungry," I admitted.

My phone rang, interrupting me, and I immediately grabbed it. Only two people would be calling me. Dad or Mase.

Dad's name lit up the screen.

"Daddy?" I said into the phone. He rarely called me when he was on tour.

"Hey. I'm headed home. There's a problem with Emmy. I need to be there. And I want you to be prepared. Things are going to blow up once they find you."

Find me? "I don't understand, Daddy. What things are about to blow up? Who's going to find me?"

"Some motherfucker leaked the info about your mom. Some new staff member at the Manor. When she saw me there, she did some digging. When you came to visit, she discovered you're my daughter. I was attacked by the paparazzi in fucking Paris tonight. I'm headed home. I don't want them getting anywhere near your mother. The bitch has been fired and escorted off the property, but the press is covering the Manor. The staff is in a panic. They'll be after you, too."

I had always been kept safe from the paparazzi because I was boring. Now my mother's existence was going to change it all. "What can I do to help, Daddy?" I asked, worried about the man I'd seen protecting the woman in that room as if she were a princess.

"Nothing. Not a fucking thing, sweetheart. Not a fucking thing. I gotta get to your mom. She needs me. I'm sorry, but you're on your own. Just be prepared—they'll find you. It'll all come out. Everything. You understand that, don't you?"

He meant my life. My secrets. My privacy.

"Yes, sir. I know."

"I'm so sorry, baby girl," he said, and the pain in his voice was honest. He really wished I didn't have to face this. But I had to figure this out on my own.

"Only thing I can think of is you can come to the Manor. I can get you a room there and you'll be safe, but they will eventually get the story. Too many people know things. It will all come out. You can hide for a while, and I'll hide you. But it's time you faced this. You aren't my little girl anymore."

He was right. It was time I faced this life. The one I'd hidden from.

"Call me. Let me know how she is and that you're safe when you get there," I told him.

"I will. Nan's story will come out, too. Be ready for that."

"Okay."

He hung up and I stared down at my phone.

"What's wrong?" Grant asked, his gaze on me.

"I . . . they know. The media know."

"Shit," Grant moved the notebook between us and slid over to me. I hadn't even realized we were parked until that moment. "You mean about your mom?"

I nodded. "Yes. My mom. Nan . . . me. They know it all. They'll come looking for me. I won't be hard to find. They already know where Rush lives. He makes the papers randomly when they need some Slacker Demon family stories for the smear papers."

Grant pulled me into his arms and held me against his chest. I had to tell him everything now. I just couldn't form words. "I won't let those fuckers get near you. I swear," he growled, tightening his hold on me.

He didn't know what they were like. This was a breaking story in the music industry. The world's most legendary rock band's lead singer was married to a woman he'd kept a secret from everyone. Even his own daughter for years.

Then there was me. Their miracle child. The child who shouldn't have lived but did. The one who might not live a long life. The one who couldn't have kids or it would kill her.

The one who wasn't whole, whose heart never worked properly. The pills I'd taken my entire life. The precautions—it would all come out. And I would be the sick girl. The one everyone looked at as if she wasn't normal. I didn't want that. Not again.

I had lived that life before, and I didn't want it again. I kept my secrets guarded for a reason. And now they were all coming out, and I had no control.

"Shh, it's okay, baby. I swear I will protect you. I swear, I will," Grant murmured as silent tears ran down my face. My life was about to completely change.

# Grant

Holy hell. This wasn't something I could fix, and I hated it. Harlow's shoulders silently shook as her tears wet the front of my shirt. Her life was about to be splashed all over the media. And I couldn't do a damn thing about it.

Rush had never had to deal with this because the world knew he existed. He made the tabloids at times, but his normal life didn't supply them with the drama they craved.

This would. Harlow would get no peace. I could take her away and hide her. We could get on a plane and leave the damn country. "Let's leave. Get on a plane and hide. We can go to a secluded island somewhere."

She shook her head. "It won't make it go away. They will find me one day and until I face it—" she hiccuped "—they will be after me. I have to face this. And I need to check on my dad. This is going to be so hard on him."

Always worrying about someone else. It was what she did. It was one of the things I loved about her. But right fucking now, I wanted her to think about herself. Kiro was used to the paparazzi. He was used to being in the media and rumors spreading about him. He had kept Harlow out of the limelight and now she was about to be thrown into it.

It wasn't like the world didn't know she existed. They just didn't know that much about her, so they ignored her. She was boring, and Kiro's exploits were a lot more fun.

"Tell me what to do and I'll do it. Just tell me what you need," I told her as my heart felt as if it was being broken with each sob.

"I need to go back to Rosemary and pack," she said, simply.

Pack? Why? "Why are you packing?" I asked, feeling the first pulls of panic.

"I have to leave. Nan will be less interesting to the media if I'm not there. I need to go back to L.A. and hide out. I'm good at that."

"I can't work in L.A. but I'll call Dad and tell him to deal," I told her.

She shook her head. "No, you don't need to come. You need to stay here and stay out of this."

I gently grabbed both her shoulders and pushed her back so I could see her face. Her tear-streaked face and big eyes stared up at me. "I'm not letting you leave me. Ever. Don't you understand that?"

She just looked at me. Emotions flashed in her eyes that I wanted to cling to, and others I hated. She doubted me . . . she doubted us. I thought we'd moved past that.

"Harlow, I won't let you leave me."

She wiped at the tears on her face. "You will," she said with a sad, defeated sound. I hated it.

"Sweet girl, ain't no amount of paparazzi gonna send me away from you. I can handle any shit as long as I have you."

Harlow shook her head and looked away from me. "You say that now. But you don't know. It isn't worth it."

She was worth anything and everything that could be thrown at me.

"I'll take you back, but I won't leave your side. I won't let you deal with this alone, and I'm not going anywhere. Do you hear me?"

A sad smile touched her face. "I know you think that, but it'll be too much. You'll know soon. It isn't what you think. Stuff will come out, and you won't be able to deal with it. And I'll understand."

She didn't trust anyone. I was losing this fight. I was gonna win her heart, dammit. She had mine, and I was gonna do anything I could to prove to her she had my heart. Telling her wasn't enough. Words were weak. I had to show her. And I would.

⌗

I kept Harlow tucked beside me. We didn't listen to the radio. I was pretty sure it was already being talked about on every station. I didn't want to upset her. This wasn't going to be easy, and I was liable to beat the shit out of someone before it was over, but I'd show her I meant it. That she was it for me.

When we rolled back into Rosemary, TV station vans and cars lined the streets. I turned around and headed for my apartment.

"What are you doing?" she asked, sitting up and looking at the paparazzi already surrounding Nan's house. They were taking pictures of her car and the house.

"Taking you to my place," I informed her.

"I need to face this now. It'll just get worse. I want them to leave so everyone in Rosemary can go back to normal."

"Harlow, if I let you out of the car and they come at you, I'll end up in jail. Do you understand me?"

She glanced at me with a frown. "Why?"

"Because I'll fucking snap. That's why."

"Oh," she replied. She let me drive to my apartment without any more questions.

When we pulled in, I felt like breathing a sigh of relief. I was afraid they had already figured out who I was and would be waiting here, too.

My phone rang when I stopped the truck, and I grabbed it. Rush's name was on the screen.

"Hey," I said, opening the truck door. I wanted to hurry and get Harlow safely inside.

"Where's Harlow?" Rush asked.

"With me."

"Where?"

"Just got to my apartment," I replied.

"Get her inside and don't fucking leave," Rush barked.

"Already ahead of you," I told him, annoyed that he thought he needed to protect what was mine.

"She knows?" Rush asked.

"Yeah. Kiro called and warned her."

"Did she know about her mother?"

"Yeah, she found out when we went to find her dad in Vegas. I was there."

"They're already talking about Harlow. Keep the TV off," Rush said.

"Planning on it. I'm taking care of her. I don't need you telling me how the fuck to keep my woman safe."

Rush was silent a moment. "Okay. Fine. But if—" he paused.

"Never mind. Call me if you need me." He hung up and I took Harlow from the truck and slipped my hand into hers, and we both started running for the door. There was no one here, and I wanted to fucking keep it that way.

When I had her safely inside, I closed the door and locked it.

"You okay?" I asked her.

She nodded and stood there and stared at me. I wasn't sure what she was thinking but I could tell she was battling something.

I took a step toward her and she threw herself into my arms. I hadn't expected that but I caught her and held her. I realized this was the first time in her life someone had made her the priority. The relief in her body as she pressed against me told me everything I needed to know. My overprotected Harlow had never been protected for her sake, but for the secrets in her family and a woman she didn't know was alive.

"From now on, you have me," I told her, and she nodded against my chest.

# Harlow

It took them only three hours to find us. Grant closed the blinds and curtains over the windows and glass doors leading out to the balcony. Cop cars were out there, too, and I knew Rush was using every ounce of power he had to get the vultures off me, but it wouldn't do any good.

Grant was locked in his apartment like an animal because of me. I hated that. I watched him as he peeked outside, and I started to hate myself. I had done this to him. I was selfish and I let him stay with me. I should have run. I should have forced him to leave me. I should have told him that his fear of caring about someone whom he could lose was very real with me. I wasn't sure how long I'd live. He could never get me pregnant. I'd seen him looking at Rush with Nate, and I knew he wanted that.

But he could never have it with me.

I was defective.

And now I was ruining his life.

Grant turned back around and saw me staring at him. He frowned and made his way over to me in a few long strides.

"I don't like the look I see on your face. Ignore that shit out there."

"I can't. You're locked in your apartment because of me."

Grant raised his eyebrows. "You think I care about that? The only problem I would have with that is if you weren't with me. But you are. And that makes this a damn nice setup."

I couldn't help but smile at the teasing look on his face. He never ceased to make me smile. "You're gonna want out soon," I told him, trying to remind him of a very real problem.

Grant didn't argue with me. Instead, he crooked his finger at me. "Get up," he demanded.

I did as I was told.

He reached out and caressed my cheek with the back of his hand. "Good girl," he cooed. "Now, take off your clothes," he said in a stern voice. It should have made me angry, but the dark, sexy undertones only got my attention in a very different way.

"What?" I asked, starting to breathe harder.

"I said to take off your clothes. I know you heard me correctly," he said slowly.

I thought about arguing but the way he was watching me changed my mind. I reached for the zipper on my skirt and pulled it down, letting the skirt pool at my feet. I grabbed the hem of my shirt with both hands and pulled it up and over my head slowly. If he wanted to play games, I decided I would, too. When I dropped my shirt to the floor, his gaze burned into me. I could almost feel the heat searing my skin. I reached behind and unhooked my bra before letting it fall forward. I let it dangle from one of my hands then dropped it in front of him.

"Panties," he said in a husky voice.

I took extra effort in shimmying out of them, then stood

there while his heated gaze warmed my body and made it tingle in all the right areas.

"No man would regret being locked away with you," he said in a low voice and reached out to cup one of my swollen, needy breasts in his hands. "Such responsive nipples. They don't even need me to touch them. Hard as candy from just my gaze," he murmured. I thought I should point out that any woman's nipples would get hard if he looked at them like that. But I didn't want to think about that. I just wanted to think about us. No one else. Just us.

"Waxing that pussy should be fucking illegal. It's unfair. A pussy already that damn perfect shouldn't be made even more irresistible. A man can only handle so much." His hand slipped down to cup my bare mound, and I whimpered. I wasn't sure what game we were playing now, but I liked it.

"Wet. Always so wet. You get wet so easily. What makes you wet? What is it I do to you that makes you wet?" he asked as his fingers slid over my moist heat.

"It doesn't take much. Just a look from you and I get wet," I told him.

A pleased smirk touched his mouth and he closed the space between us. "Just a look, really? That's gonna make it hard for me to keep my hand out of your panties. I already think about kissing you and tasting you all damn day long. Knowing your pussy is wet is gonna get you fucked in some dangerous places," he whispered as he kissed my neck.

I shivered and grabbed his arms to keep my legs from giving out under me. His hand was still working its magic over me, and I was close to having an orgasm between his naughty words and his fingers.

"You were made for me," he said, causing me to pause. What did he mean by that? It was awfully close to something else. He couldn't love me. He didn't know. He wouldn't love me when he found out.

I wanted to forget. I didn't want him to say more. I lifted my left leg and wrapped it around his hips, opening myself to him. His fingers sank inside and he groaned.

"Fucking flexible," he said, kissing me everywhere his mouth touched. My ear, my jaw, my neck. "Turn around and grab the back of the couch. Stick this sweet ass up for me," he demanded.

I didn't ask, I just did it. I wanted to do it. His hands cupped my bottom and he slapped at it gently. I cried out and he slapped it harder. "I like watching my handprint forming on your skin," he said, caressing the spot he had spanked. I squirmed, wanting the orgasm I was so close to reaching.

"My girl is wiggling. She likes it." He spanked me again, this time harder, and I cried out. "Fuck, that's pretty," Grant growled, and then his lips brushed the stinging skin. His warm tongue came out and licked the tender spot. Knowing his mouth was that close to other areas made me greedy.

"What is it you want, sweet girl? You need something else spanked?" he asked. I didn't know how to respond. I just wanted that orgasm he was causing to build. It was going to be different from the others. I felt it.

A loud hard slap hit my clitoris, and I screamed out as the release slammed through me and I began to fall onto the couch, unable to stand as my body was racked with tremors.

Grant grabbed my hips and held me up as he entered me in one smooth stroke. "I got a fucking naughty girl that likes being spanked," he panted as he controlled me, as he moved in and out of me.

I never imagined that I would like being spanked, but the way Grant had done it was wonderful. My body was still humming from the orgasm when I felt another building on top of the aftershocks. I wasn't sure I could handle another. Not like that one. He would have to hold up more than just my hips.

"My pussy. Knowing no one else has touched this pussy and it's all fucking mine drives me crazy," he growled in satisfaction, and I began moving with him, needing what he was about to give me.

Grant's hand slipped around and began rubbing my clit in a circular motion as he praised me and my body. "Come for me, baby," he said, sending me off once again. He jerked out, and I started to beg him not to stop as he roared his release.

We hadn't used a condom again, but he'd pulled out. The warmth on my back was proof. We couldn't keep doing this. I couldn't get pregnant. It was not an option for me. Ever.

"Stay still. I'll clean you up," Grant said, and he walked away, leaving me there. I just wanted to sink into the sofa, but I knew he wouldn't want his come all over his furniture.

My legs felt like Jell-O. He was back in less than a minute with a warm washcloth, gently wiping away his release. I smiled, knowing he had watched himself as he shot his come onto my body. His roar of release had been louder than the others. I knew he liked watching it.

"Guess I marked you again," he said with an amused grin as I turned to sink down onto the sofa.

"Yes, you did," I replied.

Grant's eyes ran over my body. Then he picked up his shirt

and threw it at me. "I can't look at you like that or we'll be going at it again in about five minutes."

I loved knowing he wanted me that much. I tugged his shirt down over me then pulled my legs up under me.

"If you were trying to distract me, you did a wonderful job," I told him.

"Good. Glad I distracted you, but baby, sex with you is never about anything but the fact that I love being inside you."

I liked that. It made me feel as if he needed me as much as I needed him.

"I would say let's take a shower, but I like knowing you smell like me and sex. It makes me feel like a fucking caveman. If I start beating on my chest, just ignore me." He winked and pulled his jeans up, leaving them unsnapped and showing off his sexy stomach, then sat down beside me.

"Remind me to send those stupid fuckers a thank-you note for giving me a reason to lock you up and keep you in my shirt."

I laughed and leaned against him. This was right. Everything about Grant felt right. Maybe God had made him for me. There had to be someone out there who wanted me, even if I was broken. Surely God hadn't meant for me to live my life alone.

# Grant

Harlow sat curled up in my arms with her hands in my hair, playing with it. I had considered cutting it because I'd kept it long for a while. But the way she ran her fingers through it made me decide I would keep it like this. She obviously liked it.

I wasn't sure why I'd decided to play rough with her earlier, but I'd wanted to. She always seemed so fragile, and I treated her like something precious and cherished. Because she was. I had wanted to see how far she'd go, though. I had pushed and waited for her to balk, and I would've quit. She hadn't. Sexy little ass stuck up in the air, and she'd been squirming for more. Fuck, that was hot.

I hadn't checked outside lately. Rush had called and asked if they were here yet, and I told him they were. He said they had some paparazzi camped out at his place, too. I knew I couldn't keep using sex as a way to distract Harlow. I was going to have to go out there and face those nosey shits soon.

"I think I need to go out there and talk to them," Harlow said as she wrapped my hair around her fingers.

"No," I replied, closing my eyes so I wouldn't see her eyes if she decided to beg.

"They won't go away until they talk to me," Harlow told me.

"Good, because if you keep playing with my hair, I'm flipping you over and going for round two," I warned.

Harlow tugged at my hair. "Grant. You can't use sex to keep me under control."

I smirked. "Yes, baby, I can," I replied.

A small giggle only made me smile bigger. I peeked at her through half-closed eyes. She was looking at the door with her bottom lip between her teeth. She was thinking hard about something. I wished I could read her mind. I hated not knowing what she was thinking. I was always scared that she might be planning to leave me.

"Dad said this won't go away until they have their story. I should just answer their questions. Maybe they'll leave him alone if I do. He has Emily to worry about."

She wasn't referring to Emily as her mother. I didn't understand that but I figured it was like finding out you were adopted. That biological parent didn't raise you. Emily wasn't a part of Harlow's life. Just hearing that she was alive didn't make Emily Harlow's mom.

Hell, I knew my mom and didn't even call her Mom.

"His problem, not yours," I said.

"Dad will do something stupid if he feels like she's being threatened in any way."

Her dad was Kiro Manning. He made it his life goal to do stupid shit. Did she not watch the news?

"Not your problem," I repeated.

"Yes, it is. He spent his life protecting her and me."

I didn't see it the same way. I felt as if Kiro had protected Emily because he didn't want the world to know he had a weakness. I didn't believe he was protecting Harlow. He just didn't have time for a kid. He saw Harlow's grandmother as a perfect solution and ditched her onto the woman. Granted, it turned out better for Harlow; but it was because she was lucky to have such a good grandmother—not because of anything Kiro did. The dude was a selfish dick. He ignored Nan her entire life. And then there was Mase. The dude didn't give a shit about his dad. That said a lot.

Mase, however, cared about Harlow. He had called three times already, and she had sent his calls to voice mail. He was gonna come barreling into Rosemary with his cowboy boots and his damn gun if she didn't talk to him soon.

"You need to call Mase back," I told her.

She sighed. "Yeah. I better before he does something stupid."

She started to sit up and I held her to me. "Call him from right here. I don't want to let you go," I said.

I could tell by her little frown she didn't like that. Did she want privacy? Why? What the fuck did she have to tell Mase that she couldn't tell me?

"Okay," she said and reached for her phone and dialed her brother's number.

I was somewhat mollified, but I sure as hell was going to listen to this conversation closely now. If she intended to get the cowboy to come ride in and take her off to Texas, I'd take on the whole damn state. I didn't give a fuck. She wasn't leaving me.

"Hey, yeah, I'm fine. I'm locked up in Grant's apartment," she said.

I couldn't hear what he was saying, but I could tell from the deep sound of his voice he was worried and being bossy.

"I'm going to have to talk to them eventually," she said.

"No, I haven't . . . I know that . . . not your business . . . yes it will . . . just let me handle it . . . I know you are . . . I'll call if I need you . . . promise . . . okay, love you, too. Bye." She hung up the phone and let out a heavy sigh.

"I need some alone time to think. Do you mind if I take a bath and soak a little while?" she asked me.

I wanted to soak with her but I understood she wanted to deal with all this shit, and if I was with her we'd have tub sex.

"Go enjoy yourself. I'll be right here if you get lonely," I told her.

She grinned and pressed a kiss to my mouth. "Thank you."

After this was over she would believe me when I told her I loved her. They wouldn't be weak words. She would believe them because I would have shown her just how much I loved her. There would be no doubt in those big eyes that had hooked me the first time our gazes met.

I waited until the water was running and the bathroom door was firmly closed before I got up and went to look outside again. The crowd hadn't waned any. It was still there, and so were the cops. This was bullshit. Why was a fucking rock star's private life so damn important? My phone rang and I pulled it out of my pocket. It was Rush again.

"They're still here," I said.

"They will be until she talks to them. Not sure she needs to, though," he said.

"Not going to let her."

"You seen any of the news?" Rush's tone bothered me. He knew something.

"No, why?"

"Stay away from it for right now. Give Harlow time."

What was that supposed to mean?

"I'm keeping her from it."

"You, too. Stay away from it. She needs you right now."

"Yeah, of course."

"Call if you need me," Rush said and hung up.

I walked over to the counter and grabbed the television remote and turned the volume on low. Rush was hiding something, and I wanted to know what the fuck it was. If I was going to keep Harlow safe, I needed to know what from.

# Harlow

I dried off with a towel and walked into the bedroom to look for one of Grant's T-shirts to wear. I didn't have any clean clothes here. I was surprised he let me take that long a bath alone. I wouldn't have minded him joining me after I got past the conversation I had with Mase.

He said I needed to tell Grant. They were showing pictures of me as a baby in Dad's arms as he took me from the hospital all those years ago—when the miracle baby had lived. They were talking about how, when his wife was believed dead, he'd forgotten about the child, as did the world.

Pictures of me coming and going from his mansion in L.A. had also surfaced. People who went to school with me were being interviewed. I was now the world's biggest sob story. My heart condition and my life were being broadcast to the world.

Grant would find out soon. I needed to tell him. I had congenital heart disease and should never have lived. I'd been defying every doctor's prediction since I started walking at nine months old. My parents had been told I wouldn't develop as quickly as other children my age.

The fact still remained that my heart was defective. Pregnancy would be impossible for me to handle. I took medication that I kept in my purse with me at all times. I didn't drink alcohol. I ate healthily. I took care of myself. My grandmama had made sure to do everything she was told to do in order to keep me alive.

I took a deep breath. I had to tell Grant all this. I would be going to L.A. in two weeks to see my cardiologist and have a regular testing. He would tell me how I was, and I would hold my breath until I knew no surgery was needed at this time. I was defying the odds. I intended to keep doing that.

Opening the door, I stepped into the living room. Grant was sitting on the couch with the television remote in his hand as he stared straight ahead. I glanced in horror at the television, but it wasn't on.

His blue eyes shifted to look at me, and I knew he had been watching it. The knowledge I had kept from him was there in his gaze. Hurt, betrayal, fear—it was all there.

"You know," I said simply, and walked over to get my skirt, which was now folded and resting on top of a bar stool. I suddenly felt naked and exposed.

"Why didn't you tell me?" Grant asked, with such raw emotion in his voice I felt like crumpling to the ground and sobbing at the unfairness of it all. I had wanted to be the one to tell him.

"I never tell anyone. I hate being looked at like a broken person who people are afraid to get close to," I replied, unable to look at him.

"I'm not just anyone, Harlow. You should have told me. You let me get close to you and care about you, yet you kept this huge secret to yourself." He looked almost dazed. His eyes stared at me and the fear in them was obvious.

"I was going to tell you. I just didn't know how. I was afraid to lose this . . . this thing we have."

He dropped his head and sat there without speaking. I wasn't sure if he was angry or if he was scared, too.

"I'm the same person you've always known. I just have a condition that has to be monitored. I needed to trust you before I told you about it."

He lifted his head. Disbelief in his eyes. "Trust me? Trust me? You had to trust me to warn me that falling in love with you might be a dangerous thing to do? Can you see how unfair that is? I was terrified to let myself have feelings for you because I was haunted by the idea of losing you. It controlled me. Then, when I decided to let that go and do what my heart wanted . . ." He shook his head and let out a hard laugh. "All along you were sick and you never told me."

Sick? I wasn't sick! "That is the exact reason I don't tell people. They treat me like I'm sick. I'm not sick. I've been sick and I know what that's like, but I'm not sick now. And you think me not telling you is unfair? You know nothing about fair. There are a lot of things in life that aren't fair, but protecting myself is fair. Wanting to live life and not be left out of it is not unfair."

Grant stood up and shook his head. "You can't just let people get close to you and not trust them with that kind of information. When were you going to tell me? When I fell in love with you? When I told you I loved you, were you going to say 'Oh, yeah, I may not live for long.'" He paused as pain sliced through his features, and he looked away from me. "Was that your plan?" he asked with a hitch in his voice.

"NO! I was going to tell you now. I didn't expect you. I didn't expect this thing between us, but I wanted it. I wanted you." Tears burned my eyes as I jerked my skirt on and looked around for my shoes. I had to leave. I would face the vultures out there. It was time anyway.

I hated seeing him like this. I hated seeing the fear in his eyes. Maybe I should have told him sooner. Maybe it was selfish of me to keep it a secret from him, but I already knew how things went once someone knew. I never would have known what it was like to have Grant. I didn't regret that.

"I had been planning on telling you today. I sat in the bath going over how I would tell you. I knew it was time that you knew. I didn't want you hearing it on television or from someone else." Tears burned my eyes.

"You lied to me," he said with his voice devoid of emotion. It was as if he were shutting down inside. It was how he was going to cope. He didn't intend to fight for us and make this work. He was going to protect himself. That told me what I needed to know. He didn't have to tell me it was over. I read that loud and clear.

I walked over to my phone and texted Rush.

**I need you to come get me. I'm about to walk out into this and deal with them now, and then I'm going home. Please.**

"What are you doing?" Grant asked as I slipped my phone back into my purse.

"I'm leaving. It's time for me to go," I replied, then picked up my shoes and slipped them on.

"You can't leave." He slammed his hand against the wall, "Fuck! Why didn't you tell me? I need time to process this, Harlow. You can't just leave."

I walked over to him and stood in front of him. This was it for us, and when I looked back on this day I would always have regrets. But telling Grant the truth before I left was important to me. "Because you would have treated me differently. I didn't want to see in your eyes what I knew would be there. I wanted to be near you. I wanted to know what it was like to have a guy want me. I wanted to live. My heart may not be whole, but it still beats. I'm still alive. Why should I live like I'm dead?"

I stood there and waited for him to respond. He said nothing. The emotions in his eyes as he stared back at me were too much to define. I knew he was hurt. I also knew he felt betrayed, and I hated that I had made him feel that way. But for once in my life I chose me. I wanted Grant Carter and his sweet-talking magic words. I let myself have him and forgot about the facts. Hearing him say I may not live long was like being slapped in the face. No one said that to me. Everyone who loved me talked about my life being long. They believed and had faith. Grant was already digging my grave. I couldn't let myself be near someone who expected me to die young.

"Don't go out there. Just give me a moment to process this. You just let me get close and didn't prepare me for this. I don't understand how the sweet, selfless Harlow I know could do this."

I stopped as my hand touched the doorknob. His words hurt deeper than anything else. Maybe because I knew they were true. I had been wrong. I should have told him.

"Well, now you know. I'm not the kind of girl you plan forever with. At least you found out before your heart got involved," I said.

"Can't you at least see my side of this? Don't walk out that door," Grant said, taking a step toward me.

Staying any longer would just hurt worse. Grant would tell me good-bye. I was saving myself from that memory. It was one I could do without. I hadn't told him that my heart was weak. I hadn't warned him. I had let myself live. And now I would live with the fact he couldn't forgive me for it. That he didn't have the courage to love me anyway. I opened the door to walk out into the crowd. Flashes went off and people came running toward me.

"Miss Manning, are you seeing Grant Carter?" someone yelled, and I looked over as a camera was shoved in my face. Before I could think of an answer, someone else shouted, "Miss Manning, is your mother still alive?"

That was the question I had been prepared for, but I was pushed and I stumbled forward.

"Miss Manning, where is your father? Is he still in Paris?" another voice shouted at me. I couldn't focus. There were too many of them. Too much.

"Miss Manning, can you tell us if you have seen your mother?"

"Did you know?"

"Have you been living in your father's Beverly Hills mansion since the death of your grandmother?"

My head was spinning. Questions were yelled at me, and I could hardly see over the flashes of light in my face. I shouldn't have come out here. I wasn't going to be able to do this.

"Get the fuck off her." Grant's voice broke through the tunnel of people and voices. His hand closed around me and pulled me away, and he shoved me into a truck. At first I thought it was his. Then I saw Rush sitting in the driver's seat.

"You okay?" he asked, his face hard as stone as he glared out at the people now calling out his name.

"Get her out of here," Grant said without looking at me and closed the door.

Rush backed his truck up as I watched Grant walk back toward his condo. Not once did he look back at me.

"I'm sorry, Harlow," Rush said.

"Me, too," I replied. I couldn't go back to Nan's. I needed to leave all of this.

"Can you take me to the airport?" I asked him as I pulled my purse closer to me.

"Where are you going to go?" Rush asked.

"L.A., Texas, I don't know. Dad needs me but I don't know if he wants me. I could go to Mase, but I don't want to take this insanity to his ranch."

"Grant just needs time to deal. He'll come around," Rush said.

"No. That's over. Things were said I'll never forget. That chapter is closed."

Rush didn't reply as he pulled out onto the main road that led out of town.

"He's just scared," Rush said, defending him.

"I'm gone now. Nothing for him to be scared of," I replied. "Could you get my things from Nan's and ship them to the L.A. house?"

Rush let out a loud, defeated sigh. "Yeah, I can do that. So you're going to L.A.?"

It was better for Mase if I did. "Yes, for now. I'll hide out there and help deal with Dad."

Rush nodded.

We drove in silence for a while. I tried to think about Dad

and what he was dealing with. I didn't let myself think about Grant. I couldn't. I would break down on Rush, and he didn't need to deal with that. I would have plenty of alone time once I got to L.A. Plenty of time to cry.

"I never knew," Rush said quietly.

"I didn't tell people. Dad didn't either. After Mom's accident, the world believed she was dead and they forgot about me. It was like I had died with her."

Rush's phone rang, and I hated how hope soared through me. Even if it was Grant, I couldn't get over what he'd said.

"Hey, baby . . . I'm taking Harlow to the airport," Rush said into the phone. It was partly Rush and Blaire's fault. I had seen them together and wanted to know that feeling. I had given in when Grant pursued me. Yes, he'd been pretty damn irresistible, but I'd also wanted to feel loved. I wanted to love someone freely and know the security that came with that.

But I didn't get that. My heart would always stand in the way. God hadn't created Grant for me after all. No, God had left me out. Figures. I was used to being left out in life. At least I had lived once. I had this memory to pull out and remember. Grant might not have loved me, but I had loved him. I still loved him. I knew what that felt like. I was thankful for that.

Maybe that was my gift. I had a few stolen moments of a life that I could have had if I was whole. I never had to give those memories back.

"She's upset but she's going to be okay . . . yes, I'm sure. She's tough—a lot like another woman I know . . . yeah. I love you, too . . . I'll call you when I'm on my way home. Don't shoot Grant if he comes over there." Rush grinned then hung up the phone.

He glanced over at me and his grin faded. "She'll probably call you. A lot. Be prepared."

I needed a friend. I was glad I had one in Blaire. "Okay," I replied.

Rush pulled into the private airport that Slacker Demon's jet usually departed from. I hadn't called for the jet, so it wasn't here.

"What are you doing?" I asked.

Rush flashed an ID at the gate and they opened up. "I'm getting you a private jet. You can't walk into the airport and get on a regular plane, Harlow. You'll get mobbed. When you land in L.A., I'll have a limo waiting to pick you up and get you to the house. Stay there. They'll probably be swarming outside the gate."

I hadn't thought of any of that. He was right, though. My private life was now over.

"Thanks. I hadn't . . . this hasn't sunk in yet," I said, opening my door.

Rush got out of his truck and walked toward the main office.

"Stay here, I'll be right back," he called out.

I didn't doubt Rush could get me a jet. He knew how to make the world do what he wanted. I often wondered if it was because he was raised in our fathers' world.

He never seemed intimidated.

When he came walking out, he waved me over.

I went to him, trusting him to get me home safe. My time in Rosemary was over much sooner than I'd expected.

But the memory was mine to keep.

# Acknowledgments

I've been wanting to write Grant's story since Blaire pointed a gun at him in the first few paragraphs of *Fallen Too Far*. At one weak moment I even considered Grant for Blaire. I'm really glad I gave Rush and his badass a chance though. Now that I've written Harlow I know that Grant was always meant to wait for her.

I need to start by thanking my agent, Jane Dystel, who is beyond brilliant. The moment I signed with her was one of the smartest things I've ever done. Thank you, Jane, for helping me navigate through the waters of the publishing world. You are truly a badass.

The brilliant Jhanteigh Kupihea. I couldn't ask for a better editor. She is always positive and working to make my books the best they can be. Thank you, Jhanteigh, for making my new life with Atria one I am happy to be a part of. The rest of the Atria team: Judith Curr for giving me and my books a chance. Ariele Fredman and Valerie Vennix for always finding the best marketing ideas and being as awesome as they are brilliant.

The friends that listen to me and understand me the way no one else in my life can: Colleen Hoover, Jamie McGuire, and Tammara Webber. You three have listened to me and supported me more than anyone I know. Thanks for everything.

*Take a Chance* was my baby. I had grown to love Grant and Harlow before I even started writing it. Without readers who aren't afraid to be honest with me during the beta reading, I wouldn't have been as happy with *Take a Chance*. Natasha Tomic pointed out exactly what was missing to me after she read it, and I knew she was right. It was the icing I needed for this story and I love her for it. Thank you, Autumn Hull and Natasha Tomic for being my eager readers and never holding back a punch.

Last but certainly not least:

My family. Without their support I wouldn't be here. My husband, Keith, makes sure I have my coffee and the kids are all taken care of when I need to lock myself away and meet a deadline. My three kids are so understanding, although once I walk out of that writing cave they expect my full attention and they get it. My parents, who have supported me all along. Even when I decided to write steamier stuff. My friends, who don't hate me because I can't spend time with them for weeks at a time because my writing is taking over. They are my ultimate support group and I love them dearly.

My readers. I never expected to have so many of you. Thank you for reading my books. For loving them and telling others about them. Without you I wouldn't be here. It's that simple.

Blaire told her side of the story in *Fallen Too Far*.
Now it's Rush's turn. Read on for a sneak peek at the
highly anticipated follow-up to *Fallen Too Far*, *Never
Too Far*, and *Forever Too Far* by #1 *New York Times*
bestselling author Abbi Glines.

# *Rush Too Far*

Available from Atria Books in eBook
and trade paperback in May 2014

They say that children have the purest hearts. That children don't truly hate because they don't fully understand the emotion. They forgive and forget easily.

They say a lot of bullshit like that because it helps them sleep at night. Such sayings make for good, heartwarming clichés to hang on the walls, to bring out a smile in people passing by.

I know differently. Children love like no others. They have the capacity to love more fiercely than anyone else. That much is true. That much I know. Because I lived it. By the age of ten I knew hate and I knew love. Both all-consuming. Both life-altering. And both completely blinding.

Looking back now, I wish someone had been there to see how my mother had sown the seed of hate inside me. Inside my sister. If someone had been there to save us from the lies and bitterness she allowed to fester within us, then maybe things would have been different. For everyone involved.

I never would have acted so foolishly. It wouldn't have been my fault that a girl was left alone to take care of her ailing mother. It wouldn't have been my fault that the same girl stood at her mother's graveside, believing that the last person on earth who loved her was dead. It wouldn't have been my fault that a man destroyed himself after his life became a broken, hollow shell.

But no one saved me.

No one saved us.

We believed the lies. We held on to our hate, and I alone destroyed an innocent girl's life.

They say you reap what you sow. That's bullshit, too. Because I should be burning in hell for my sins. I shouldn't be allowed to wake up every morning with this beautiful woman in my arms, who loves me unconditionally. I shouldn't get to hold my son and know such a pure joy.

But I do.

Because, eventually, someone did save me. I didn't deserve it. Hell, more than anyone it was my sister who needed saving. She hadn't acted on her hate. She hadn't manipulated the lives of our family members, not caring about the outcome. But her bitterness still controlled her, while I had been delivered. By a girl . . .

No, she wasn't just a girl. She was an angel. My angel. A beautiful, strong, fierce, loyal angel who had entered my life in a pickup truck, carrying a gun.